EGMONT PRESS: ETHICAL PUBLISHING

Egmont Press is about turning writers into successful authors and children into passionate readers – producing books that enrich and entertain. As a responsible children's publisher, we go even further, considering the world in which our consumers are growing up.

Safety First
Naturally, all of our books meet legal safety requirements. But we go further than this; every book with play value is tested to the highest standards – if it fails, it's back to the drawing-board.

Made Fairly
We are working to ensure that the workers involved in our supply chain – the people that make our books – are treated with fairness and respect.

Responsible Forestry
We are committed to ensuring all our papers come from environmentally and socially responsible forest sources.

For more information, please visit our website at
www.egmont.co.uk/ethicalpublishing

The Shell Magicians

Kai Meyer

Volume 2 of 3

Translated by Anthea Bell

EGMONT

EGMONT

We bring stories to life

First published in Great Britain 2007
by Egmont UK Limited
239 Kensington High Street, London W8 6SA

First published in Germany 2004
under the title *Die Muschelmagier*
by Loewe Verlag GmbH, Bindlach, Germany

ISBN 978 1 4052 1636 4

1 3 5 7 9 10 8 6 4 2

A CIP catalogue record for this title is available from the British Library

Typeset by Avon DataSet Ltd, Bidford on Avon, Warwickshire
Printed and bound in Great Britain by the CPI Group

CONTENTS

THE ATTACK

The voice of the Acherus roused her.

Jolly woke with a start. She felt as if her skull had struck something hard, her headache was so bad. She was lying on a scratchy raffia mat, and a woollen blanket lay in an untidy heap beside her. A narrow strip of daylight fell through the window opening roughly hacked in the side of the cave, but it couldn't drive away the shadows around the rumpled bed where she had been tossing and turning. She must have knocked the jug of water over in the night, and the contents had evaporated in the oppressive heat. Not even the rock walls around her could cool the stuffy air.

The scream of the Acherus.

She'd heard it, she was sure she had.

But now there was silence again – or no, not silence, only the distant murmur of the Caribbean Sea, the whispering of

1

the wind, the faint roar of the breakers. And . . . yes, voices. Very far away.

Where was she? What was she doing here?

It took her a moment to remember. But then images came back to her mind, most of them just as painful as the headache raging behind her brow.

They had gone overboard. In the middle of a fierce sea battle, she and Griffin had found themselves in the water as murderous cannon shots were fired and gunpowder smoke swirled in the air. Jolly remembered looking for Griffin in the rough seas and, with the last of her strength, dragging him to the rocky shore of an island. When the air cleared, their ship was gone.

And their companions had disappeared along with the *Carfax*: Munk, Captain Walker, the pit bull man Buenaventure, Soledad the pirate princess and the Ghost-Trader. They might have dissolved into thin air along with the gun-smoke.

'Jolly! You're awake!'

Bending low, Griffin came through the cave entrance. The pirate boy could just fit through the narrow opening. Like all the caves offering shelter on the island, this one was hardly larger than a small ship's cabin. But once the two of them had been given food and water, their dismal refuge in the rocks had seemed like a palace.

'I . . . I heard something,' Jolly managed to say hoarsely as Griffin crouched down beside her. 'The Acherus, I think.'

For a split second alarm chased over the boy's features. Then he grinned, and shook his head so hard that his many little blond braids whirled around his head like a wreath.

'You were dreaming,' he said gently. 'There's nothing on this island. Or at least, no Acherus or anything that could set the Maelstrom after us.'

He was probably right. Jolly had dreamed a great deal since this venture began.

Again and again, she saw images of the endless kobalin armies lying in wait beneath the waves all the way to the horizon. She felt the dead fish that came raining down from the sky on her skin, she smelled the foul breath of the Acherus. And yet the evil that had conjured up these terrible events was no easier to understand. The Maelstrom and the Mare Tenebrosum were still hidden behind their own creatures – unimaginable, incomprehensible, and all the more dreadful for that.

'Agostini told me to fetch you,' said Griffin. 'He wants to take us up on the bridge with him. Coming?'

She nodded vigorously, but immediately pulled a face as her headache made itself felt again. All the same, she was glad of any kind of distraction. She stood up, swaying slightly, washed briefly at the spring of water in a rocky crevice, and then hurried out into the open air with Griffin.

The bridge-builders were camping in a number of tiny caves like air bubbles in the lava rock on this side of the island. Jolly and Griffin had come ashore to the north, where the slopes of the conical mountain were covered with old, petrified tree trunks and the ground was yellowish-grey. Here in the south, however, a layer of solidified lava several miles wide covered most of the extinct volcano. It must have rolled down from the crater thousands of years ago, gradually cooling on its way to the water. Time and the weather had carved a branching maze of cracks and crevices into the rock, offering the inhabitants of this wilderness shelter from both the heat and the much-feared typhoons.

It was now four days since the two shipwrecked mariners, hungry and thirsty, had stumbled on the camp pitched by Agostini the bridge-builder and his men. They had spent the long hours here waiting around doing nothing. Jolly was almost relieved to see no sign of the *Carfax* on the horizon even on the second day, and then the third. It looked more and more as if their friends had gone on to the starfish city of Aelenium without them. Well, good riddance, thought Jolly snippily. She might be a polliwiggle, but she wasn't anxious to face the Maelstrom. She just wanted to go on board the next ship that put in here for supplies and get back to her old life as a pirate at long last.

'There you are!' cried Agostini, as they left the labyrinth of rocky crevices and reached the cliffs.

The master bridge-builder strode to meet them, waving his long arms imperiously as he gave orders to workmen in passing, took a scroll of paper from one of them, inspected it, handed it back, spat tobacco juice, bit into a banana and adjusted his broad-brimmed hat – all without ever slowing down.

Agostini was always doing at least three things at once, and not because he was short of time. It was probably his nature to be busy with something, talking, constantly on the move, designing new plans or revising old ones. The man was all activity, as if an anthill had taken human form.

Today, for the first time, he was going to take Jolly and Griffin up to the unfinished bridge with him.

He turned on his heel as he reached the couple and walked back to the cliff-top with them, across a surface of porous, ash-grey rock covered with tents, workshops and dark-skinned men. A dozen or so of them, born on various different islands, were working for him.

Agostini had long, flowing hair and wore something that might have been patched together from a shabby Spanish

5

uniform, an English naval captain's outfit, and the traditional costume of a French farmer. Never mind: it served its purpose. His tousled grey locks fell to his shoulders beneath his slouch hat, looking much the same as the faded, limp feathers tucked into its red hatband.

A group of bridge-builders scattered, jabbering something, as Agostini reached the building site with the two young people.

The master bridge-builder stopped beside Jolly and Griffin and for once stood still for a moment. He took a deep breath. Jolly followed his eyes to the spectacular wooden structure reaching out from the edge of the lava rocks and into the distance.

When she and Griffin had first seen the bridge they could hardly believe their eyes. It spanned a whole arm of the sea between this island and the next. It was still incomplete, but the sight of the gigantic construction was already enough to take your breath away.

Agostini's bridge was indeed amazing: two hundred paces long, ten paces wide, a crescent curving high above the water without a single pier to hold it up, plain and unadorned, designed only for utility and yet with an elegance that made the bridge look like an ornament in itself.

It consisted of an intricate filigree framework of planks

and boards. During the next few weeks they would be covered, but meanwhile the workmen picked their way over the wooden struts like tightrope walkers, always just a step above the abyss. The bridge ended in cliffs far above the water on both sides of the channel. At its highest point, the vault rose as much as the height of twenty men above the surface of the sea.

It was a grand but obviously crazy structure. What made a man build something like this in the middle of nowhere? Who was to use the bridge when it was finished? Why go to such vast expense to link two desolate islands that lay far from all civilisation and were not on any trade routes? Agostini hadn't answered any of their questions.

Jolly suspected that he was simply mad. However, the bridge-builder had taken her and Griffin in and given them the necessities of life. Little as Jolly liked being stuck in this desolate place, they depended on him for help until they could get off the island.

The wind blew in their faces as they left the land behind and stepped on to the wood of the bridge.

'It was finished this morning,' Agostini told them. 'The workers have closed the final gap.'

A little alarmed, Griffin looked down through the spaces between the planks at the abyss. Like Jolly, he had grown up

7

on pirate ships. He moved as easily as she did on the yards of a sloop. But this, for reasons that weren't entirely clear even to them, was something different.

They had to take care where they placed their feet on the narrow struts. For Jolly in particular, falling to the surface of the sea would be fatal. As a polliwiggle she could run across the water – and the waves felt as hard as stone. Hitting them would break every bone in her body. But even for Griffin, to whom water was only water, a fall from such a height would end badly.

They walked along the side of the bridge, holding the balustrade with one hand. A few of the islanders leaped nimbly past them – no wonder, since most of them had been working on the framework of this bridge for over a year.

It was some time before they approached the highest point of the arched bridge. Jolly was so deep in thought that she never noticed them gradually leaving the workmen behind. But now, when she looked up, she saw that they were alone with Agostini.

Out of politeness, Griffin put a few questions, but Jolly was hardly listening. Only when he asked how the wood stayed in the air without any piers to support it, and Agostini replied, 'By magic,' did she prick up her ears.

Magic? But only polliwiggles could work shell magic, and

of the two polliwiggles still left alive obviously only Munk had the gift. Jolly lacked the patience for it, and the skill too, even though the Ghost-Trader had said she was wrong there. But Munk was far away. By now he and the others had probably reached Aelenium.

So who exactly was Agostini? What did he know about magic?

She was on the point of asking more questions when the master builder stopped. They were in the middle of the bridge now, and a drop of a hundred and twenty feet or more yawned below them.

Agostini put both hands on the rail, closed his eyes and breathed deeply. His long hair fluttered in the wind like ashes in a breeze.

Griffin and Jolly exchanged a glance.

Far away, they heard howling. Alarmed, Jolly spun round, but it was only the stormy wind blowing through the narrow clefts between the rocky islands. The roaring of the rough sea was flung back in whispers from the cliffs, and the echo reached them even out here.

Jolly ventured another question. 'What use is a bridge like this? I mean, what will it do out here at the end of the world?'

The bridge-builder smiled, but he didn't look at Jolly. His glance travelled over the water to the other islands. The panoramic view looked as if someone had applied layers of grey and brown paint to a blue canvas.

'It will do what all bridges do,' he said mysteriously. 'It leads from one place to another.' This was the first time he had spoken so calmly and quietly. Jolly had to strain her ears to hear him.

Griffin shifted uneasily from foot to foot. His anxious expression silenced Jolly. What business of theirs was it? It was probably best just to enjoy the breathtaking view for a moment, and then turn back to land.

'The other island over there —' Jolly pointed to the far end of the bridge and the wooded hill rising beyond it — 'why didn't you camp on that one? It looks much more comfortable, with all those trees.'

Something rang an alarm bell at the back of her mind, an idea connected with what she had just said. Only a moment later did it become clear to her.

The trees . . . all those trees. Of course. It looked as if not a single trunk had been felled. Only on the volcanic island, but not . . .

Not over there!

And yet the trees of the island couldn't possibly have supplied enough wood to build this gigantic bridge. When she thought about it soberly, all the trees of the entire island group would hardly have been enough.

'Jolly?' Griffin had noticed that something was bothering her. 'What's the matter?'

She did not reply, but looked down at the wood beneath her feet in silence. At first sight there was nothing unusual about it. She crouched down and ran her fingertips over the surface. It felt smooth, although it wasn't polished, and it was fibrous, almost like reeds or bamboo.

'This isn't ordinary wood, is it?' She raised her head.

That mysterious smile was still playing around Agostini's lips. 'No,' he whispered.

Griffin looked from one to the other of them, and then took Jolly's arm. 'Let's go back.'

Jolly was still staring at the master builder. 'Where does this bridge lead?'

Griffin looked at her, wide-eyed. 'Where?' he repeated in surprise.

'He knows what I mean.'

Agostini nodded. 'Not to the other island, anyway.'

'But –' began Griffin.

Jolly interrupted him. 'Designing this bridge wasn't your own idea, was it? Someone gave you orders. And most of the wood too.'

The bridge-builder nodded again. Raising his right hand,

11

he began fiddling absent-mindedly with the brim of his hat. 'You arrived too soon,' he said. 'But never mind, little polliwiggle, it will all work out now.'

She had never told him about her special gifts.

'Come on, Jolly.' Griffin was tired of hearing the two of them discuss something he didn't understand. 'I'm going back on my own if you don't –'

This time he was interrupted not by Jolly but by uproar on the lava cliffs behind them. His head turned abruptly. Jolly followed his gaze.

The islanders were running and leaping towards the rocks, where a large crowd had gathered. Slowly, a circle formed around something that couldn't be seen from this distance.

'What's that?' asked Jolly.

Some of the workmen screamed, and the crowd broke up here and there. Many of the men looked up at the heavens, as if expecting to see something unusual. But the azure Caribbean sky was as empty and blue and endless as ever. Other islanders fell on their knees, bowed their heads, and spread their arms wide in prayer.

Something slapped down in front of Jolly's feet.

'Oh no, not again,' she said grimly through gritted teeth.

Dead fish fell on them as if out of nowhere, striking the wooden struts, sliding off and disappearing into the depths.

Silver, scaly bodies, octopuses, spiny pufferfish, crabs with red pincers, bloated bodies without eyes and limbs, they all came raining down from the cloudless sky, pouring over the bridge, the cliffs and the surrounding sea, a sinister shower of corpses.

'Let's get out of here!' shouted Griffin, turning to run.

'Little polliwiggle,' whispered Agostini. And even more quietly, he repeated, 'It leads from one place to another . . .'

A shimmering body glanced off the bridge-builder's shoulder, but he didn't even flinch.

Jolly was about to join Griffin and run for the land, but after only a few steps they both stopped.

Griffin drew his breath in sharply. 'My God.'

Jolly couldn't utter a sound. They saw the whole crowd of islanders scattering as the men fled in all directions, a few of them even running back to the bridge. Little could be seen through the hail of dead fish, but that little was enough for the friends to see why the workmen were panicking. Small, dark shapes had appeared among them. Figures striking out with arms that were much too long, uttering cackling cries.

Jolly tore herself away from the sight, leaned over the rail of the bridge and looked down into the water. The sea was churned up by the impact of thousands of fish falling into it; the waves seemed to be boiling. And from below, shapes were rising through the water, dark shapes moving in the waves like seaweed. Hundreds of them.

'Kobalins!' Griffin leaped back from the rail as if one of the fearsome beings had appeared right in front of his face.

Jolly's voice was so hoarse that it could hardly be heard through her frantic gasping. 'And something else too.'

Griffin ducked away from a dead inkfish, and was hit on the back of the head by another corpse. He grimaced. 'Something else?'

She nodded. Jolly had seen such a rain of fish twice before. The signs were unmistakable: a creature of the Maelstrom must be somewhere near. A beast like the Acherus that had killed Munk's parents.

'But why are the kobalins attacking the workmen?' Griffin was staring at the cliffs, where more and more dark figures were now attacking the islanders, a black, glittering wave of misshapen, wet bodies, their limbs outsize and far too scrawny, their mouths snapping. 'Kobalins don't come up on land!' The way he said that sounded pathetically helpless. 'Ever!'

'They do now.' Jolly pushed away from the rail and glanced anxiously down through the framework of the bridge at the water below. The crests of the waves were now swarming with kobalin heads. 'Their leader's driving them ashore. They must be more frightened of him than of the land and the air.'

Agostini had climbed up on the balustrade, raising both

arms, his head thrown back. 'Go along, little polliwiggle,' he whispered, for no reason that she could see. 'You're expected.'

Jolly had not seen him climb on the balustrade, and she didn't know how he could stand there without holding on to anything. But his words froze the blood in her veins. What on earth did he mean?

A deep humming emerged from Agostini's throat. A gust of wind blew the hat off his head, and now his grey hair fluttered around his skull like swirling smoke.

Griffin seized Jolly's arm. 'The kobalins are following the islanders up on the bridge! Come on, we must get away from here!' He pointed to the far end of the bridge, where the wooded hills of the second island could be made out beyond the rain of fish pelting down.

'No, no!' Jolly held him back. 'Wait!'

Griffin looked over his shoulder at the volcanic island. Kobalins were crowding up on the framework of the bridge now, scrambling, swinging hand over hand, leaping. They reached the fleeing islanders and threw them over the balustrade into the depths. Once they hit the water they sank among the dead fish at once, never to surface again.

'They've seen us!'

'Of course,' she said. 'After all, it's because of us they came here.' It was an obvious conclusion to draw, but even as Jolly put it into words she doubted it again.

'We *can't* go to the far end,' she cried, trying to shout above the sound of dead fish raining down while ducking to avoid them at the same time.

'Why not?'

'What exactly did Agostini say just now?'

Griffin stared desperately at her and then at the bridge-builder, who was still standing on the balustrade in his attitude of humble worship. He looked less and less like a human being; his proportions were distorted, as if his outspread arms were growing towards the sky.

'What did he say when I asked him where the bridge led?'

'"Not to the other island."'

'Not to the island,' repeated Jolly, trying to make herself think. Keep calm! Put your mind to it!

Griffin's eyes were wide as he looked at her. 'But where else would it . . .? I mean, if it doesn't lead to the island, then . . .' He stopped short, shaking his head.

'It's a gateway. Or a crossing. Or a . . . well, a *bridge*,' she said helplessly, since nothing else occurred to her. 'Agostini did build a bridge, but it doesn't lead to the island, even though it may look like it. There's really something else over there. Perhaps another world.'

'The Mare Tenebrosum?'

'It's possible, don't you think?'

Griffin's features hardened; his expression was grim. 'They're coming. We *have* to get out of here.'

Jolly still didn't move. Then she took a step towards Agostini, who was still humming and whispering as he stood in the rain of corpses. He didn't even look at her.

The kobalins were coming closer. They weren't as fast on foot as in the water, and the height of the bridge seemed to intimidate them even more than its curious material beneath them or the strange element of air. Yet the snapping, hissing, screeching throng was menacing enough to show her that Griffin was right. They had to get away.

As she ran she felt as if someone else were running for her, as if she were being carried forward by something and made insensitive to her own horror.

Only for a few paces. Then she stopped again. Griffin was staggering and looked like slipping off the bridge, but with her help he saved himself at the last minute.

'Look ahead there,' she said tonelessly.

They were closer to the other island now, and yet it seemed more indistinct than before, fraying at the edges like smoke. At the same time the air was growing darker, not with clouds, but as if the light were being sucked out of the blue Caribbean sky.

'What's that?' asked Griffin.

The kobalins uttered shrill, raucous screams in unison as they came up behind. They were only forty paces away now.

'Come on!' cried Griffin, looking back over his shoulder again.

'We can't . . .'

'Are you going to let them tear you to pieces?' He seized her arm and pulled her on. 'They only have to throw you off the bridge like the others. But the impact will break your neck – either that or the kobalins in the water will finish you off.'

The darkness in the sky had spread. There was dusk not only above them but beside and ahead of them. The hump-backed island grew taller and broader and then dissolved, drifting away in all directions.

A screech alarmed them and made them both spin round. Something was racing towards them with outstretched arms, teeth bared, webbed fingers bent like claws.

'Watch out!' cried Jolly.

Griffin ducked. At the same time he drew his dagger from his belt. The blade flashed in the last glint of blue sky shining above the bridge behind them like light at the end of a tunnel. The kobalin avoided Griffin's thrust, flailed its arms wildly, and came to a halt, legs apart, on two wooden struts.

Its ugly face with far too many bared teeth turned watchfully from right to left, again and again, while its horde of companions came up after it.

Jolly snatched her own knife from her boot, turned it swiftly in her hand, grasped its point and with a smooth movement flung it at the creature, just as Captain Bannon had taught her. The blade went into the monster's chest with a hollow thud. One last high scream, then the kobalin lost its balance and fell through the planks to the depths below.

Jolly spun round and gratefully took Griffin's outstretched hand. As they raced on along the bridge, it crossed her mind that she was unarmed now.

The kobalins were left behind, as if what light remained held them captive.

The island at the end of the bridge was not an island any more, but a throbbing heart of darkness, stretching and growing, pulsating as if it were alive. The bridge seemed to have got longer. They ought really to have reached the end of it by this time. But the structure still led on and on, curving down now, making it more difficult for them to keep a foothold on the struts as they ran. And if they didn't, their own speed would carry them away and off the bridge.

'They . . . they're not following!' Griffin's voice almost cracked.

I don't know whether that's a good sign or not, thought Jolly, but she said nothing. Her throat felt raw, and there was a bad taste in her mouth, something between crushed peppercorns and rotten meat.

Suddenly the view cleared, and the darkness became a deep, starless night, like a dome spanning the stormy horizon of the sea.

A sea that hadn't been there just now. With no islands in it, without a trace of land. A sea of black, oily water. The crests of the waves were crowned by dark foam that seemed to consist of millions upon millions of tiny living creatures, small crustaceans, maybe, or water insects.

There was no light at all behind them any longer. The part of the bridge along which they had come led straight into the endless night of this place and was lost in the darkness. The kobalins had disappeared; they couldn't follow them here. Or perhaps they *dared* not?

The end of the bridge ahead led down to the water in a gentle curve. The waves broke against its intricate framework, washed over it and away, leaving dark smears.

Huge bodies moved below the surface, elongated bodies as broad as Spanish ships of war. Sometimes something leaped from the waves further off and slapped down again, but you could hardly see what it was in the darkness.

An ancient ocean, seas that might have existed at the beginning of the world, and yet different, stranger, more terrifying. A grey shimmer lay over the water, showing the vague outlines of turbulent breakers and waves as high as houses.

Jolly and Griffin stopped dead, hand in hand, and stared out at the abyss of timeless black and the deep sea.

They were looking at the Mare Tenebrosum.

A BRIDGE OF FIRE

Jolly felt as if someone had seized her by the feet and turned her upside down. She could hardly cling to the wooden framework of the bridge. Her body was shaking and swaying; her mind seemed lost in a bewildering void.

Griffin was holding her hand (or was she holding his?) but their fingers were cold, as if the emptiness above that endless, black ocean were sucking all the power out of them, using it to give life to its own fearsome creatures.

In the distance lightning flashed over the foaming water, above a horizon that, absurdly, seemed to be much further away than the horizon in their own world. Or was *everything* on a larger scale here? The distances, the darkness, the mountainous waves.

The living creatures.

Jolly and Griffin were still standing there, unable to move. And where would they go anyway? The bridge led about thirty paces further down before it disappeared into the oily waves of the Mare Tenebrosum, black sea-spray breaking over it. It was surrounded by gigantic shadows that glided through the water, circling close to the foot of the structure. Sometimes it seemed to Jolly that she heard angry roaring, dull and long-drawn-out, like the sound of calls and cries from below the surface. But the crash of the waves was deafening anyway. And the wind, sighing and howling as it swept around the wooden framework of the bridge, some-times seemed to be whispering to her too – words in strange languages, cold and terrible.

The place stank of rotting seaweed mingled with the stench of dead fish. But there was another smell too, one that Jolly couldn't place at once.

'Vanilla,' said Griffin, as if he had sensed what was going through her head. Perhaps she had spoken her thoughts out loud without noticing. 'It smells of vanilla.'

She nodded silently, because she was afraid her voice might sound as pitiful as his. The sweet vanilla scent in the middle of all these horrible vapours made the smell even more unbearable. It reminded her that there might be something better and more beautiful, but it was right out of reach in this place.

'We can't go on,' Griffin managed to say. Every word

passed his lips with difficulty, slow as a snail crawling out of his throat.

Still none of the kobalins had appeared behind them. The bridge was empty, an endless arch vanishing somewhere in the blackness. But every time lightning flashed, they saw that the bridge really did go on into infinity, thin as a thread, thin as the finest hair, yet as clear to see as if all the rules of visibility had been suspended. The view in this world went on forever. Did it go on and on in time as well, into the past and the future? Was the Mare Tenebrosum really both an ancient ocean at the beginning of time and the state to which everything would return some day?

They were still standing there wondering what to do, holding each other's hand tight, disturbed, amazed, overwhelmed by the sheer otherness of this deep black ocean . . . standing there and resigning themselves to death . . .

. . . when the bridge ahead of them caught fire.

Flames shot up through the struts. The sudden bright light hurt their eyes. A wave of heat swept over them.

The bridge was burning!

The dark spray at the foot of the wooden structure retreated like a living creature, forming a watery crater. At the same time a scream rose from the depths of the sea, not from the invisible creatures down there this time, not even from the mysterious masters of this world, but from the Mare Tenebrosum itself. Fountains as tall as towers rose into the air at a strangely slow pace, as if they were freezing in time, formed wonderful patterns in the blackness, and then ponderously collapsed. Once the spray looked almost like a gigantic mouth with watery fangs opening round the bridge, only to fall back into the sea.

Meanwhile the flames at the end of the bridge were rising higher and higher, crawling along the planks like glowing swarms of ants, rapidly devouring the strange fibres of the wood – the wood that Jolly now suspected came from plants at the bottom of this ocean, strange growths flourishing in places as cold and dark and empty as the chasm between the stars. Agostini must have used materials provided by the masters of the Mare Tenebrosum to carry out his project – no, *their* project.

A bridge between worlds, much smaller than the Maelstrom, one that was also to break through the barrier, but less conspicuous. The perfect eye of the needle through which those beings that were to prepare for the rule of the Maelstrom could pass.

Were there more such gateways in remote parts of the Caribbean? Even all over the world?

Jolly had no time to follow this train of thought. Griffin

snatched her back. While she was looking into the flames, transfixed, the fire had come closer. Griffin hauled her away with him, and then they leaped and ran back the same way as they had come, towards the invisible crossing between this world and their own.

The darkness retreated, their surroundings shifted, and once again Jolly thought that perhaps they were also moving through time, coming back from the very beginning of the ages to their own short, limited lifespan.

The bridge ahead grew shorter, shrinking to its original dimensions. The bodies of the kobalins stood out from the confusion of images and colours and sounds, leaping rapidly about on the struts of the wooden framework. But the creatures took no notice of the couple returning to them from the mists of other times and other worlds. Fire was their natural enemy, hostile to their native element.

The bridge was blazing on this side of the crossing too. The black smoke from the flames darkened the sky, so that they hardly noticed as they passed between the two worlds. The smoke bit into Jolly's lungs, and she coughed. At the same time the heat hit her like a blow, and she felt as if the ends of her hair were frizzling and her eyebrows were smouldering.

The flames were everywhere – behind them, in front of

them, even on both sides, dancing along the balustrade like an army of glowing fiery devils.

Agostini was still there too. He stood in the midst of the flames as if they couldn't hurt him. His clothes were burning, and the brim of his hat blazed around his head like a grotesque halo.

But not a muscle moved in his face.

Or what was left of his face.

'A shape-shifter,' said Griffin, as matter-of-fact as if he mingled with such creatures every day. 'A wyvern!'

Jolly managed to take her eyes off what had once been Agostini for a second and looked blankly at Griffin. 'A what?'

'A wyvern. I've heard of them. In the seaports they say —'

A scream interrupted him. Agostini's skull was circling on his neck; his burning hat fell off and disappeared into the wall of flames. The bridge-builder's head had no human features left, wasn't even of human size — it was pumping itself up, it doubled, became a long oval of swarming dots that reminded the horrified Jolly of the living sea-spray of the Mare Tenebrosum. And indeed Agostini's body now consisted of tiny beetle-like crustaceans, none of them larger than the nail of her little finger. They swayed in confusion, formed distorted images of human limbs, then abandoned even that memory of their former body, and finally, in the shape of a kraken with many arms, slid out of the burning scraps of Agostini's clothes.

At first Jolly thought the creature – or the swarm of creatures – would fall on her and Griffin and attack them, but the being's tentacles twitched back and forth in the air. Something seemed to alarm it, for it suddenly collapsed, and poured itself through the gaps in the bridge into the depths below.

Jolly had no time to think about Agostini and what had become of him. The fire almost surrounded them now. Burning kobalins leaped the balustrade in panic, broke through walls of flame and disintegrated like hot fat, until Jolly and Griffin were alone on the bridge.

'Back to the volcanic island!' cried Jolly faintly – anything rather than stand there doing nothing until the fire reached them.

She knew how poor their chances were: their way to land was blocked by a sea of flames, and the other way, to the Mare Tenebrosum, was cut off by the hissing, roaring fire. Anyway, she'd rather burn than go back again, or even take another look at that world of horror.

They ran past the burning balustrades. More and more tongues of flame went licking down to seize on the wooden framework of the floor. Not much longer and the bridge would collapse beneath their feet.

What had looked from a distance like a solid wall of flames turned out to be a labyrinth of separate fires. It was possible that they might yet make their way through it. If the bridge held. And if the blaze didn't go on spreading at such breakneck speed.

'Griffin!' cried Jolly. 'You must jump. Hitting the water won't hurt you.'

'What, and leave you alone?'

'Stop acting the hero and jump, will you?'

He shook his head as he ran. 'What good would that do me? The kobalins are waiting down there.'

'They've gone by now. They're even more afraid of the fire than we are.' She wasn't sure whether that was true. For whatever had induced the kobalins to come on land could still force them to lurk there, waiting in the water.

Was the wyvern their commander? Hardly, for after all, the kobalins had attacked the islanders while he was out on the bridge with Jolly and Griffin. The attack had probably taken the shape-shifter by surprise too. Someone or something had changed its plans without letting Agostini know.

But then who had set the bridge on fire?

They reached the last third of the bridge. The wood creaked and crunched beneath their feet. It was still about fifteen feet above the sea here, much too far for Jolly to jump. Looking at the gaps between the planks, she saw the water through swathes of black smoke. The swarming kobalin heads were gone, but whether gone entirely or just submerged she couldn't tell. And then there was the wyvern. It might be lurking below the surface.

When they came to the last part of the bridge, just before it reached the cliffs, they could go no further. The planks and beams were blazing. The heat was almost unbearable, and now it came from all sides.

'This is it,' gasped Griffin.

'Griffin,' repeated Jolly, 'you *must* jump!'

He was going to argue again, but the words stuck in his throat. Something dark shot up behind him and over the balustrade, making for them. Out of the corner of her eye Jolly thought she saw mighty wings as dark as the kobalins' leathery skin. It looked as if a part of the Mare Tenebrosum had followed them, and was now hovering over them like a giant bat.

The shadow landed on the planks between them, wings still spread – though they weren't wings at all – and a voice shouted, 'To me! Quick!'

Darkness flew over them, enveloping them. It was fabric, dark, coarse fabric, and there was a warm, musty smell under it, but it kept the heat off. Beneath the fabric was a tall body, and above the body the face of a one-eyed man.

The Ghost-Trader held Jolly in his right arm, Griffin in his left arm, both firmly wrapped in his flowing robe.

'Where have you –'

Jolly didn't finish her sentence. The ground disappeared from beneath her feet. At first she thought the bridge had collapsed and she was falling into the void. Then she realised that it was nothing like that.

The burning bridge was still there below them – or above them? Beside them? At any rate, it was gone, and Jolly, Griffin and the Ghost-Trader were flying safely down towards the water, now changed by the firelight into a sea of lava.

She had seen the Ghost-Trader take such mighty leaps before, in the harbour of New Providence when the Spanish fleet burned the pirates' lair to dust and ashes. Now he had done it again. It wasn't flying, it wasn't hopping, but something entirely different and superhuman, something he did as easily as anyone else would take an ordinary step.

He let Jolly slip out of his embrace. She came down on the waves, fought to keep her balance for a moment and then finally stood still. The blazing bridge was about twenty feet away, a gigantic, glowing crescent with an inferno of dark smoke behind it. Not long now before the whole crazy construction collapsed like a house of cards.

And they were not alone in the water, although Jolly was the only one who could stand upright on it with her feet on the waves. Strange creatures had gathered around them in a circle, beings that at first glance bore some resemblance to horses, except that they were larger and only half of their body rose above the waves. The lower part was below the surface. Their rough, wrinkled skin shimmered in all colours of the rainbow. They had blunt horns instead of ears, round fishy eyes, and no limbs; their entire bodies consisted of a single broad fishtail that was not smooth but horny, with irregular ridges. Oddly shaped saddles on their backs allowed their riders to sit up straight. Each of these strange animals reared at least six feet out of the water. Jolly suspected that the hidden part of their body was as long again.

The men who sat on these gigantic sea horses were dressed in plain leather clothing studded here and there with what looked like stone. Or coral.

'The riders of Aelenium,' the Ghost-Trader called down to them from the back of a sea horse. His own mount had been waiting for them among the others, its pointed skull as white as ivory, its horns the colour of amber. The creature's lidless eyes were deceptive; it was really observing its surroundings with watchful intelligence.

Now Jolly understood why the Trader had put her down on the water: he needed both hands to get Griffin into the saddle in front of him. Only then did he stretch a hand out to Jolly.

'Come up!' he told her urgently. 'Hurry!'

She grasped his hand, let him pull her up and place her behind him in the broad, curved saddle. Straps wrapped around her waist as she settled there, holding her secure.

'We're off!' cried the Ghost-Trader to the company of sea-horse riders. The men were armed with swords and spring-lock pistols. Most of them had their loaded guns in their right hands, while their left hands held the sea horses' reins.

Jolly pressed close to the Ghost-Trader's back. She still didn't know where he had come from and who these other people were, but she was enormously grateful to them for turning up just in time.

'The kobalins,' she managed to say, all in a rush. 'Where are they?'

'They dived down.'

'But they weren't alone!'

'No.' With a vigorous movement, the Trader turned his sea horse. The other animals followed the movement, maintaining the protective formation around them. 'The hippocamps have picked up the scent of something.' He must mean the sea horses.

Jolly looked around her. Her gaze flickered over the other sea-horse riders, but they blurred before her eyes like something that wasn't there at all.

'Hold tight!' called the Ghost-Trader as his hippocamp gathered speed again. Jolly doubted whether any ships could move as fast as these creatures.

The sea-horse formation raced through the labyrinth of islands, leaving the burning bridge far behind. It had almost disappeared beyond the cliffs and rocks when a terrible grinding, exploding sound announced its end. Jolly looked over her shoulder, but her eyesight wasn't keen enough to make out any details. All she saw was a distant, glowing streak that suddenly collapsed on itself, to disappear the next moment in a seething confusion of black smoke and white water vapour.

'It's over,' said the Ghost-Trader, although she guessed at his words more than she actually heard them. The waves were crashing over the horny skin of the sea horse's chest. White foam sprayed into Jolly's face, leaving a salty film on her lips.

She couldn't believe he had really said *over*. A voice inside her whispered that it wasn't true. He wanted to reassure her; he was keeping something from her.

For in reality, this was only the beginning.

'Where's the wyvern?' asked Griffin, in a voice that sounded as faint as her own.

'Gone,' replied the Trader. 'Shape-shifters are cowardly beings when the crunch comes.'

There was something else too, thought Jolly again, but she was too exhausted to find the words for it.

Something else.

Griffin's voice sounded thin in her ears, carried on the wind that was lashing into their faces more and more violently. 'It's stopped raining dead fish. Does that mean . . .'

'Yes,' said the Trader. 'Whatever it was, it's gone. For the time being. We don't know exactly why. When the warriors of Aelenium appeared and started the fire, the kobalins did nothing to stop them. Far from it — as soon as we attacked they retreated.'

Jolly tried to understand what his words meant. 'But the kobalins are under the Maelstrom's orders. Why would it let the bridge be destroyed? After all, it was sent to prepare a way for the masters of the Mare Tenebrosum.'

The Ghost-Trader shrugged his shoulders, and sighed. 'The Maelstrom's strength and force are growing day by day. As in a game of chess, every move in this war has its purpose, even if we don't always know what that purpose is.'

Once again Jolly summoned up all her reserves. 'War?' she asked, in a faltering voice.

Now the hippocamps were moving over the rough sea towards their distant and invisible destination so fast that Jolly's surroundings blurred.

The Ghost-Trader looked over his shoulder, but she saw only the blind half of his face, the black patch covering his useless eye.

'The great battle for Aelenium,' he said.

THE STARFISH CITY

The hippocamps never tired. They swept across the deep blue sea like whirling dervishes, they seldom needed to rest, and they didn't sleep at all – or perhaps they regained strength without losing speed, which seemed to Jolly even more splendid and extraordinary. She herself slept, but only briefly and restlessly in the cramped space of the saddle, and her sleep brought no real refreshment.

The journey passed without any incidents. No more was seen of the Deep Tribes. The Maelstrom appeared to have changed its plans. Once they had left the labyrinth of reefs and rocky islands behind, Griffin had changed to Walker's sea horse, and was now sitting behind the captain in the straps of the curiously shaped saddle. Walker was talking to him, but at that distance Jolly couldn't hear what he was saying. Perhaps he was just trying to reassure and hearten Griffin, which was a strange idea, for when the boy had stowed away on his ship not so long ago the pirate captain had wanted to throw him overboard.

Walker had tied back his shoulder-length hair into a short ponytail. He still had on the scarlet breeches he had been wearing when they first met, and obviously not even Princess Soledad could persuade him to take the gold ring out of his nose. Jolly herself had half a dozen rings in each ear, and a pin holding two silver balls in the skin just above her nose. But she still thought Walker's nose-ring looked ridiculous.

Soledad, daughter of the murdered pirate emperor Scarab, was riding ahead of Walker in the sea-horse formation. Like the captain, she had additional straps to hold her secure in the saddle. Neither of them, after all, had had any practice in riding these amazing creatures, but Jolly noticed that Soledad managed more elegantly than Walker. Unlike him, she had experience of horse-riding on land. Her long hair, black as a raven's wing, fluttered loose in the wind, and sometimes she gave Jolly encouraging glances or a smile to cheer her up.

During these long hours Jolly often thought about their destination: the city of Aelenium. She had no clear idea of it, but she knew it was a kind of floating city anchored by a long chain somewhere in the Atlantic, north-east of the Virgin Islands. The inhabitants of Aelenium could be described as guards who had kept watch over the captive Maelstrom for hundreds of years – before it broke free to gain new and terrible power.

But so far the Maelstrom had kept away from the city. Jolly had no idea why it was waiting so long to attack; all she knew was that Munk and she were the only people alive who could stop it.

The fate of Aelenium depended on their survival. In the long run, if the Ghost-Trader was to be believed, so did the future of the entire world, for only if the Maelstrom was prevented from breaking down the borders between this world and the Mare Tenebrosum would they all be able to go back to their old lives.

She thought of the day when it had all begun. At a single stroke, she had lost her foster-father Captain Bannon and his whole crew with him. Jolly had grown up on Bannon's ship. He had been both mother and father to her, as well as the best teacher she could imagine. But every trace of him she had chanced upon since, every hope of finding him, had come to nothing. And although she wouldn't admit it, the events of the last few days and weeks had pushed her grief for the loss of Bannon further and further to the back of her mind.

The sun sank in the sea twice and rose again twice before dense mist appeared in front of them. Jolly's muscles tensed when the riders guided their hippocamps straight into it.

For some time they seemed to be floating through a grey void, until at last they were through the mist and saw Aelenium ahead.

Jolly missed a breath. She had never seen anything like it. The only towns she knew were shabby little settlements around the harbours of the Caribbean, with badly built, crooked streets full of hovels and tumbledown houses, along with sinister taverns, warehouses, and the businesses run by receivers of stolen goods, sellers of rum and tattooists.

Aelenium, on the other hand, looked as if a part of the sky had taken shape here, an iced cake of a city with higgledy-piggledy coral structures, tall as a small mountain and with countless towers and balconies, pointed roofs, extraordinary bridges and platforms. Everything here seemed to be made of coral, white or pale beige, sometimes shot through with streaks of chocolate brown or amber. The windows and doors were tall and narrow, and many of the buildings so finely chiselled that they reminded Jolly of beautiful Chinese porcelain. Bannon had once captured a whole ship's cargo of porcelain artefacts from China.

But . . . buildings? Had any of this actually been *built*? It looked more as if most of Aelenium had grown, like a miraculous coral reef. The city was a mighty starfish shape, with the points of the star reaching out into the sea. The citizens used them as natural landing stages. Most of these points, at least on this side of the city, were covered with low houses; only in the centre of the starfish did the buildings become larger, clambering up around a flattened cone to reach dizzy heights. The mountain itself had steep sides of the same pale material as everything else here, with many streams of water running down them; some flowed calmly through narrow channels, others cascaded over ledges and vertical rock faces like waterfalls.

'Impressive, isn't it?' said the Ghost-Trader, looking over his shoulder, but Jolly couldn't even answer. Impressive seemed to her the wrong word. Aelenium was much more than that: a miracle, a spectacle, something entirely incredible.

And she noticed something else: above the towers of the city, under the cloudless blue of the sky, winged creatures were flying – mighty rays, moving through the air like the smaller members of their species swimming through the depths of the sea. A rider sat on each of these flying rays. They were the city's soldiers.

The sea horses brought the homeward-bound company in to land at the side of one of the starfish points. It was obvious that even the guardsmen were exhausted by the long ride. Walker jumped down from his saddle to hurry over to Soledad and help her dismount – but his knees gave way and he fell full length on the ground. Some of the riders laughed, but Soledad gave him a sympathetic look; she knew that she would probably do the same once she tried standing on her own feet again after days in the saddle.

Someone lifted Jolly down and set her on a coral platform. Griffin was brought over to her. His hand reached for hers, but neither of them said a word.

The *Carfax* lay at anchor very close. It had suffered badly in the sea battle, and now carpenters and ship-builders were busy everywhere about its hull and in the masts and rigging, working side by side with the sloop's misty crew of ghosts.

Looking away from the *Carfax*, Jolly gazed in astonishment at the city. It was like a fairy tale come true.

Two birds flew down from Aelenium's sea of rooftops and settled on the Ghost-Trader's shoulders. Smiling, he greeted the two black parrots. Hugh and Moe usually followed him everywhere he went; it was strange that they hadn't been with him. Hugh's eyes were yellow, Moe's bright red, and anyone who looked at them quickly realised that both birds were strangely intelligent.

New faces appeared round Jolly. Many looked at her curiously, some whispering things like, 'Is that her?' and, 'Rather skinny, don't you think?' Jolly was hardly listening, and when she did she acted as if she didn't notice how discourteously she was being inspected and discussed, as if she weren't there at all.

Then a tall, broad-shouldered figure with the head of a dog emerged from the crowd, striding towards them. Buenaventure the pit bull man flapped his crooked ears and then gave a toothy grin. He took hold of Walker, who had now been helped to his feet, hugged him vigorously and slapped him so hard on the back that the captain almost collapsed again. Then he saw Jolly, uttered a yell of delight, and took her in his arms too.

'I'm damn glad to see you back with us, little Jolly! Damn glad!' Then he turned with his doglike smile to Griffin, who grinned wearily. 'Glad to see you made it too, young snot-nose.'

The two of them shook hands – Griffin's hand disappeared almost entirely in the pit bull man's huge paw – and then Buenaventure turned his back, evidently to show them something. He was wearing a rucksack out of which peered the head of a bizarre creature, half caterpillar, half beetle, but as long as a man's arm. Under the horny plate that covered most of its head a kind of mouth opened.

'My lady Jolly,' announced this creature unctuously (he had never called her that before). 'I consider myself more than fortunate to see you and your bold companion again.'

'Bold?' enquired Griffin, frowning. They really weren't

used to this kind of tone from the Hexhermetic Shipworm, master of ten thousand curses and even more insults.

'I bid you welcome to Aelenium,' continued the Worm, undeterred, 'and would like to take this opportunity of reciting a few modest lines that I have written with great poetic enthusiasm in honour of your arrival.'

'Oh no!' groaned Jolly.

'What, now?' said Griffin.

The Shipworm coughed audibly and was about to begin when the flat of Walker's hand came down on his horny plate.

'None of that!' said the captain, who had made his way over on his still-shaky legs. 'Forgotten already? No poetry, no verses, not when I'm around.'

'Who cares for you!' said the Worm indignantly, letting his dignified formality slip for a moment. 'That may have been the rule aboard your dirty, stinking pirate ship, but not here in the wonderful city of Aelenium, where they know how to appreciate great poems and works of art.'

Buenaventure looked down at Jolly over his shoulder. 'The folk here think highly of him. *A spring of lovely language*, they call him, and *Maestro Poeticus*.'

'And *Wonderful Worm,* don't forget that one,' said the Shipworm.

'Only six days away,' muttered Walker, 'and I have a worm

44

running rings around me the moment I get back.'

'A Won-der-ful Worm!' repeated the Shipworm, turning in the direction of the captain and emphasising every syllable. 'You just remember that, barbarian! *Prince of Poetic Song,* someone called me. And *Master of Melodious Music.*'

Walker made a sound that was neither poetic nor melodious.

'Huh!' said the Shipworm. He coughed again, and began:

Heroes return from a great deed,
To cries of joy and minstrel's lays.
Their friends to victory they'll lead,
Driving away sorrowful days.

My lady and Sir Griffin true
Now freed at last from durance vile,
Will soon rejoice both me and you
By —

'Ouch!' howled the Worm. 'That hurt!'

'So did your verses,' said Walker.

'No one hits a poet!'

'I do!' The captain came so close to the Hexhermetic Shipworm that his nose was almost touching the creature's horny plate. 'I've murdered children in my time, I've abducted women, I've crippled – well, cripples. So who's going to stop me roasting a Worm alive and *eating* him, eh?'

'Eating him?' asked the Worm, sounding subdued.

'With salt and pepper. And a dash of red wine vinegar.'

'Walker.' Soledad gently put her hand on the captain's shoulder from behind. 'He meant well.'

'Not to me, he didn't,' said Walker grimly.

Jolly looked at Griffin and sighed. 'Welcome home,' she said.

They entered one of the coral palaces over bridges and up flights of steps. High corridors led further into the heart of the city. Their way took them under slanting ceilings that were never symmetrical, and past walls from which all kinds of angular structures grew. At close quarters, they were unlike anything an architect would have thought of.

Aelenium was a coral, the largest ever known, made of ancient particles that had settled on the back of the gigantic starfish and grown with time, layer upon layer of fantastic deposits which at some point had taken shape as something more like a termite mound than a city built by human hands.

Pathways here always seemed longer than necessary, suites of rooms led apparently nowhere, and there were halls with not a single angle in them, only swellings, curves and bays.

'Where's Munk?' Jolly's conscience suddenly pricked her. She ought to have asked about him before.

'Working,' said the Ghost-Trader briefly.

'Working?'

'Perfecting his talents. Working at shell magic.'

'Why wasn't he there when we arrived?'

The Trader was silent for a moment. Then he said, 'Perhaps no one told him.'

'But the others all knew!'

Griffin touched her arm. 'Perhaps he didn't *want* to come.'

'But that's –' Jolly stopped short, and did not contradict him after all.

'Munk has learned a great deal more in these last few days,' said the Ghost-Trader, who had not failed to notice her disappointment. 'You'll have to work hard to catch up.'

She didn't reply, but thought she herself might have something to say about the way she spent her time. Polliwiggle she might be, but she wasn't a shell magician like Munk and had no intention of becoming one.

She wanted to be a pirate, the greatest, most feared woman freebooter in the Caribbean. And she wanted to find out what had happened to Captain Bannon and the crew of the *Maid Maddy*. Other people could put their minds to the Maelstrom and the masters of the Mare Tenebrosum. Munk, for instance.

And the Ghost-Trader himself. Jolly didn't like to have anyone telling her what to do and what not to do. Least of all did she want to hear any more prophecies.

'Where are we going?' she asked, fearing welcome parties under coral domes, with wise men and women greeting her as if the fate of the world really did depend on her.

'I thought you'd both want to rest first,' said the Ghost-Trader. 'So now we'll show you to your apartments. Sleep for a few hours, and then we'll see.'

Apartments. Jolly nodded, lost in thought. She thought of Munk as she had last seen him: his face flushed with fever, bending over his collection of shells, constantly forming them into new patterns to work magic.

Like someone possessed, she thought, and the idea made her uncomfortable.

I'm not like him.

I'll never be like Munk.

She must have slept for a long time, because when she woke up her clothes were lying on a stool beside the bed, washed and dried. Her linen trousers, however, had been replaced by a pair made of leather, astonishingly light and comfortable to wear. There was twilight outside the high window with its pointed arch, but whether it was morning or evening she couldn't say. Never mind – what mattered was that she had slept her fill. The Ghost-Trader had given her some kind of herbal infusion with an unpleasant flavour to drink before she lay down. And whether she owed it to the mysterious brew, or to hours of rest, she certainly felt refreshed and ready for a little exploration. Only her behind still ached from the long ride, and when she looked in a mirror she saw bruises there as big as coconuts.

A little later she left her bedroom, a place much higher than it was wide, its vaulted ceiling shot through with a pink shimmer that she could see only from certain places in the room. The door was wooden, like all the furniture, which made her extraordinary surroundings a little more real. Human beings lived here, not angels or fairies. People from many different countries who had come to Aelenium for a wide variety of reasons.

Griffin had been given the room next to hers, but when she knocked there was no reply. He must still be asleep.

So she set off alone through the city, following the Ghost-Trader's instructions not to climb any higher up, and when she came to crossings and forks in the road always to choose the downward path – like that, he had said, you could be almost sure not to get lost in Aelenium.

Jolly thought this advice rather strange but soon forgot

about it, for the sight of the city demanded all her attention. She soon realised that Aelenium was by no means the compact mass it had looked from a distance. In fact, most of the houses, even the palace where she had slept, were rather small and filigree-like. Beyond and among them, often under them or on bridges built over them, ran a maze of alleys, pathways and streets. Even if you were going only a short distance, you often found yourself in the open. There were many different scents in the air. Jolly's way took her through markets with stalls of fresh fruit, past windows from which delicate perfumes wafted, or simply to balconies high above the sea where you could breathe in its salty tang. She realised how long she had taken sea air for granted.

The people of Aelenium were not like the riff-raff living in the seaports. Not that Jolly had ever minded the riff-raff – after all, she was one of them herself. But she couldn't help admitting that everything here was rather more comfortable and in better order than the grubby alleyways of Port Nassau, or the rundown slums of the Jamaican ports.

For one thing, obviously not too many people lived in Aelenium; there couldn't be more than a couple of thousand. She saw few men, and supposed most of them were being trained to defend the city. The women and children wore simple but clean clothes, and if there was anything that didn't quite fit the picture of a fantastic idyll, it was the fact that most people went about their business out of doors as quickly as possible, looking anxious.

They seemed to know that the starfish city was in danger. Evidently the coming war against the Maelstrom and the powers of the Mare Tenebrosum was no secret in the coral streets and houses. In spite of all its beauty and its outwardly peaceful appearance, this city was preparing for a siege.

They must all know what defeat would mean: the complete destruction of Aelenium and the death of its people. In view of that, Jolly thought it surprising that there was still an atmosphere of peace and calm. But then she remembered Port Nassau when the Spanish armada threatened it: hardly anyone there had thought of the danger. All of them, pirates, traders and trollops, just went about their dubious business. Why should it be different here? The people of Aelenium might be better behaved and rather more refined, but all human beings were probably the same when they faced an inevitable fate.

Jolly had a lump in her throat as she wandered around the bridges, stairways and terraces of Aelenium. She was coming to understand why it was so important to the Ghost-Trader to save this place. The Trader was old, much older than any of them could understand, and it was the superhuman aura about him that sometimes frightened Jolly. Had he found peace in this city, only to see that peace menaced by the masters of the Mare Tenebrosum? Was that why he was ready to make any sacrifice for the sake of victory over the Maelstrom?

She shuddered at the thought, and clutched the balustrade of the balcony from which she was looking down into the depths. Below her, beyond the roofs and towers and minarets, lay four of the mighty starfish points, standing out against the dark surface of the ocean in the evening twilight like white fingers. Sailing boats and hippocamps circled the floating city, and the air was full of the mighty flying rays with their armed riders, ever watchful, always on the lookout for the smallest sign of an attack.

The wind whistled keenly through the narrow rifts in the coral, murmuring like strange organ music. Jolly swept back her hair. Lost in thought, she looked from the waves to the wall of mist that surrounded Aelenium, a ring of vapour protecting it. Wisps of mist hovered and drifted, forming into fairy-tale shapes, or sometimes menacing gargoyle faces that you saw only if you looked for long enough.

You're brooding, Jolly told herself. And you're making the mistake of looking on the dark side. Aelenium isn't lost yet. There may still be a way to save this city.

It depends on you, whispered the voice inside her. It's all up to you.

She shook her head as if to rid herself of the idea like a troublesome fly, but it didn't help. The Ghost-Trader had imprinted his message too deeply on her mind: only the two polliwiggles could save Aelenium from downfall. And with the city the whole Caribbean, everything that Jolly knew and loved.

'Jolly!' A cry startled her. She was almost glad of it, even if her heart missed a beat.

'Jolly, up here!'

She looked up, and saw a huge shadow above her, triangular like the point of a giant's lance, its wings rising and falling with deliberation, as if they were still swimming through the deep sea.

The ray majestically glided down until its two riders were level with the balustrade, separated from her only by a few feet of empty air.

'Jolly . . . thank heavens, you're all right!'

One of the riders was d'Artois, captain of the Flying Ray Guard of Aelenium and master of the hippocamps. He had been one of those on the bridge; Jolly recognised him. However, it was not d'Artois who had spoken but the thin, fair-haired figure sitting in the saddle behind him.

Jolly let out her breath, and a smile stole over her lips.

'Munk,' she said, relieved. 'Where the devil have you been hiding?'

POLLIWIGGLE MAGIC

'Come on, get up here!'

Munk's face was flushed, but it seemed to be with excitement now, not fever, and certainly not with that horrible shell magic. She stared at him across the gap as if she were seeing a ghost.

Deep down inside she was still angry with him for not coming to welcome her when she arrived. But when she saw him sitting there in front of her on that monster's back, obviously in much better shape than when they parted a week ago, she was more than ready to forgive him.

Munk had lost both his parents when the Acherus devastated his island, but now he could clearly feel happy again. His eyes were shining with delight, which was more than Jolly had dared to hope for.

'Get up there?' she asked nervously. 'Are you crazy?'

D'Artois pulled on the reins of the flying ray to bring it

even closer to the balustrade. Behind Jolly, the creature's wing-beats sent straw and a few faded flowers whirling up into the air from a small square walled with white coral.

'I *can't* get up there,' she said.

'Of course you can,' said the captain.

He gave a shrill whistle. Jolly ducked as the ray flew over her and came down in the square with a dull thump. It had no feet, no claws like a bird, and Jolly suspected that it usually landed on water. Here, however, it simply settled on its belly, lowered its wings to the ground, and waited patiently.

Munk reached a hand out to her. 'Come on. There's room for three.'

She was still hesitating. 'I don't know . . .'

'These rays can carry up to five of us,' said d'Artois, smiling. 'And they're gentle beasts, much easier to ride than the hippocamps.'

'My behind's still sore from them.'

Munk sighed. 'You don't usually make such a fuss.'

Jolly gave him a sharp look, then pulled herself together, climbed carefully over the ray's pointed tail, and sat down in the saddle behind Munk. He was right about one thing, anyway: the ray really did have room for several riders on its back. And there were loops to secure each rider's hands and feet separately, so that they didn't even have to hold on to each other.

All the same, for a moment she moved very close to Munk and put her arms round him. 'Good to see you again!'

His face went the colour of a ripe tomato, and his grin reached from ear to ear. He took her hands and held them tight. 'I've missed you.'

'Hey!' cried d'Artois. 'I'm still here too, you know!'

Jolly let go of Munk and settled herself on the smooth leather saddle. She put her hands and feet through the loops, and couldn't suppress a brief groan as her bruises reminded her painfully of the state of her behind.

'Ready?' asked the captain. Jolly nodded. 'Off we go, then. Hold tight!'

He whistled again, several times, and immediately the ray rose a few feet above the ground, beating its wings gracefully, turned between the buildings and went gliding out into the empty air. The movements of its mighty body were so smooth that Jolly felt as if she were sitting in a boat on a calm sea. But her legs could feel muscles as thick as a man's arm beneath the creature's smooth leathery skin.

The wings prevented her from looking straight down into the abyss. It was like travelling on a flying carpet. Only if she looked over her shoulder could she see past the ray's tail and down to the depths below, but the sight made her so dizzy that she quickly turned back to look ahead of her. D'Artois' long hair was blowing out in the air in an almost horizontal line, like her own. The wind in their faces was cooler than she had expected, but that was because the sun had long ago disappeared behind the mists. Only the upper rims of the bright layers of air still shone softly, like entangled gold leaf.

The coral rooftops of the city were left fifty and soon sixty paces behind. Then the captain steered the ray into a curving flight that took them around Aelenium in a spiral. For the first time Jolly saw the other side of the starfish city and discovered that one of its peaks was missing, while two others fell abruptly to the sea as if someone had struck them with a gigantic fist. The houses on the remains of these peaks were destroyed and the ruins blackened with soot, as if a great fire had raged here not very long ago.

'What happened down there?' she asked.

'Creatures of the Maelstrom,' replied d'Artois briefly. 'An attack. We beat it off.'

'No one here likes talking about it,' said Munk. 'It was a couple of months ago that –'

'Five,' the captain interrupted him.

'Five months,' said Munk, as if he had been living in

Aelenium himself at the time. 'A troop of kobalins invaded under cover of the mist, led by . . . well, by what exactly?'

D'Artois looked morose; he didn't like discussing the subject. 'By something with no name. Larger than the largest ship ever seen. And more dangerous than the giant krakens.'

Munk looked back. 'Captain d'Artois and his men beat it back. And the kobalins too, of course. But there were many dead, and you can see what almost happened to the city.'

Jolly nodded sadly.

'Since that attack, rays have been patrolling below Aelenium, protecting the anchor chain,' said d'Artois. 'The Deep Levels were abandoned long ago, but now we're not so sure that they're still empty. Divers go searching the halls and grottoes, but they're too large and intricate for us to be certain. If something really has settled down there, it may just be waiting for an opportunity to strike.'

'What are the Deep Levels?'

'The city under the city,' Munk said before the captain could answer. 'There are coral structures underneath the starfish as well as on its surface. It's like a mirror image of Aelenium.'

'Countless coral grottoes and caves,' said d'Artois. 'Once they were safe, and nothing but a few sharks and moray eels swam down there. But in times like these? Who knows?' He sighed. 'All the same – we're doing our best to fortify the underwater city.'

'How many soldiers are there in Aelenium?' Jolly asked.

'Not enough. A few hundred.'

Jolly remembered the armies of kobalins she had seen two weeks ago from the *Carfax*. A mighty procession of thousands upon thousands swimming out into the Atlantic, where the Maelstrom was gathering its forces.

Aelenium didn't have the faintest chance if it came to a battle between men and kobalins.

'I know what you're thinking,' said d'Artois, as they flew around the city a second time, gradually losing height. 'But we will fight when the time comes. We have no choice.'

'Jolly, look!' Munk's sudden cheerfulness sounded a little too deliberate to be genuine. He wanted to take her mind off the subject. 'The merchants' quarter is down there – see those bazaars?'

'Yes.'

'And over there, a little higher up, the libraries lie. We have to go there tomorrow morning.' He pointed to a group of tall coral domes clinging to the cone-shaped mountain. Several streams of water running down the mountainside fell into basins and canals set among the library buildings, turning into sparkling waterfalls and pools full of exotic plants.

'And there,' said Munk a little later, 'are the buildings of the Council of Aelenium. Right beside them are the Guard's barracks. And lower down is the poets' quarter. Well, painters and musicians live there too.' He laughed softly. 'You should have seen them when the Hexhermetic Shipworm turned up. They sent a delegation to the Council to make sure he was given a house of his own among them. And special rations of wood. He's very popular here.'

'The Prince of Poetic Song.' Giggling, she repeated the Shipworm's words.

'Your Worm is a great poet,' said d'Artois gravely. 'You ought not to make fun of him just because he's smaller than you are.'

Munk laughed. 'You see? They all feel that way here. Terribly understanding and kind . . . *just because he's smaller than you are*,' he joked, imitating the captain. 'That's probably why the Ghost-Trader is so fond of Aelenium – all the people are so nice.'

'But nasty enough to throw you off this ray if you don't watch your tongue, my young friend.'

Munk glanced over his shoulder at Jolly and made a face, but said nothing.

'We're going to come down at a steeper angle now,' said the captain. 'So hold on tight.'

Jolly slid a little way forward as the flying ray went into a kind of nosedive. For a moment she felt so sick she thought she was about to throw up. Only when d'Artois turned the creature to a horizontal position about three paces above the surface of the water did her stomach settle. The handholds to which she was clinging were damp and slippery.

D'Artois slowed the ray's flight until it was gliding above the waves at a comfortable speed. Down here the darkness was almost complete, except for the flickering lights of Aelenium as they gradually came on and were reflected back from the black surface of the water.

Jolly felt a sudden pang at the memory of the Mare Tenebrosum. A deep black, lifeless ocean. Almost like . . . no, not like this one. This was the Caribbean Sea, and she could run over its waves as easily as other people ran on dry land.

Munk took his feet out of the loops securing them and began clambering down from the saddle, swaying slightly.

'Are you out of your mind?' she asked.

'Just watch this.'

'You don't have to try impressing me,' she snapped. 'If you fall on the water from this height you'll break every bone in your body.' Anyone else would probably have been all right, but Jolly and Munk were polliwiggles. Jolly was surprised that the captain was letting Munk fool about like this – after all, the fate of Aelenium depended on him far more than on her.

'You tell him!' she demanded, looking at d'Artois. 'The idiot will fall.'

'Wait,' said the captain. He let out a long whistle, and the ray moved into a gliding flight with its wings held completely still.

Munk was now standing on the saddle with both feet, legs apart. 'Watch this!' he told Jolly. 'I'm going to show you what I've learned over these last few days.'

'How to break your neck?'

Munk turned to one side and walked away over one of the ray's outstretched wings. It bore his weight, and the great flying ray didn't even sway as it hovered.

'Munk, for heaven's sake!' She put out a hand to hold him back, but he was already out of reach, and now he walked to the far edge of the wing as if it were a wooden platform, not part of a living creature.

'The trick is to dive in with your hands and head first,' he said.

'Dive in?' What was he talking about? Polliwiggles couldn't dive. Seawater was like stone to them. He'd hit his head on the surface if he tried it. 'Stop being so stupid!'

Munk gave her a smile that was a little too arrogant for her liking. Then he looked ahead of him again, bent his knees slightly, leaned forward – and dived head first off the wing of the ray.

Jolly screamed as she saw him go down. Then the ray was above the place where he had fallen, and Jolly craned her neck to keep Munk in sight. But the water was too dark for her to see where he had hit it.

'Fly back,' she demanded. 'Turn round! Quick!'

'Don't worry,' replied d'Artois. 'He's all right.'

'Oh yes?' She was still straining her eyes to stare at the dark waves, expecting to see Munk's broken body on the surface any moment. 'We're polliwiggles! A trick like that can kill us!'

'*Can* – but doesn't necessarily have to,' said d'Artois, guiding the ray in a wide curve back the way they had come. 'Not if you do it properly.'

'Are you telling me . . .'

'There's a teacher here in Aelenium who knows all about what you and Munk can do and what you can't. He's not a polliwiggle himself, but he knows the old traditions.'

'Old traditions?' There was scorn in her voice. 'The first polliwiggles were born after the great earthquake in Port Royal. That's just fourteen years ago. So these traditions of yours can't be all that old, right?' She heard him speaking, though she could think of hardly anything but Munk. Munk who was more than probably dead, drifting somewhere down there in the darkness.

'Wrong,' the captain told her. 'I admit I don't know all about polliwiggles, but one thing I do know for certain: they were around earlier, many thousands of years ago – at the time when Aelenium was set to keep watch over the Maelstrom.'

'And fine watchmen you turned out to be!' she said bitterly. It didn't give her half as much pleasure as she had hoped to wound him, but at the moment it somehow felt the right thing to do. Even if only to take her mind off Munk and what d'Artois had just said.

'We have failed as watchmen, that's true,' agreed the captain, and his voice had lost some of its steady confidence. 'However, it seems to me that our wise teachers know you polliwiggles better than you know yourselves.'

She couldn't think straight, couldn't listen to this – not until she knew what had become of Munk. 'Fly lower.'

To her surprise, he did as she asked.

'Jolly!' cried a voice from the darkness. 'Here I am!'

She moved into Munk's place on the saddle so that she could peer ahead and see past the captain better. 'I can't see you!' Her voice sounded rough and husky.

'Don't worry about him,' said the captain. 'He's all right.'

Her glance moved over the glittering surface of the sea. And there – yes, it was Munk!

He was *swimming* in the water. Only his head and arms showed above the waves.

Jolly's heart missed a beat. 'But this can't –' She broke off, because she couldn't believe the evidence of her eyes.

Munk could *swim*. He was down there – *in the water*!

That was impossible. He was a polliwiggle, like her. Polliwiggles don't swim in salt water. Polliwiggles walk on it. Anything else would be like a normal person suddenly sinking into a paved road.

The ray swept above Munk's head, and once again d'Artois turned it into a wide, curving flight.

'You can do it too,' said the captain. 'The important thing is to do exactly what he did. Let your hands and head go into the water first.'

'That . . . that doesn't make sense.'

'It depends on speed. Ever tried passing your finger through a candle flame?'

'All children do that.'

'Well, did you burn yourself?'

'Of course not.'

'Why not?'

'Because I passed my finger through the flame too

fast . . .' She hesitated. 'Too fast for it to burn.'

'Exactly.' D'Artois nodded, but he still wasn't looking at her. 'It's just the same with polliwiggles and the water. If you pass through the surface fast enough, so fast that you don't notice it, you're all right. No harm will come to you. And once you're in the water you're just the same as anyone else. You can swim if you want to, because the surface of the water offers you no resistance from below, only when you're above it. And as I said, not even then if you're fast. That's why you go in head first.' After a short pause he added, 'At first Munk wouldn't believe it any more than you do. But he's learned to accept that it's possible.'

Jolly tried to put her ideas in order. 'You want me to try too?'

'Can you swim?'

'Of course. I've swum in lakes and rivers. Polliwiggles walk only on the sea, they can't do it on fresh water.'

'Right. Then try.'

'I'm not tired of life yet, thanks.'

'Believe me, you can do it. And you just wait – because it gets even better.'

'What do you mean?'

'One thing at a time. First the dive. Then Munk will tell you what to do next.'

'I really don't know about this.'

'Jolly!' Munk shouted from the water. 'It isn't difficult. Honestly!'

'Have you ever dived into water head first?' asked d'Artois. 'I mean in a lake?'

'Of course.'

'You can do the same here.'

She still hesitated, but then she plucked up all her courage. With her heart beating fast, she stood up on the saddle. The ray stretched its wings again so that she could walk along them. But did she really want to?

'I can't come down any lower, or your dive will be too short and too slow,' the captain explained.

'Very reassuring. Thanks a lot.'

He looked back and grinned. Swaying, she made her way over one of the ray's wings as it glided on. The creature was flying horizontally again, right towards the place where Munk was dog-paddling in the water.

'Ready?' asked d'Artois.

'May I decide that for myself, please?'

'Of course.'

She bent her knees, still undecided, at the same time fearing that the wind blowing in their faces would simply sweep her off the ray before she had a chance to jump of her own accord.

Three, she counted in her mind.

Her neck hurt. Her back hurt.

Two.

Not to mention her poor behind.

One.

Jolly dived. It wasn't a perfect dive or particularly graceful, but all the same it took her down head first.

The surface of the sea raced towards her, met her fingertips – and swallowed them up. She went under. Her breath stopped for a moment. A scream burst from her mouth, sprayed bubbles of air round her face, and rushed up and away with them.

All was dark around her. Empty. Cold.

She was drowning.

She could swim, yes, but not now. Not here. Not in salt water. It was plain impossible – she was a polliwiggle!

'Jolly.'

Munk's voice. He was beside her in the water.

How could she hear him? Why could she see him so clearly?

Good heavens, she must be dreaming.

'All right?' he asked, taking her hand. Her legs were still flailing frantically, but gradually she calmed down and nodded.

They weren't on the surface, they were under the sea. Yet they could move as if the water offered no resistance, both of them sinking slowly as if carried down by an invisible hand. When Jolly moved her arms and legs, however, it was like walking on land.

No resistance.

What on earth was going on?

'I was just as surprised myself at first,' said Munk. He was letting himself drift down beside her, further and further into the depths. Jolly followed him, and found to her surprise that she could still see him distinctly. Yet they must be too far from the surface by now for light to make its way down. All was black around them. It was as if she could suddenly see in the dark like a cat.

'You'll get used to it,' he said. 'Or no, that's not right. You don't really get used to it, but you adjust to it. It even gets to be fun.'

'How come I can hear you in the water?'

'Because we're both polliwiggles.'

'And how come we can move as if we had air round us instead of water?'

'Because we're polliwiggles.'

'And why don't we drown?'

He opened his mouth, but she got in first.

'Because we're polliwiggles,' she said. 'Of course.'

Munk smiled, looking strangely pale in the darkness that,

for reasons she couldn't understand, wasn't darkness any more. At least not to polliwiggle eyes.

'Is that the only explanation anyone can find in these amazing *old traditions* d'Artois was talking about?' She wanted to sound sarcastic, but she didn't succeed. There was no point in denying something that she was experiencing at this very moment.

The way they sank into the depths wasn't diving. The water wasn't like ordinary air either, because if so they'd have been falling now. No, they were hovering, a slow, relaxed movement, and when Jolly tried to swim a stroke or so towards the surface she drifted a little way up. Munk stayed with her, but he held her back before she could rise any further.

'I've been right down,' he said.

'To the bottom of the sea?'

He nodded. 'Not under Aelenium, it's too deep for me here. For now, anyway. But d'Artois took me on a sea horse to a place where the water is shallower, two or three hundred feet.'

'You've been *two hundred feet* under the sea?' She opened her eyes wide, and only now did she notice that the salt water didn't sting them.

'Yes, and it was . . . well, great, in a way. But weird too.'

'Because of the kobalins?'

'No, not them. I didn't see any. I suppose d'Artois picked a relatively safe place. And there were divers there as well. Wait till you see those things they dive with here . . . never mind, what I mean is the look of it down there was weird. Plants are found only quite far up, and after a while it gets so dark that nothing will grow. It's all grey and bleak and sort of . . . sad. There are fish, but that's all.'

'And you can breathe normally?'

'It doesn't make any difference. None at all. We polliwiggles can run over the sea-bed as if we were going for a walk on land. And we can see under water in the dark for several hundred feet ahead — I've tried it. It's as if it were evening, with dusk coming on very slowly, except that the light never changes. To our eyes it's eternal twilight down here.'

She wasn't sure if she still thought all this was fascinating. It was beginning to scare her. A foreboding was gradually coming over her, an idea of what might yet await her on the path ahead — if she decided to take it.

Once again she told herself that she would never, never let anyone order her to face the Maelstrom and fight it. None of this — Aelenium, the polliwiggle magic — none of it was her world. It wasn't what she wanted.

She wanted to avenge Bannon, be a pirate, be a famous woman sea-captain. That was what she wanted.

As for running over the dark sea-bed to seal the spring through which the Maelstrom could come . . . just thinking of it made her head ache. Not to mention the fact that her stomach was playing up again.

Munk could read her face. 'Enough to scare anyone, right?'

'Yes . . . enough to scare me anyway.'

'Me too.'

'We don't have to do it. Have you thought of that?'

'A hundred times a day,' he said, and nodded, while they went on hovering down. 'It's nothing to do with what the others say either . . . but Jolly, this place is my new home.'

'I thought you wanted to turn pirate with me.'

He smiled sadly. 'You don't have to *turn* pirate, Jolly, you're a pirate already. You grew up with pirates. But how about me? That's what I always dreamed of, yes. But all that time at sea these last few weeks . . . it wasn't at all the way I'd imagined. It's not for me. Aelenium is different. The libraries, the people . . . I want to stay here, Jolly. Whatever happens, I belong with them now.'

For a moment she wondered whether anyone had been leaning on him – was he just repeating what he'd been told to say? But then she saw the determination in his eyes, the hard look that she'd seen there once before. When the Acherus killed his parents. Munk had made his own decision.

'Whether you come with me or not,' he said, 'I'm going to the Rift. Alone if I must.'

The Rift. That was the place, somewhere in the deep sea, where the Maelstrom sprang from a mighty shell. A slender column of water growing ever broader and more murderous on its long way to the surface. Or so the Hexhermetic Shipworm claimed, anyway. And if Munk spoke so confidently, the teachers of Aelenium must have confirmed it.

Jolly avoided his eyes. She knew what he expected her to do now. He was waiting for her to say: yes, I'll come with you.

But she couldn't. She simply couldn't bring herself to do it. Not out of fear – although a great deal of fear was churning about inside her. No, she couldn't do it because she wasn't sure whether she really wanted to. She still had a feeling that the girl hovering deep down in the sea here with Munk, the girl who had joined the Ghost-Trader and come to Aelenium, was quite different from the Jolly who had grown up on Captain Bannon's ship and had been sure, all these years, that some day she'd be just like him. She'd be a notorious freebooter sailing the Caribbean Sea.

The Rift. The Maelstrom. Aelenium. They were words out of a fairy tale, a dark bedtime story.

'Come on,' said Munk, who must have guessed what was going on inside her. Was he disappointed? If so he didn't show it. 'We have to swim this way.'

He said 'swim', but that wasn't really the word for it – it was more like flying through an element that to anyone else would have been water, but for them had no more density than the sky and the wind.

'You have to do swimming strokes. Yes, just like that . . . careful, slow down! The water doesn't offer any real resistance here, remember.'

All the same, Jolly swung her arms back too fast and moved at great speed. The stroke took her a long way forward, four or five times the length of a man.

'Oh no!' she said, kicking in the water to steer herself back and turning two accidental somersaults in the process. 'This looks easier than it is.'

'Just a matter of getting used to it.'

But did she want to get used to it at all? Life had been simpler when she was still walking *on* the water, not darting about in it like a fish.

It took her several more attempts before she finally succeeded in moving forward steadily and with reasonable confidence.

'Where do you want to go?' she asked.

He grinned. 'Where do you think?'

Doubtfully, she looked ahead of them again. After two more strokes, something emerged from the darkness far in the distance: a colossal, colourless wall of branching coral. Above them bizarre, sloping formations fanned out, ending underneath the starfish. Only now did Jolly realise that for some time she and Munk had been below its huge pointed tentacles. When she looked further down the wall of coral, she saw that the mighty structure tapered on and on down into the depths like a giant icicle.

So this was the underwater city of Aelenium. The Deep Levels that d'Artois had mentioned.

'You want to go there?' she asked, without looking at Munk.

'Don't *you* want to know what you're going to fight for?'

She couldn't take her eyes off the fantastic shapes now emerging more and more clearly from the darkness. Munk had said the underwater city was like a reflection of the upper part of Aelenium. But that wasn't entirely accurate. The underside of the coral was much rougher, in a more natural state. Jolly had assumed that the city on the surface had grown rather than being built, but now she saw that the truth was somewhere between the two. The people of Aelenium had worked the coral mountain with great skill to shape it into houses and streets and squares. In its raw, unhewn condition, however, this part of it showed what the upper part of Aelenium had probably once been: a rampant, branching, dangerous structure of peaks, jagged points, and knife-sharp edges. The most gigantic coral in the world.

D'Artois had mentioned the sharks that lived here. And moray eels. And something else.

Something might perhaps have settled down here, he'd said. Something that was just waiting to strike.

All of a sudden the water felt very much colder.

UNDER THE WATER

The closer they came to the Deep Levels, the better Jolly learned to get around in the underwater world. You saw in a different way here. The intricate, roughened surfaces of the corals looked to her pale grey, sometimes shot through with a trace of colour as they were on the surface. But the shadows among them were far darker down here, so deep a black that every crack, crevice and hollow became a menacing abyss. A monster could lurk in every hole, a kobalin behind every ledge. In one way her new ability to see in the dark gave her a welcome sense of security in these unknown regions of the sea, but in another it made her more afraid of what might be waiting for her down here.

She felt that every one of those branching, shadowy structures was watching her, and asked Munk if he felt the same.

'It's worst to start with,' he replied. 'And your fears probably never go away entirely.'

'And you actually *want* to go down to the Deep Levels?'

'I've been here before, with some divers.'

Munk floated through an irregular opening in a wall of coral. 'Try to move slowly. If you get up too much speed in these tunnels and grottoes you'll soon find yourself sticking to a wall.'

Or impaled on a coral spike. 'Very encouraging.'

Munk looked over his shoulder and smiled cheerfully. 'I'm with you.'

'Oh, that makes me feel a lot safer.'

Me and my big mouth, she thought.

She followed him – very slowly, indeed cautiously – down a tunnel inside the coral mountain range. For reasons she didn't understand her vision seemed more limited in here. The end of the irregular tunnel lay in total darkness. Rifts and crevices branched off it on both sides, and sometimes there were openings as large as arched gateways.

Jolly lost all sense of how long they had been moving through the labyrinth of the Deep Levels. Munk led the way as confidently as if he had often been down here. Usually they swam along between the floor and roof of the tunnel, but sometimes they came down on the coral floor and walked. Munk was right: they really could move as easily on the sea-bed as on the surface of the water. They could walk, jump and even run. The only difference was that Jolly felt she got out of breath faster down here. She didn't even like to think that she was taking salt water into her lungs instead of air.

And yes, the salt . . . they weren't entirely immune to it. By now she had a strong, salty taste in her mouth. It didn't just make her thirsty, after a while it made her queasy too. She supposed it would have been crazy to expect no downside to all this.

'You get used to that too,' said Munk, when she complained of her queasiness. 'And there are a few other uncomfortable things. The water pressure, for instance. We don't really feel it, but after a while you get backache as if you'd been dragging heavy sacks around for hours. And when you come up you sometimes have a headache. Forefather says the brain doesn't understand why it suddenly isn't under pressure from all sides, or something like that.'

'Who's Forefather?'

'Our teacher. You'll meet him tomorrow.'

'Did *he* tell you all this?'

'Yes. But Forefather can only talk about it. He isn't a polliwiggle himself, although he knows all about us. Well, almost all. I think he knows every book and every scroll in the libraries of Aelenium by heart.'

Jolly was going to ask a question, but Munk stopped at a place where the tunnel branched. Rather crestfallen, he looked round. 'Hm. I think we're lost.'

Wonderful! 'Lost?'

He lifted an eyebrow. 'We've come off the right path. Taken a wrong turning. Climbed through the wrong hole.'

'I *know* what getting lost means!'

'Then why ask?' He grinned again, looking pale and wan to her underwater vision. 'Anyway, I was only joking. I know just where we are.'

'Very funny.'

He scratched the back of his head repentantly. 'Sorry.'

'Can we go up again now? I just can't wait to feel the headache and the backache.'

He sighed – something else that sounded very strange under water – then nodded and went on again. After a dozen or so more bends, coral halls and shadowy hollows they came to a broad shaft leading vertically upwards.

'There,' he said briefly.

They pushed off and glided up the shaft with ease, going a good deal faster now. Perhaps Munk wasn't quite as self-confident as he made out after all.

The walls of the coral shaft were irregular, so they had to keep avoiding the sharp edges of outcrops and shelves. Once

Jolly pulled Munk aside just before a sharp coral blade could slit his back open.

'Thanks,' he murmured, and she wasn't sure if he had really been scared or was secretly annoyed because she had protected him, not the other way around. He liked himself in the role of leader, that was obvious. The fact that he knew more than she did was making him feel superior. And careless too.

The shaft seemed endless. Jolly hadn't realised quite how far down they had gone into the deeps. The clefts and crevices in the walls made confused patterns of flickering shadows. Some of those clefts were large enough to shelter sea creatures, and Jolly kept waiting for a head to emerge from the darkness, its jaws wide open to show teeth of vast length.

But perhaps d'Artois and his men had done a thorough job of flushing intruders out of the Deep Levels.

At last a fissured roof appeared above them, and the shaft turned sideways into the horizontal. Jolly and Munk stopped for a moment.

'I thought this shaft came out in the city,' said Jolly anxiously. She was no longer trying to pretend she wasn't afraid of all these empty caverns and tunnels.

Munk frowned. 'So did I, as a matter of fact.'

'Do you mean to say you *really* don't know where we are now?'

'It can't be that bad. At least we've come a long way up.'

She made a face.

'We'll just go on along the shaft. It's sure to lead to the outside air some time.' He took her hand to encourage her. 'If necessary we can retrace our tracks.'

'Go down there again?' She glanced at the abyss that narrowed to a dark, shadowy point far below her. 'Definitely not.'

Did the darkness go on further down at the foot of the shaft? Her heart missed a beat, and then thudded against her ribcage like a fist.

Was something climbing up to them from down there?

'I want to get away from here,' she said.

He followed her glance, looking down. Did he see it too? Could he *feel* it coming closer?

'All right,' he said, and drew her behind him along the now horizontal shaft. 'We can hurry if you like.'

They had left the abyss behind, but at the moment that wasn't very reassuring. Jolly kept looking back to the bend in the shaft and the darkness lurking there like an oily black puddle.

They swam faster, moving forward at a good speed now. That wasn't wise, Jolly knew, and if they weren't careful their uneasiness would turn to hopeless panic. But she couldn't help herself now, and she could tell that Munk felt the same.

A sound came to her ears, a scraping, splintering sound, as if something were pushing its way along the shaft after them, something with a body too large for it that was breaking off coral crests and ledges. But when she looked back once more the tunnel was empty, and there was no sign of anything back at the distant bend either.

Imagination, she told herself. You'll just send yourself crazy.

'Can you hear that too?' asked Munk.

'Yes.'

Without another word they put on even more speed. Fear made them careless, and they kept colliding with coral growths and protruding outcrops.

'There's a way out ahead!' cried Jolly.

'Not far now,' gasped Munk, though gritted teeth.

About a hundred feet ahead of them the walls of the shaft came to an end in a grey oval. They couldn't see what lay beyond it – it was dark there, and the polliwiggles' underwater vision met with nothing in between to help them work out the distance. If they were in luck the open sea lay ahead. Unless it was just another hall in the coral labyrinth of the underwater city.

Once again Jolly looked over her shoulder. The water behind them seemed hazy, like the air above a burning ship, but she still couldn't see any real reason for alarm. If something had followed them from the depths, it seemed to have given up the chase.

'It *is* a way out!' cried Munk triumphantly.

They raced towards the oval opening, and now Jolly saw that he was right. Like two cannonballs, they shot up through the opening to find themselves in the middle of the ocean again, with a very different kind of abyss below them, bottomless yet not half as terrifying as that eerie shaft.

But couldn't whatever had been following them have been looking for a way out itself?

They were climbing towards the surface, swift as hornets moving to attack, when Munk suddenly said, 'Look over there.'

She froze inside as her glance followed his outstretched arm. But there was nothing to frighten her.

To their left, the anchor chain of Aelenium passed right through their field of vision at a slant. It emerged from a confused mass of steel and corals on the underside of one of the starfish points and ran down, stretched taut, to be lost from view in the dark grey of the sea several hundred feet away. The chain itself must measure about thirty feet across, and every link was the size of a house. Seaweed and other water plants drifted in invisible currents. Where the metal of the chain showed between them it was covered with dark brown rust.

'How long is it?' Jolly asked.

'It's three thousand feet to the sea-bed here.'

'As much as that?'

'The Rift is almost ten times as deep.'

For a second she held her breath. *'Thirty thousand feet?'*

Munk nodded as they swam towards the edge of one of the starfish points. 'That's what Forefather says, anyway.'

Jolly said nothing as they completed their upward climb. She was trying to imagine a depth of thirty thousand feet. That was almost –

Six miles!

They were expected to dive six miles down to the bed of the ocean and seal the source of the Maelstrom there?

She couldn't imagine the depth, the darkness and the loneliness that must reign down there. Yet a breath of it touched her, making her shudder inwardly.

They came up through the surface of the water close to one of the starfish points, and climbed out into the dry. By now it was deep night in the city. The coral slopes of Aelenium were sprinkled with hundreds of lights, and the wall of mist was invisible in the total blackness.

Six miles.

Through icy cold, through the dark. Through a landscape unlike anything they knew on the surface.

For the first time tears came to Jolly's eyes at the thought of the future. She didn't want to cry, not in front of Munk, not in front of anyone. But she did cry all the same, sobbing softly to herself, and wouldn't let him comfort her.

Wet through and silent, they climbed uphill through the city, along empty streets and across deserted squares. In many places it was as dark as if Aelenium itself had already sunk into the depths.

Jolly's tears didn't dry up until she saw the coral palace ahead of her again. Griffin was somewhere in there. She had to talk about all this to someone — someone who wasn't a polliwiggle. Someone who had no responsibilities in this terrible war.

Someone who wasn't Munk.

THE PLAN

Once Jolly reached her room she took off her wet clothes, dried herself, and slipped into the garments that had been laid out ready for her – another pair of close-fitting leather trousers, black this time, a comfortable sand-coloured shirt with a broad belt, and high, laced sandals. She also saw a silver-embroidered waistcoat and put it on over the shirt.

No one here had yet tried giving her skirts or a dress. They simply didn't seem to think of her as a girl.

Yet just at the moment she wouldn't have minded if they did: she could have made herself out helpless and naive, and no one would really have expected her to tackle the Maelstrom. But everyone in Aelenium seemed to take it for granted that she would accept the challenge.

Munk was right about the backache, but her head still didn't hurt, although it was full of thoughts, impressions and images, all moving at such speed that they merged into flickering, whirling confusion. She didn't know what to think. Or where to turn.

She never got around to looking for Griffin, for there was a knock at her door just as she finished dressing. A maid-servant standing outside in the passage asked Jolly to follow her to the Assembly Hall of the Council.

'At this time of night?' asked Jolly, but the only answer was a shrug of the shoulders.

She followed the young woman up stairways and over bridges to a high porch. It must have been approaching midnight when they arrived, and two guards with expressionless faces, carrying muskets on their backs, let them in.

Beyond the porch, in a wide hall with a vaulted coral roof, Jolly's companions were waiting for her – and so were some other men and women, people she didn't know. Most of them were sitting around a long table, but some stood together in groups talking.

Princess Soledad was leaning against a white coral pillar, one knee bent, deep in conversation with Walker. The pit bull man stood beside them, looking bored and rolling his eyes silently every time the captain said something to Soledad. When Buenaventure saw Jolly, he moved away from the two of them with a sigh of relief and strode fast towards her. His boots hammered on the coral floor as if he were trying to break pieces out of it with their heels.

'Thank heavens, Jolly . . . those two will send me crazy with their flirtations!'

She returned his smile, and noticed that he wasn't carrying the rucksack with the Hexhermetic Shipworm. Obviously Aelenium's new prince of poets hadn't been invited to this meeting.

Instead she saw Griffin, who looked up at that very moment. He had been sitting with his feet on the table, looking bored. Now he jumped up with a happy grin and quickly came towards her.

Griffin and Buenaventure, she thought, feeling an unexpected warmth rise in her. If there were a couple of people to whom she'd unhesitatingly trust her life, it was those two.

And perhaps Soledad, but the princess's aims still seemed to her a little dubious. Soledad wanted to bring down Kendrick the pirate emperor and claim her father Scarab's rightful inheritance. But what price was she prepared to pay? Would she ever value anything more highly than the throne of the Caribbean pirates?

Then there was Walker, a pirate himself, a man who could sail a ship like few others. Walker was here mainly for just one reason: he was speculating on the gold that the Ghost-Trader and Jolly had promised him.

With a sudden sensation of heat, she remembered that Walker must still believe the half-finished tattoo on her back was part of a treasure map. She had told him that tall tale to win his help in her search for Bannon.

It was true that Walker also had another motive: he hoped to win the princess's affection, and she obviously wasn't going to turn him down straight away – Jolly still couldn't work out whether that was out of genuine liking for the captain or to make sure of his support.

And last there was the Ghost-Trader, who was now standing at the head of the table beside a man wearing the clothes of a European nobleman, not ostentatious but made of fine fabrics. His cloak was embroidered with the same pattern as Jolly's new waistcoat, and she wondered whether this similarity had some deeper significance.

Was she so highly valued as a polliwiggle that she was allowed to wear the same symbols as the rulers of this city? She felt flattered, even though she knew that was foolish.

Of all those present, the Ghost-Trader was certainly the most inscrutable. He was a living mystery, a man who could sometimes be friendly, almost fatherly, and then again was cool and calculating when it served his strange purposes. He was the only one of the friends who didn't have new clothes; as usual, he wore his dark, floor-length robe, but he had put his hood back to show his thin face. His narrow-lipped features, with that one piercing dark eye, helped to make him look even more sinister than perhaps he really was. The black parrots Hugh and Moe sat on his shoulders, copying every movement of his head in a rather unsettling way.

Jolly turned to Griffin and Buenaventure, who were now beside her as if waiting for instructions or advice. They both seemed to feel as uneasy and out of place in this strange gathering as she did.

They had hardly exchanged a couple of words when the door behind them swung open again, and Munk came in.

He was wearing a dark, long-sleeved jacket with silver embroidery like the patterns on Jolly's waistcoat and the clothing of the nobleman at the end of the table. Munk was giving the support of his arm to an old man in a long robe who also had to walk with the aid of a stick. This must be Forefather, the teacher of the polliwiggles.

Munk gave Jolly a smile, but before she could return it a gong was struck in the depths of the hall, and all conversation died away.

'Please sit down, my friends,' said the nobleman at the end of the table, turning to those standing around it. 'Now that our two polliwiggles have arrived, we are all here.'

All eyes turned to Jolly and Munk. Forefather gave a quiet murmur of satisfaction. Several of the men and women present were whispering surreptitiously to each other. Her doubts returned: she'd never be able to live up to these people's expectations.

Those who were not yet seated moved towards the table. Munk was making for the chair to Jolly's right, but because he was giving Forefather his arm Griffin got there first. Buenaventure sat down on her left.

Looking morose, Munk placed the old man at the opposite side of the table and sat down beside him. Jolly met Forefather's eye, and smiled nervously when he nodded to her. His lined features looked still and relaxed; there was an aura of calm about him that did her good.

Walker took the chair next to Buenaventure, then looked Soledad's way and indicated the empty chair beside him with an enquiring glance. The princess fluttered her eyelashes at him, but sat down between two women who frowned as they inspected her. Obviously the noblemen and ladies of Aelenium weren't used to mingling with pirates.

The nobleman at the end of the table waited until they were all seated, and then spoke again. 'I am Count Aristotle Constanopulos. My grandfather came to Aelenium from

Greece many years ago with a fleet of ships. He was permitted to stay and initiated into the secrets of this city. The Council chose him as its leader, and after him my father had that honour. I myself have now been serving Aelenium for twenty-four years.' For a split second his gaze flickered, but then he was in control of himself again. 'It was under my rule that the Maelstrom broke its chains and achieved new power. I bear the responsibility for this catastrophe, and I will —'

'Forgive me, Count,' the Ghost-Trader interrupted him without rising to his feet, as would probably have been usual. 'You are not to blame for this misfortune. No one could have stopped the Maelstrom.'

Count Aristotle smiled sadly. 'It is kind of you to make excuses for me, but I cannot agree with you. It has always been the task of Aelenium to keep the Maelstrom imprisoned in the Rift, and for whatever reasons it has now gained strength, that happened during my term of office.'

The Ghost-Trader was about to contradict him again, but the count cut him short with a gesture. 'That's a fact, my friend,' he said. 'But we will not discuss it any further today. This company has to take more important decisions.'

Jolly was surprised to see the Ghost-Trader bow to the count. It didn't seem like him to nod agreement and keep his mouth shut. But perhaps it was all part of his wisdom: he knew when it was better to respect someone else's opinion.

'Some of us already know what lies ahead, and how we must withstand it,' said the count. 'But I think we owe it to the two polliwiggles to call things by their right names once more.' So saying, he looked at Jolly and Munk, and fell silent for a very long time as he scrutinised them. Jolly felt as if his gaze were going deep into her eyes, and finding something very surprising far behind them.

'It all began with magic,' said the count, and the Ghost-Trader at his side nodded thoughtfully. 'Magic is only another word for the power that streams through our world, flowing through the veins beneath its surface as blood flows through the human body. It is this power that keeps us all alive, although only a few discover its secret and hardly anyone understands it. And this power, this magic, comes to the aid of the world when it is threatened, as it is now. Just as happened once before, many thousands of years ago.'

Jolly sensed that Forefather was still watching her. Munk looked her way again too. She briefly returned his glance, and saw to her surprise that he flushed red, and then smiled.

'That was when the Maelstrom first threatened to break down the borders of the Mare Tenebrosum and open up the way into our world for its masters. And it was the people of these islands who then succeeded in averting the danger and locking the invader in a vast shell at the bottom of the sea. Today we call the place where the shell lies the Rift. The Maelstrom was held securely there for a long time, for the veins of magic come together in the Rift, and they kept it under control.

'But at that time, even so, some of the creatures of the Mare Tenebrosum managed to get into our world by way of the Maelstrom before it was sealed off. That is how the ancestors of the kobalins came over, so we are told. There were human beings who made alliances with them, and so the kobalins got their present form.'

Walker, visibly ill at ease in this company, spoke up. 'Are you saying the kobalins are half human?'

Some of the nobles looked angrily at the captain, but Count Aristotle nodded patiently. 'A certain amount of human blood does flow in their veins, yes. No one can say just how much. Are they mainly of this world, or do their origins lie in the Mare Tenebrosum? I don't know, and I doubt whether anyone else here knows the answer either.' His glance went to the Ghost-Trader, who shook his head and said nothing.

'But we're not concerned with the kobalins at this moment,' said the count after a short pause. 'I mentioned them only to point out what we may expect if the Maelstrom opens fully.'

He picked up the earthenware goblet standing in front of him and drank from it. 'The kobalins came here because the barrier between the worlds fell for just a moment, perhaps for only a few seconds, perhaps for the space of a single heartbeat. No one can imagine what might come across if the Maelstrom ever lies open for an hour. Or a day.'

'Or forever,' added the Ghost-Trader, and his parrots nodded wisely.

'Or forever,' the count repeated. 'Back in those times, in the first war against the Maelstrom, there were polliwiggles too. Although I assume they had some other name then. The world opened the veins of its magic and let a little escape, and where it spread among humanity polliwiggles were soon born. Just as they were fourteen years ago.'

'The earthquake,' murmured Jolly softly, but in the silence that followed the count's words everyone in the room could hear her.

Aristotle nodded. 'The great Port Royal earthquake. It was felt not just there but deep on the sea-bed too. Down in the Rift. The shell opened and the Maelstrom escaped. The magical veins crossing one another there were shaken, some of them lost power, and the strength of the shell waned. That was the terrible consequence of the earthquake, but there was a good one too, for the world keeps everything in balance. Around Port Royal, where the quake came to the surface, magic seeped out of the burst veins and made new polliwiggles. Their predestined task was to repair the devastation in the Rift.' He made a derisive sound. 'No one could guess that yet again humans would have nothing better in mind than to misuse polliwiggle magic for their own ends. You all know what happened. A murderous hunt began for the polliwiggles and their families, and that is why only two of them are here among us, the last survivors of that massacre.'

Jolly knew the story. Munk's father had told them about it. But hearing it from the count sent a shiver down her spine yet again. Recently she had reluctantly found herself wondering whether Bannon had told the truth when he claimed to have bought her as a small child in Tortuga slave market. Suppose he had been one of those who hunted the polliwiggles, murdered their parents and abducted the children? After all, he had been profiting all these years from her ability to run over the water.

No, impossible. Not Bannon.

She was glad when Count Aristotle went on with his speech and gave her something else to think about.

'The polliwiggles are predestined to take up the fight

against the Maelstrom. With the help of shell magic –' he gave Jolly and Munk a piercing look – '*you* must shut the Maelstrom up in its shell at the bottom of the Rift again, sealing the gateway to the Mare Tenebrosum.'

Soledad raised her slender hand. 'May I ask a question?'

'By all means, Princess,' said the count.

Soledad registered his courtesy with satisfaction. Not everyone regarded the daughter of a pirate emperor as a princess, and many would probably have spoken to her with less civility. 'I'm wondering why Aelenium is anchored not directly above the Rift but here, many miles away.'

Count Aristotle nodded, as if he had often heard that question before. 'Aelenium is a floating city, held in place only by its anchor chain. But the length of such a chain, however strong it may be, has limits – otherwise the currents would tear it apart. So the sea-bed below the city must be no deeper than it is here, where Aelenium lies today. A hundred feet more and there would be a danger of the links in the chain breaking. But the Rift is very much deeper. This was the nearest possible place to anchor Aelenium, even though we are almost two hundred miles from the Rift.' The count looked at Soledad. 'Does that answer your question, Princess?'

'There's something else troubling me too. If the chain is as fragile as you say, then surely it will be one of the first targets of any attack.'

'We're aware of that danger, and we are doing our best to protect the chain. Divers patrol its links, as far as possible anyway. We don't know exactly what it's like at the bottom of the sea. The divers can't go down to such depths.'

'But we can,' said Munk.

The count frowned.

Munk gave him no time to object. 'Jolly and I need practice. Before we go down to the Rift –' he glanced at Jolly, not quite sure of himself, but with a spark of triumph – 'we could make sure that all's well down at the far end of the chain.'

'Too dangerous,' said the Ghost-Trader, shaking his head so vehemently that up on his shoulder Hugh strutted a single bird-step to one side. 'We mustn't risk your lives unnecessarily.'

'Quite right,' agreed Count Aristotle, and there was a murmur of agreement from the rest of the Council too.

Jolly was glad, but she saw Munk's features harden. She was coming to realise that he enjoyed the power of polliwiggle magic, and indeed positively basked in other people's recognition of his qualities. He was annoyed to have his offer turned down.

Griffin had noticed too. 'Our friend Munk is sulking,' he whispered.

Jolly nodded, but said nothing. To Griffin, Munk might appear defiant, maybe injured, but she was afraid that the unexpected rejection of his idea hit him much harder. She didn't like the way the magic was changing him. She didn't like it at all.

And what about her? Was she immune to it? What would become of her if Forefather took charge of her and initiated her into the mysteries of her origin?

'Our plan is this,' the count continued. 'For some days now our soldiers have kept finding kobalin scouts in the sea. It seems that it won't be long now before they begin to attack Aelenium. Our preparations for battle and the siege of the city are making fast progress. The building of barricades began long ago. But training the polliwiggles comes before everything else – and that is your task, Forefather.'

The old man nodded in agreement, but still he said nothing.

'In twenty days' time at the latest, perhaps sooner, the sea horses will take Jolly and Munk as close as possible to the Rift. From there on the two of you are on your own, for none of us can accompany you to the place where you are bound. You will have to go down to the bottom of the sea and finish the last part of your journey on foot. The eye of the Maelstrom will be turned on the battle for Aelenium, and it will not be expecting its adversaries to approach over the sea-bed. And that's our chance. Your chance.'

There was unconcealed sorrow in his eyes now, and his voice sounded sad. 'I know what I am asking you to do. You will be alone down there in the dark, with only each other to depend on. No one can prepare you for the dangers there – no one knows what they are. If all goes well then you will face no worse than a hard march to reach the Rift. If not . . . well, we can't tell in advance.'

Jolly blinked. Suddenly she felt dizzy, as if she had lost her way and found herself in a dream. All at once the border between reality and madness was blurred.

She felt Buenaventure lay his great paw on her hand.

'They are children,' he told the assembly in his booming voice. 'Only children.'

Count Aristotle lowered his gaze, took a deep breath, and then looked up again. 'We all know that. But if the fate of the world rests on the shoulders of children, then they must bear that burden. We didn't make the choice.'

The pit bull man growled something that was lost in the sound of other voices. Suddenly everyone was talking at once. Soledad was speaking to the Ghost-Trader. The nobles were in lively discussion of the situation among themselves. Forefather was talking to Munk, and Walker was getting worked up about heaven knew what. Even the parrots were screeching.

Only Jolly said nothing. A dead, black landscape opened up before her mind's eye, an underwater mountain range riven by deep crevices like gaping mouths in the earth's crust. Nothing green, no plants, only greyness and deep shadows. She was more afraid than she had ever been in her life. Not even the Acherus had frightened her so much.

Griffin bent close to her ear, but she realised what he had said only when he looked at her expecting an answer.

'Let's get out of here,' he had whispered. 'First thing tomorrow. We'll go away and everything will be all right.'

But perhaps that too was only a part of this waking dream, this confusion of reality with the strange and the terrible.

For nothing was going to be all right, as she knew perfectly well.

Nothing would ever be the same again.

A VISIT BY NIGHT

Forefather's voice was dry and cracked.

'Try again,' he said. 'You can do it. You only have to want to do it.'

Jolly stared at the three shells lying on the ground in front of her. Their opened mouths seemed to be grinning at her with malice.

'There's no point. I can't do it and I don't even want to.'

'That's the excuse of someone who is afraid of herself.'

'Nonsense.' But she didn't look at the old man as she said it, for deep inside the truth was dawning on her. Forefather was right. She really was afraid of herself – of what she might find out about herself if she explored the unknown regions of her mind any further. She felt as if she had set out on a strange sea without any compass or sea-chart, knowing for certain that murderous reefs and currents lurked below the waves.

'Try it!' the old man told her again.

They were in Forefather's bookroom, a part of the library that he had to himself. It was a hall with irregular walls, like almost all the rooms in Aelenium. That made it almost impossible to put up bookshelves, so thousands upon thousands of volumes were stacked on the floor, some in great mounds like funeral pyres, others meticulously arranged in towers and citadels of books, circular or horseshoe-shaped, piled volume upon volume like bricks in a wall. If you wanted to take out one of the lower books you had to move fast: you took hold of it with your left hand while holding a second volume in your right hand, ready to push it swiftly into the gap before the entire structure could collapse.

Jolly wouldn't have believed that Forefather, frail as he was, could be so skilful, but he surprised her the very first time he did the trick. His bony fingers were as deft as a pickpocket's. Neither Munk nor she could move the books with such agility. 'Like this,' he had explained, 'there's never any disorder. All the books lie where they ought to be, and there are no new piles to be put back in place every few weeks. For every book the library lets you have, it demands another. A fair exchange.'

Forefather insisted that all these mountains of books were sorted into a precise order, and when he wanted any one of the volumes he knew where to find it.

'Jolly.'

His voice brought her out of her thoughts.

'You can do it. Trust me.'

She looked away from her three shells and up at him. His face was as brown and lined as the keel of a ship. He seemed to her to be nodding, but he was perfectly motionless as he looked at her. It was his eyes speaking to her. Like no one else she knew, Forefather could communicate by glances alone. He had the most speaking eyes she had ever seen. Sometimes she wasn't even sure whether he had really said the words she thought she heard coming from his mouth.

He was standing beside her, his back bent, leaning on a staff made of a whale's rib, his brow furrowed in a constant frown.

'You did it before,' he said thoughtfully. 'Now work on it. Work on yourself.'

Jolly sighed, closed her eyes and tried to concentrate on the three shells. In the darkness behind her eyelids, they looked like those circles of fire you see if you've been staring at the sun too long.

'You must sense them,' whispered Forefather.

She imagined her fingers feeling for them, reaching into the open mouths of the shells, which were much larger in her mind than in reality. She put her hand inside — not her real

106

hand, the one in her thoughts – felt the magic beneath her fingertips, and pulled it out like a long thread coming loose to undo a seam. Then she joined thread after thread in the centre of the space between the shells, until she could feel that the link was made.

'Very good,' said Forefather.

She opened her eyes and yes, there it was: a glowing pearl hovering among the shells just where she had tied the magic threads in her thoughts.

'Now try controlling it.' The old man's voice was both soft and insistent. 'You have picked up the tool, now use it.'

Jolly never took her eyes off the hovering, shining pearl. She had awoken the magic of the shells and made the pearl – the first step in all shell magic. Now she must direct the magic at some particular thing: an object, an action.

'What shall I do?' She tasted salty sweat on her lips.

'Decide for yourself. It's in your power.'

A book, whispered her inner voice. Choose a book, take it out and replace it with another before the whole stack can fall.

In her mind, her fingers felt for a heavy folio volume with a cracked leather back a good ten paces away from her. This one, she thought. This one.

The pearl glowed even more brightly, dazzling her.

The book moved; the pile of volumes shook. It was as tall

as a man. Then the book slowly made its way out of the carefully built structure of spines. With a rustle, it moved further and further out.

Now another, she thought. Any book.

She reached for a second book, one right at the top of the pile and much the same size as the first. It slowly hovered down, carried only by her thoughts.

Now! Do it now!

The folio volume glided out of its place, slid over the floor and opened. It was as if a ghostly hand were turning the pages. They fluttered as they would in a stormy wind.

The stack was tottering.

The second book fitted into the gap left by the first.

Yes! Jolly thought. Done it!

But the stack was still unsteady. She had rammed the second book into the opening too hard, and now it was upsetting the balance of the skilfully built tower of books.

The pages of the first book rustled harder than ever, as if brought to life by Jolly's magic.

The top books of the stack slipped and fell.

Jolly uttered a curse.

'The pearl!' cried Forefather. 'Don't give up now!'

Jolly glanced at the glowing pearl that was still hovering among the shells. She concentrated again, but there were doubts in her mind now. She didn't succeed. Too late.

The stack of books tipped over. Hundreds of volumes swayed, then slipped, and finally fell.

And remained suspended in the air.

Did I do that? Jolly wondered. Her eyes went to Forefather, but he gently shook his head.

The books were hovering in the air like a swarm of wasps unable to decide whether to attack. They were quivering, very slightly. Then one by one they slid back into their original places. The stack was rebuilt as if of its own accord, book above book, and a few minutes later the tower was standing entirely intact again.

The fluttering pages of the first book came to rest, and it lay there open.

Jolly looked over her shoulder and saw Munk sitting a little way off with a dozen shells arranged in a circle in front of him. A very slight smile was playing around the corners of his mouth. It was Munk who had kept the tower of books hovering in the air. His magic had restored what she had spoilt. Her failure was his triumph. And not for the first time.

'The pearl,' Forefather reminded her again.

With an angry exclamation, she turned to her three shells, picked up the glowing pearl with the fingers of her mind, and flung it into the open mouth of a shell much more violently than necessary. The shell seemed to make an indignant sound as it snapped shut, swallowing the magic pearl. The other two shells closed too.

Forefather nodded thoughtfully, but even his eyes were silent now. Jolly clenched her fists, exhausted and breathing hard.

This was the third day of her training.

And her twenty-second failure. She'd been counting.

She could now dive head first into the sea and move under water very easily. She had begun to enjoy the time they spent in the ocean, not just because her first alarm was dying down – it also made a welcome change from the hours of teaching in Forefather's bookroom. She was expected to go there as soon as she got up, have breakfast with Munk and the old man, and then begin her daily exercises. They went on until evening without any interruptions worth mentioning, apart from that hour or so in the water. Generally d'Artois came for her, sometimes one of the other guards who rode the great rays.

It gradually turned out that Jolly was the better of the two polliwiggles at moving under the water. She flew – to her it was more like flying than diving – in rapid loops and spirals, could turn much faster than Munk, and learned how to rise or fall half a mile within a few minutes without feeling sick or dizzy.

Munk didn't say or do anything to show that he begrudged her such progress. On the contrary, he encouraged her to try ever more daring manoeuvres, and kept her hoping to do better with the shell magic soon.

Her first real success in the magical exercises came on the fourth day, just after the midday meal. With the help of a magic pearl, she managed to make Forefather's whalebone staff rise to the high vault of the library ceiling, where it rotated fast around itself, balancing three books on each end and never dropping one of them.

Forefather was lavish with his praise, and Munk grinned as proudly as if he had done the trick himself. She was coming to feel closer to him again, perhaps because they spent so much time together. Or perhaps it was also because she hardly saw Griffin at all these days.

Once, when they met briefly in the evening, Griffin told her that d'Artois had sent him as a pupil to one of the masters of the stables. The man taught Griffin how to control and ride the sea horses. He had already ridden through the wall of mist twice with a troop of guardsmen, he told Jolly with enthusiasm, and then they raced across the open sea beyond. By his third day he was allowed to go on patrol regularly, particularly as he had shown the soldiers that he could use a blade and a gun as well as they did.

For now Griffin had given up his plan of leaving Aelenium. Jolly and he hadn't said another word to each other about it. She sensed that he was happier here than he would admit, and perhaps it was the same with her. So both of them, in their own ways, were not discontented with the course of events, apart from the fact that they could spend so little time together – which suited Munk very well.

Jolly knew all that. She could see the misunderstanding gradually arising between herself and Griffin – a misunderstanding about why they were really in Aelenium. And she sensed Munk's relief that she and Griffin hardly saw anything of one another.

What's going on? she wondered once, at the worst possible moment, just as she was preparing to dive into the depths from the back of a ray. What's happening to us?

But she suppressed any answers to such questions. The further away she could push the uncomfortable truth, the better she became at mastering shell magic.

On the fifth day, by the power of thought alone, she switched the position of books in three different parts of the library all at the same moment, and made the heavy leather-bound volumes hover through the coral dome like the seagulls gathering around the towers and high gables of Aelenium.

She didn't think about the Rift, or the grey lava mountains on the sea-bed. She didn't think of the Ghost-Trader, and only seldom of Griffin.

As a polliwiggle she was quick to learn, and Forefather gave her all the praise he could. In spite of everything, however, Munk was still the more skilful magician. She could keep three books hovering in the air at once; he did the same thing with six. She sent a stormy wind sweeping through the ravines of books in the library; he made lightning strike and turn a whole pile of folios to ashes. She made the ghostly crew of the *Carfax* dance a jig; with nothing but vapour, he conjured up images of kobalins baring their teeth.

It was a contest, certainly, and to all outward appearances they were friends trying their strength against each other. But in fact envy of one another made its way into what they did – envy of Munk's greater powers, envy of Jolly's agility under the water, envy of every word of praise from Forefather, even of the appreciative cries that sounded from the windows of Aelenium when they walked along the city streets.

On the fifth evening Jolly went to visit Griffin in his room, but he wasn't there, and she was told that he was now a full member of the Flying Ray Guard and had gone on a night patrol over the ocean. Then Jolly realised that she was even envious of Griffin for his freedom and his work with the

sea horses. She had always liked animals, and would rather
have spent her time in the stables than in Forefather's dusty
bookroom.

On the sixth day, however, at sunset, there was a knock at
her door. 'Your tattoo,' said Griffin. He was standing out
there in the torchlight. 'It isn't finished.'

'I know,' she said.

'If you wanted . . . I mean I could do it if you like.'

She smiled, and peeled her shirt off over her head before
he was through the doorway. 'I thought you were never going
to ask.'

He had brought what he needed. Black ink. A long needle,
not too sharp. A cloth. Even a bucket of warm water that he
had fetched from one of the kitchens.

Bare to the waist, Jolly went over to her bed, which was
close to the window with its pointed arch. She wasn't shy
with Griffin. The old trust between them was suddenly back
as if it had never been in doubt. She pushed the covers and
pillows aside, lay on her stomach and linked her hands under
her chin. From here she could look out at the red-gold sky
and watch the riders of the flying rays on their rounds above
the city.

Griffin sat down beside her, put the bucket of water next

to the bed, and moistened the cloth. He rubbed it gently over Jolly's back, following the course of the half-finished tattoo and then dabbing her skin dry.

'If you know it shows a coral it's quite easy to recognise,' he said.

'Trevino did it. The cook on the *Maid Maddy*.' She hesitated for a moment and then, sadly, went on. 'Just before the *Maddy* sank. I saw Trevino collapse after he was bitten by the spiders.'

'Did he often do tattoos for the crew?'

'Sometimes. He said tattooing someone is like laying out the cards for them. You have to find a theme that means something to that person, maybe something that could be important later.'

'I never thought of that.'

Jolly looked out pensively at the evening twilight. 'A coral . . . that didn't occur to me until a few days ago, but it's obvious really.'

'You think Trevino foresaw that you'd be coming here? To a coral city?'

'Perhaps it was just a coincidence.'

'Rather an odd one, then.' Griffin dipped the tip of the needle in the black ink and made the first prick to get the colour under her skin. 'Does that hurt?'

'I've been through worse.'

He smiled. 'I know.'

They said nothing for some time, while he filled shapes and shadings into the irregular outline sketched by Trevino on her back. He kept dabbing ink and perspiration off her skin, and made an approving sound now and then, as if he were pleased with his work.

'This will take a few days,' he said.

'If it gives us a chance to see each other more often – well, take your time.' She felt his eyes on the back of her head. Perhaps he was hoping she would turn round so that he could see if she meant it seriously. But she kept looking out into the sunset. Fiery light bathed the pale coral walls of the room in yellow and red. The bedclothes glowed as if they were in flames.

'I'd like to ride sea horses too,' she said as the sky gradually grew darker above the wall of mist. 'It must be great.'

'Do you still have your blue bruises?'

She chuckled. 'I'm not about to show you *those*!'

'Well, mine must be twice the size anyway, and almost black,' he said, laughing.

'Interesting idea.'

'D'Artois and his men must have skin as thick as a turtle's shell on their behinds.'

She liked the way he made her laugh. She hadn't had nearly enough fun these last few days. Forefather was always in deadly earnest, and oh, so *wise*. And Munk, even if he was closer to her now, was still grimly pursuing his desire to perfect his abilities.

But Griffin . . . well, he was Griffin. A pirate and a trickster, with a loud mouth too. Sometimes, anyway. And from time to time he was the way he was today. Himself, yet somehow quite different. As if everything she'd secretly liked about him before was suddenly much clearer. Had he changed? Or did she just see him differently?

'The whole city is talking about you two,' he went on after a pause. 'About its two saviours, their rescuers and –'

'Please stop that, Griffin.'

'What, the needle?'

'All this stuff about saviours and rescuers. We're certainly not that.'

'Well, Munk for one makes me feel he doesn't mind the idea.'

'He likes himself in the part. And he enjoys the attention. But you can understand that, can't you? Apart from his parents and a few travelling traders, he hasn't met a human soul for fourteen years. And now the whole world seems to revolve around him.'

'Then he'd better take care he doesn't . . . oh, never mind.'

'Doesn't what?'

'Well, if everything revolves around him . . . if he's at the centre and enjoying it, then he's something like a maelstrom himself, don't you think?'

She conjured up a picture of what Griffin was saying and had to admit, reluctantly, that he had a point.

Wasn't that the greatest danger threatening them: suppose they themselves became what they were trying to oppose?

'I've talked to Forefather about it,' she said.

'About Munk?'

She shook her head. 'About what's happening to us. How we're changing. How nothing matters except living up to other people's expectations – and what we really expect of ourselves isn't important any more.'

The needle pricking her back stopped for a moment.

'What is it?' she asked, trying to look up at him over her shoulder. He was working by the light of several candles now. Night had fallen outside the window.

'But it's true,' he said quietly. 'You really are special.'

'Just because I'm a polliwiggle? Because my parents happened to be in the right place when I was conceived? That doesn't make me special.' She was talking herself into a rage, although she knew that in a way she was pretending. She had thought a lot about all this over the last few days. 'Other people are specially good at riding. Or drawing. Or learning other languages. I can run over the water. Strictly speaking there's no great difference, and it's not a question of talent. I simply *can* do it, understand? I never had to work at anything to be able to walk on the sea. I don't even have to make any effort.'

The needle was still motionless.

'That's not what I meant,' he said calmly. 'I said *you* were special. Not your abilities. Just you, Jolly.'

She felt warmth spreading through her, and tried to turn to him, but he held her back with one hand.

'No, don't do that. You'll smudge all the ink.'

She stayed lying on her stomach, but craned her neck trying to look at him. 'You said that rather nicely.'

He smiled, and it was the first time she had known him almost embarrassed. 'Oh, it's the pirate school of elegant conversation,' he said. 'Some of us just have it in our blood.'

'Sure,' she said, grinning. 'Come here.'

'I'm already –'

'I mean come closer.'

He leaned forward, closing his eyes. She raised her upper body to kiss him. As she touched his lips it felt like needles pricking every pore of her skin. But it didn't hurt, it just tingled. She felt hot and cold at the same time, and there was something new in her, new and utterly confusing.

He opened his eyes and looked at her as they kissed. She couldn't remember ever having been so close to another human being.

'Jolly —' he began, but a sound interrupted him. He hastily turned round. They both looked at the far end of the room.

'I . . . I knocked,' stammered Munk. He was standing in the open doorway, looking pale as a ghost. 'But no one said anything . . . so I . . . I mean . . .'

He fell silent and stared at them: Jolly bare to the waist on the bed, Griffin very close to her with one hand on her back.

Then he turned abruptly, left the door open, and ran off.

'Munk, wait!' Jolly called after him.

Griffin heaved a deep sigh, took the cloth out of the water — it was cold by this time — and dabbed her back clean with it. She wriggled impatiently and rubbed her face with one hand, but then sank back on her stomach and stayed there.

Griffin looked at her in surprise. 'Aren't you going after him?'

Jolly rolled over on her back. 'Would that change anything?'

FOREFATHER

Forefather was sitting in his armchair explaining the world to Jolly. She was alone with him in the high-ceilinged bookroom.

No one knew where Munk was. She had knocked on his door that morning, but he hadn't opened it. And the door was locked. None of the servants had seen him. Forefather was as surprised as she was that Munk hadn't turned up for lessons.

Soledad had warned her. Jolly ought to have known it would turn out like this sooner or later. On the other hand she couldn't bring herself to deny her own feelings just to keep Munk happy. That in turn would only have made *her* angry with *him*. All things considered, she admitted to herself with a sigh, there was a lot of anger about.

'The world,' said Forefather in his sonorous, memorable voice, 'is not really *one* world but consists of many. Some say that all those different worlds lie side by side, and touch each other now and then. But I would say they are arranged one above another, like round discs. Think of a pile of plates. That's the universe.'

She had other things to think about than imagining worlds as crockery, but some of what he was saying came through to her.

'Then one plate would be our world,' she said, 'and the Mare Tenebrosum would be another. Do you think there are a great many more?'

'Countless numbers.'

'Yet our world is so big . . . and so hard to understand.' To him that might sound as if she were thinking of blank places on a map, unknown continents and distant lands. But she really meant something quite different.

'You may not be able to count all the stars in the sky, but that doesn't make them any fewer, does it? No one else is interested in what humans can understand and what they can't. Every world has to deal with its own struggles, each has its own difficulties.'

She didn't care about any of that just now. She had a world to save – and a friendship too. And didn't they depend on each other? How was she to explain *that* to anyone?

Forefather went on, without noticing the tears rising to her eyes. 'Most people imagine the past and future of our world as a line that begins somewhere and will end, some day, at a distant point somewhere else. Or not such a distant point, depending who you ask.' His smile was as mischievous as a child's, and a little sad at the same time. 'But in fact time moves in a circle where there is no beginning and no end. Time is only the rim of the plate and keeps coming back to itself. The world is made up of repetitions.'

'I don't understand.'

'Your struggle against the Maelstrom, for instance. Others have done the same before, thousands of years ago. The same adversary — a similar battle. And if you look back at history and tradition, there have always been individual people whose task it was to preserve the world from the worst of fates. Has any of them ever failed yet?'

'Maybe I'll be the first.' She ran her fingers nervously through her hair. 'That certainly makes me feel a lot better.'

He shook his head. 'Listen to me, Jolly. Everything repeats itself. *Everything.* We just don't necessarily notice. Time is a circle racing at mad speed around the plate, again and again.'

'So how does knowing that help me?'

'You say you're only an ordinary girl. But that's not so. Or at least, not any more.' He raised one hand. 'No, wait! Listen! The worlds will never intersect of their own accord. Some claim they do, even your one-eyed friend. But the truth is that there are no points of intersection. Only beings who live in those worlds can make the link.'

'So?' She was beginning to feel impatient. What was he getting at?

'Most people never cast a glance at other worlds. They don't understand the connections; they don't even try. They are sufficient to themselves and literally never look over the rim of the plate. But there are exceptions, those who do risk a glance, and sometimes much more. They are painters, poets, artists, shamans – they look over the edge and describe what they have seen to others. But not even they are able to cross over themselves. They can see events and images, they can say what they have seen, but they can't really visit those other worlds. That is reserved for only a very few. The chosen. People like you, Jolly.'

He made another gesture to stifle her protest. 'And that's what makes you unique whether you like it or not. You have the power to break away from time as it races by, to leap from the rim of one plate to the rim of the next. You and Munk – and the Maelstrom. For it too is a living creature, and it too has been chosen.'

'Are you saying that we polliwiggles and the Maelstrom are – are like each other?'

'As alike as siblings.'

Griffin's words surfaced from her memory. Munk was turning into a maelstrom himself, he'd said. She shuddered.

'And that's not all,' said Forefather. 'Even if it is difficult for you, you must try to understand these things. Every perception of those other worlds, every deliberate venture into them, has its dangers too. Sometimes they can mean downfall. Perhaps for Aelenium. But sometimes they help us to reach something higher. Jolly, you will become someone else, you already *have* become someone else, in order to fight the Maelstrom.'

She stood up. 'I don't know if I've understood any of that,' she said. 'But it frightens me.'

'It needn't. Just because it's a new idea and you may have to think it over for a while, it doesn't have to make you insecure.' He pointed to the door of the hall. 'Off you go now if you like. Go somewhere you can be alone. Think about what I've said. Lessons are over for today.'

She didn't protest, just nodded to him and left the library. Forefather's glance followed her until she had closed the door behind her.

'Jolly!'

She spun round and saw Soledad striding fast towards her over a coral platform on the western side of Aelenium. Not far from here the steep cone of the mountain came to the maze of buildings and streets at the centre of the starfish city.

Hundreds of gulls were circling around the towers, but their screaming was drowned out by the roar of waterfalls cascading down channels in the coral mountain.

In her explorations Jolly had discovered that this place was where the storytellers of Aelenium met. They sat cross-legged on rugs or furs, some on raised rostrums, and gathered small groups of listeners around them, mostly children, for the adults were busy with preparations for the defence of the city.

Jolly had wandered from one storyteller to another, picking up fragments of their stories here and there: fairy tales and fables, as well as incidents from the history of the city, the Caribbean and the beginnings of colonisation there.

'I was looking for you.' Soledad smiled. 'The old man said you were sure to be somewhere up here.'

Jolly hadn't exchanged a word with the princess for several days, or indeed with most of her friends from the *Carfax*. For the first time that made her feel guilty.

'I had things to think about,' she said.

'Oh.' Soledad put her head on one side and raised her eyebrows.

'Don't look like that!' Jolly forced herself to give Soledad a hesitant smile.

'Is it about Griffin and Munk?'

'You don't let go, do you?'

Soledad looked at her undecidedly, then shrugged her shoulders. 'That's your business. I'm not going to interfere. And it's not why I wanted a word with you.' She came closer to Jolly and took her hands. 'I want to say goodbye.'

'You're leaving?'

'Only for a few days, if all goes well.'

'What are you going to do?' Jolly had thought it would be she who had to say goodbye when the time came for her to set out. The thought of it had been haunting her for days.

Soledad let go of her hands. 'I want to finish what I began in New Providence. I'm going to avenge my father. Kendrick must pay at last for usurping the pirate throne – and pay with his blood.'

Jolly stared at the princess. She had known that sooner or later Soledad would set out in search of the pirate enperor again, but over the last few days she'd simply forgotten it. Or suppressed the thought. Like so much else, she reflected. Like her own feelings, and her search for Captain Bannon.

'Where do you expect to find Kendrick?' she asked.

'There's been a rumour going around for months of a great assembly of all the leading pirate captains of the Lesser Antilles,' said the princess. 'Kendrick is planning to meet them. The pirates of those parts have never accepted anyone as emperor. My father himself and his predecessors tried to gain control of them, but they form their own community, and only the decisions of its council have any authority among them.'

'But why a meeting with Kendrick, then?'

Soledad pushed back a strand of hair. 'It seems he's going to make them an offer they can't refuse. I've no idea what he's planning. My father got nowhere with them, they were so obstinate, and I doubt whether that devil will do any better.'

Jolly frowned. 'So do you know where the meeting place is?'

Soledad grinned. 'To be honest, it's probably easier to get into the Spanish viceroy's treasury than find that out. But I do have a plan.' She looked earnestly at Jolly. 'I won't get another opportunity like this in a hurry.' Jolly was about to say something when Soledad went on. 'Someone else is going to that meeting too. Tyrone.'

'Tyrone!'

'Astonishing, eh? It looks as if he's going to leave his lair in the Orinoco delta to come.'

'But Tyrone . . . he's not one of them any more. He broke with the others.'

This news was indeed sensational. Tyrone was a legend, a

pirate feared even by the other captains of the Caribbean. When he was cornered years ago by a Spanish armada, he fled to the mainland and went up the Orinoco River on a raft with what remained of his crew. Apparently all the pirates were killed and eaten by cannibals – with the exception of Tyrone, who had managed to convince the savages in some mysterious way that he was a messenger from their gods. Since then there had been persistent rumours that he had made himself ruler of the Orinoco tribes of Venezuela, recruited new crews, and was making plans to attack the islands of the Caribbean with a mighty fleet of pirates and cannibals.

Most people dismissed this story as an old wives' tale. Even Bannon had thought that Tyrone as well as his crew had probably died at the hands of the cannibals.

And now Tyrone was coming to the meeting of the Antilles captains? It was almost as incredible as if the Devil himself had announced that he would be there.

Jolly took a deep breath. What Soledad was planning was nothing less than to stir up a whole hornets' nest. 'We need you here,' she said, looking into Soledad's dark eyes.

'No, you don't,' the princess told her. 'You're the only one who matters. And Munk. The rest of us have no part to play. Compared to you two, even the Ghost-Trader is unimportant.'

'But . . .'

'He's coming with me. In fact it was he who came up with the idea of how to find the meeting place.'

Jolly stared at her. 'The Ghost-Trader? But . . . he can't just leave us in the lurch!'

'No one's leaving you in the lurch, Jolly. With a little luck we'll all of us be back here before you set out.'

'All of us? You mean . . .'

'Walker's coming too. And no, before you ask, Buenaventure and the *Carfax* stay here. Walker, the Trader and I will ride hippocamps.'

It was unusual for Buenaventure and Walker to part, even for just a few days. But at the moment Jolly didn't stop to think about that. 'Why is the Ghost-Trader going with you? It can't make any difference to him whether Kendrick is pirate emperor or not.'

Soledad agreed. 'It wouldn't, in any other situation. But if the captains will listen to me, perhaps I can show them what danger we're all in – they and their crews included. If they believe me, I'll be back with a whole fleet to support us in the war against the Maelstrom.'

Jolly made a face, and didn't even try to hide her bewilderment. 'You're going to let all the pirates of the Caribbean know about Aelenium? And where the city lies at anchor? What do you think will be the first thing they do then?'

'I know the risk. That's why it's so important to have the Ghost-Trader with us. He'll be able to judge whether we have a chance or the whole plan is madness.'

'But they'll come here with their ships, and then Aelenium will have to fight on *two* fronts. The pirates will plunder the city and leave its ruins for the Maelstrom.'

Soledad stroked Jolly's hair. It was the first time she had ever allowed herself a gesture of such intimacy. 'You're clever, Jolly. But don't underestimate me. I learned a lot from my father. I know how to talk to these fellows, and what you have to promise to get them eating out of your hand. Their own survival is at stake too – they just don't know it yet.'

'It's crazy all the same. What does Count Aristotle say? And the Council?'

'They realise it's a chance. Perhaps the last. You two will need time to reach the Rift. And even if you and Munk do succeed in sealing off the Maelstrom, it's still more than likely that Aelenium will be attacked first. In that case we'll need all the help we can get.'

Jolly realised that she wouldn't be able to dissuade the princess. Soledad's plan had been made some time ago, and no one had told her and Munk.

'When are you starting?'

'At once. That's why I was looking for you. I wanted you

to hear it from one of us, not the old man or one of those pompous idiots on the Council.'

'What about Munk?'

'You tell him.'

'And what about Griffin?' Jolly felt her heart suddenly beat faster.

Soledad heard her tone of voice, and grinned. 'Griffin?'

'Is he going with you too?'

'No, Griffin's staying here. Don't worry.'

The blood rose to Jolly's face. She felt as if she'd been caught doing something wrong.

'Look after yourself, Jolly.' Soledad drew her close and gave her a hug. 'Remember what I told you. You and Munk will have to rely on each other down there.'

'Munk's furious with me.'

'He'll calm down again. He's probably sitting around somewhere sulking. Men are like that, believe me.'

They looked one another in the eye. Jolly blinked away a tear before it could trickle down her cheek.

'We'll be back, whatever way it turns out,' said Soledad.

'Yes,' said Jolly faintly. 'I'm sure you will.' She took a deep breath, as if the burden on her shoulders suddenly weighed twice as heavy as before. 'I'm scared.'

'We're all scared.'

Jolly shook her head. 'Not of the Maelstrom or the kobalins. I'm scared of being down there alone with Munk. He . . . he's my friend, but . . . oh, I don't understand what's going on myself.'

'Don't you trust him any more?'

'I wish I knew!'

'And that's worse than anything, isn't it? Uncertainty.'

Jolly hugged her again. 'Oh, Soledad, I'd rather go down there with anyone else. With any of you.'

The princess held Jolly's head close to her shoulder, and said nothing.

THE TRUTH ABOUT SPIDERS

The Ghost-Trader's plan was both crazy and brilliant. At the heart of it was a story being told all over the Caribbean.

A few months ago one of the most powerful captains of the Antilles, a certain Santiago, had been marooned by his men on an uninhabited island. The crew had mutinied because they felt that their captain had cheated them over the division of loot (and anyone acquainted with Santiago knew that their feelings had certainly not deceived them). The men made for an island that was little more than an isolated sandbank and put their treacherous captain ashore there. At his own request they had given him no provisions but a large barrel of rum — and that too was entirely in line with Santiago's nature.

No one shed a tear for him when the story went the rounds

of the seaport taverns. As a heavy drinker, a tyrant and a confidence trickster, the captain did not have many friends among the leaders of the Caribbean pirates.

The whole thing would have been quickly forgotten had not the crew of another ship, whose course had taken them within sight of the island, rekindled the rumours soon afterwards. These men, standing at their rail, had clearly seen the gigantic barrel of rum on the beach – and two legs sticking out of it. Obviously Santiago, the victim of his own intoxication, had fallen into the barrel head first and drowned miserably in rum.

Since then, so the story went, the barrel with the body inside it had stood like an ominous memorial on the shore of the island. Even the most hardened pirates shuddered when the tale of Santiago's end was told in the taverns. To be sure, they laughed at his unquenchable thirst, but secretly the thought of that lonely barrel of rum with the pirate's boots sticking out of it gave many of them gooseflesh. Santiago was not the first pirate to fall victim to an insatiable thirst, but the manner of his death was unique. Soon there was talk of a curse that the captain had uttered while drunk, washing it down with his last mouthful of rum.

But no matter how many stories went the rounds, it was certain that Santiago had been one of those who knew about the secret meeting of the Antilles captains with Kendrick the pirate emperor. The Ghost-Trader's plan, then, was that he, Soledad and Walker would ride to the island on sea horses, conjure up Santiago's ghost, and get it to tell them where Kendrick and the pirates were to meet. For while the living might well fear the consequences of doing so and keep their mouths shut, Kendrick's threats couldn't hurt a dead man. The Ghost-Trader felt sure that his plan would succeed.

Then the three of them would continue their journey from Santiago's island to the captains' meeting place, for the spies d'Artois had sent out suspected that their encounter with Kendrick and Tyrone was to be soon. So haste was advisable, not only for fear of the Maelstrom's attack, but also because the meeting might otherwise be over before the companions arrived there.

Soledad told Jolly all this while they were walking along the streets of Aelenium together, under the shade of the awnings stretched from building to building. It took them almost half an hour to reach the hippocamp stables down by the waterside. Walker and the Ghost-Trader were already waiting for them there.

The sea-horse stables were in a large coral complex on the shore of one of the starfish points. Grooms were hurrying about, many of them in groups of two or three, dragging large baskets full to the brim with tiny, freshly caught fish. Others were rolling along waist-high tangles of dried seaweed and twining plants formed into balls; they had been harvested from plantations on the walls of the underwater city and the links of the anchor chain. Both were needed as fodder for the sea horses, for despite the animals' stamina they were susceptible to deficiencies in their diet, and as Jolly had learned from d'Artois they were apt to catch chills in cooler waters. That was one of the reasons why the sea horses never moved beyond the Caribbean Sea.

The interior of the stables had a central footbridge several hundred feet long, with water flowing into basins in the floor on both sides of it. The hippocamps were splashing about in these basins, often under water but sometimes side by side above the surface. Their large, circular eyes curiously observed the men and women busy cleaning the basins, laying new channels to pipe water in, or scrubbing down and feeding their charges. The place smelled of seaweed, salt water, and the grooms' wet clothing. Only the smell of fish that you might have expected in such a place was almost entirely absent, for hippocamps have an earthy aroma, a little like shoreline silt and damp stone.

Walker and the Ghost-Trader were waiting for Jolly and

the princess beside one of the basins. Three saddled hippo-camps were rocking peacefully in the water. Grooms were holding the reins, patting the creatures' horny skins and whispering soothingly to them.

Walker grinned at Jolly, while the Trader nodded thoughtfully and just murmured, 'Hm, hm.' Perhaps he had feared that Jolly would disapprove of her friends' journey and refuse to come to the stables with Soledad. His two parrots were nowhere to be seen; they were staying in Aelenium as observers so that if the city were attacked they could fly swiftly across the sea and warn their master.

Walker took Jolly in his arms, and she was surprised for a moment by the strength of his hug. 'Don't let those idiots get you down, little one! Remember, in better times you and I would be robbing this whole place, driving those folk with their mincing ways into the sea and sinking the city.'

Jolly made her fiercest, most piratical face and nodded.

'And another thing,' said Walker before he let her go, 'if one of them turns his nose up at you, just break it for him. Punch it right in the middle! Understood?'

'Understood!'

Soledad too hugged her again. 'We've come far together, all the way from Kendrick's lair on New Providence to here, right?'

Jolly grinned. 'Right.'

The princess tapped her gently on the shoulder. 'Ah, who'd have thought it?' She took a deep breath, and for a moment looked as if she were going to add something, but then shook her head and stepped back to let the Ghost-Trader come forward.

'Take care of yourself,' he said, crouching down in front of Jolly so that his one eye was level with her face. 'You're a brave girl. And no matter what Munk can do with the shells – he needs someone like you to go on the journey with him.'

'And I'll need *him* down there in the Rift.'

'If all goes well we'll be back before you set out,' he said. 'If not . . . well, the two of you are the only ones who can do it.'

He patted her on the shoulder and stepped back without embracing her. The three of them mounted their sea horses, waved once more, and then guided the creatures towards an opening in the coral wall. No one else had come to see them off. Jolly suspected that the official goodbye had already been said, maybe in the count's Council Chamber or in some other hall of the great coral palace. But why hadn't Buenaventure turned up? And Griffin?

She pulled herself together and went along the central footbridge to the way out of the stables. Under the arched gateway she stopped, shaded her eyes with one hand, and looked out over the water. She saw the three riders on their hippocamps growing smaller and smaller in the distance before they disappeared into the surging wall of mist. A last streak showed where they had entered the vapours, but only briefly, and then it all merged into monotonous grey again.

Jolly stood there for a long time, ignoring the grumbling of the grooms, though she was in their way. Grief filled her, as if she had seen her friends for the last time. The whispering of the waves sounded like an invitation to run out over the sea after them, away from Aelenium and the people who lived here, away from the Maelstrom and the Mare Tenebrosum, away from a responsibility she didn't want.

What would Griffin think of her if she simply stole away? Would he take her for a coward? Perhaps.

But suppose she had a good reason, one that weighed more heavily than her fear? Suppose she remembered her real aim, as Soledad had remembered hers?

Would he understand her?

Yes, she thought, Griffin does understand me. I'm sure he does.

Suddenly she had an idea, and she was surprised that it hadn't occurred to her much earlier. She cast a last glance at the wall of mist, then quickly ran up flights of steps and along alleys to the palace. Eagerly, she rushed into her room and searched her possessions for the little box containing the dead spider, the sole proof that she hadn't imagined the attack of the venomous spiders on the *Maid Maddy*. Not that she distrusted her own memory. Yet it was a good feeling to have evidence of that disaster in her hand – even if the evidence had eight legs and ugly bristles.

Taking the box and the spider, she hurried on to the Great Library, not Forefather's bookroom but the main building. And there she began her search.

The spider had a Latin name that Jolly had to take apart into separate syllables in order to read it. When she said it out loud to herself it still sounded as if she were spelling it instead of saying a whole word.

It had been late in the afternoon before she finally reached this part of the library. Armed with a ladder and a telescope, she searched hall after hall from the lower stacks of books up to the highest. Only when she was almost on the point of giving up did she step by chance through a narrow doorway, and behind it she found the section for books on Living Jungle Creatures and Diseases of the Gut in Tropical Climates – obviously not a subject that the wise of Aelenium bothered about much.

After her long search, it was almost like the finger of Destiny pointing when she found the book with the information she was after lying on the very top of a pile, right beside the dusty reader's lectern. It had been written about thirty years ago by a monk who – so Jolly gathered from a small note in the appendix – had lost his life in a shipwreck not long after finishing it.

On page 427 she found the first clue that just might give her information about Bannon's fate. She compared the striking markings of the dead spider in the open box with the illustration in the folio volume.

According to the book, the species of spider to which the dead creature in her little box belonged came from a region on the coast of South America. Not just any coast, not just any region – but the very place that Jolly had already heard about today when she was talking to Soledad.

The Orinoco delta.

The part of the jungle to which the legendary Captain Tyrone had fled, and where he apparently still ruled over cannibals and pirates today, a terrible despot.

Coincidence? Possible but extremely improbable.

The spiders that had been hidden in the reefed sails of the Spanish galleon waiting for the pirates of the *Maid Maddy* as they boarded her, the spiders that Jolly had escaped only by the skin of her teeth, while all the rest of the crew fell victim to them – they came from Captain Tyrone's cannibal kingdom.

In her alarm Jolly took a deep breath, inhaled a large amount of dust and coughed for half a minute before she calmed down again. Then, once more, she compared the light brown pattern of the dead spider with the illustration. There was no doubt of it. She went through the text again, but there was nothing in it to suggest that this species of spider was found anywhere else.

It all fitted. The ambush, the spiders, Tyrone's sudden readiness to make common cause with the pirates again after so long.

But why all this? Why would a man like Tyrone set such a trap for Bannon? What was his interest in the crew, the ship – or Jolly?

Supposing Tyrone had actually had his eye on the polliwiggle on board Bannon's ship – did that mean there was some link between him and the Maelstrom? Or was there something she had overlooked?

At least one thing was certain: now she had a clue. For the first time since the terrible attack of the venomous spiders, Jolly felt genuine hope. If Tyrone had set the trap for them, there really was a chance that he had given Bannon and his men the antidote in time. Always assuming he had an interest in getting his hands on Bannon alive.

Jolly closed the book. A cloud of dust rose, veiling everything. When it settled again, the room in the library was as quiet and deserted as it had been for all those years before.

By night the sea around Aelenium was as black as a bottomless abyss. The ring of mist swallowed up much of the starlight, so Captain d'Artois had given orders to kindle huge fires on rafts. They were to light up the night and warn the defenders of any kobalin attacks. The blazing platforms drifted over the dark water, but the circles of light they cast were nowhere near large enough to illuminate the entire surface. It was like trying to overcome darkness with a handful of glow-worms.

Jolly took cover behind a stack of timber. The repair work on the *Carfax* was finished, but remains of the material and tools still lay close to the place where she was tied up. The sloop was lying by the shores of the starfish point beside a dozen fishing boats, towering above their low masts.

While she studied the moorings intently from her hiding place, it struck Jolly for the first time that the ship had something majestic about her, and she felt guilty about her plan: Walker had inherited the sloop from his mother, a much-feared woman freebooter whose urn he kept like a relic in the captain's cabin. It was wrong to steal the ship. But after all, Jolly was a pirate. Walker would understand. At least for a second – before he smashed her skull in.

Jolly knew there were soldiers everywhere in the dark. Later in the afternoon, d'Artois' men had come upon a troop of kobalins in the mist, keeping watch on the city from the shelter of its vapours. They now knew that the Maelstrom's warriors were inexorably coming closer. The guards posted on the shores of the city and in the lookout towers were doubled.

Jolly's plan was madness, and she knew it. It was impossible for anyone to leave Aelenium unnoticed. She could only hope that no one would suspect she was on board the *Carfax*. Then she might have a day or two's start before anyone came to the right conclusions. Even so, the sea horses were still fast enough to catch up with her. But perhaps they'd realise that Jolly wasn't right for what they wanted her to do. After all, Munk was still there. He was the bolder of the two polliwiggles, and the more powerful magician; he could have been just made to fight the Maelstrom.

She felt a sharp pang at this idea, and couldn't help remembering what the Ghost-Trader had told her when he said goodbye. However she tried to get around it, the fact was that she was leaving Munk in the lurch. He would have to go down to the depths and make his way to the Rift alone.

Stop that! Don't make it harder for yourself than it is already!

She tried to take calm, regular breaths. When she had herself fairly well under control she looked round one last time, then scurried over the open space by the harbour to the moorings, bending low. The gangplank of the *Carfax* vibrated as she went aboard. Her steps on the wood sounded hollow.

Once past the rail she ducked down into cover again and looked back. Not a human soul in sight. If there were any soldiers nearby they would probably just be looking at the water, not at the moorings. None of them would expect anyone to steal a ship.

Only the cone of the mountain with its hundreds and hundreds of pinnacles, towers and bridges seemed to be leaning over her if she looked up at it long enough. Then she felt as if it were slowly and endlessly tilting over, and she had to fight an urge to turn and run. Even in the dark she couldn't entirely shake off that feeling. Or perhaps it was just her anxiety in case someone was looking down at her from up there.

She bent low again and crossed the deck. It smelled of fresh wood shavings, tar and carpenter's glue. The craftsmen of Aelenium and the ghostly crew of the *Carfax* had done a good job, so far as she could see in the dark. Although Jolly hadn't met ghosts anywhere else in the city, mingling with those misty beings seemed to be nothing new to the people of Aelenium.

Jolly had tried giving orders to the faceless ghosts earlier, but she had failed. After her lessons with Forefather, however, she knew what she had to concentrate on in order to control them, and she had shown it only two days ago in a contest with Munk.

Now she went up to the bridge, undid the ropes securing the helm, took hold of the wheel and concentrated. Her lips formed silent words known only to herself, words that held no meaning for anyone else. Magic, she now knew, was a very personal matter. There was no established magic art that everyone could use; there were no firmly fixed spells and incantations. Magic books and scrolls? All nonsense. You shaped your own spells for working magic. The words and syllables came from deep inside you. Even shell magic worked on a similar principle, except that it was far more powerful and its effects were much more dangerous.

Jolly's call to the ghosts passed over the planks of the *Carfax* like a gust of wind, clung softly around the masts, crept up the cables and shrouds. Like an invisible force, it danced over the yards and brought the lost souls of all who had died aboard this ship under Jolly's command.

It was only a few moments before their misty outlines and silhouettes rose from the wood of the vessel, fraying at the edges and with blurred faces that made it impossible to tell them apart. Soon they had gathered everywhere on the main deck and the bridge, surrounding Jolly and the ship's wheel. A ghost was even wavering as unsteadily as a wisp of vapour up in the crow's-nest of the new topmast.

Jolly's gaze moved once more over the deserted pier of Aelenium, and then she gave her orders. She had never steered a ship all by herself before, let alone commanded a whole crew. But she couldn't afford any doubts now. Bannon had taught her everything he knew about seamanship. All she lacked was experience.

The ghosts manned all the important positions on deck and in the rigging. Nothing could be heard but the rattle of the sails unfurling, the creaking of the taut cables and the winch of the anchor chain. In a few minutes the *Carfax* would be ready to put out to sea.

'Haven't you forgotten someone?'

Jolly spun round. Behind her, in the shadow of the rail, a lean figure was sitting cross-legged. A circle of small, bright dots shimmered on the dark wood of the deck.

'Munk!'

He sighed slightly. 'Yes, only me. A pity, eh?'

'What do you mean by that?'

He looked up at her. 'You'd rather it had been someone else.'

Her eyes flashed. 'Stop that nonsense. This is not the time for –'

'Why aren't you taking Griffin with you? Now that the two of you are getting along so well together.'

'This is my business. Not Griffin's. Not yours either.'

'Hm,' he said, putting his head on one side as if he had to think that over. 'I think you've overlooked something.'

She wondered whether she should just tell the ghosts to throw him overboard. She had no time or patience for an argument of this kind now. Certainly not with someone who was acting like an injured little boy.

'The Rift,' he said, unerringly finding her vulnerable point. 'So you want me to finish the job by myself.'

'I have to find Bannon. That's what I was going to do from the first, and you know it.'

'What about Aelenium? The people here and all over the Caribbean? Me and – oh, what the hell, and Griffin too, for all I care? Don't you mind about any of us?'

'I have to do what I have to do.'

'Good heavens, Jolly, can't you think of anything more original to say?' He got to his feet, walked carefully around the circle of shells on deck, and stopped very close to her.

'Admit it. You're scared silly. Bannon's just an excuse to run for it.'

'I'm not a coward.'

'Oh no? And how do you think what you're doing at this moment looks?'

She put her finger to his chest as if it were the barrel of a pistol. 'You're jealous, that's all it is! I'm scared, you're right about that, but so are you. And I'm not leaving Aelenium because I'm afraid.'

'You want to find Bannon – that *pirate*,' he said scornfully. 'How noble!'

She stared at him, and couldn't guess what his thoughts were. 'It's not so long ago you wanted to be a pirate yourself.'

'That was earlier. And I was different then.'

Jolly looked at him. Yes, he was right. He had been different. 'And do you like yourself the way you are now?' she asked softly.

His eyes narrowed to slits, and suddenly she was glad she couldn't see every shade of expression on his face in the dark. His voice sounded cold, and was shot through with seething anger. 'It's not about that, Jolly. It's destiny. *Our* destiny.'

Jolly had gooseflesh. A few days ago she had still thought the change in him was because of his parents' death. But she had been wrong. It was this city and the expectations of its people that had changed him. *Saviour*, the cold thought came to her. *Destiny*.

'Do what you want,' she said. 'Save the world if you think you can. And I wish you luck.'

He seized her wrist. 'We have to do this *together*. Just the two of us.'

'I'm not the heroine all these people think I am.' She tried to release her hand, but his grip was too tight. Jolly lowered her voice to a whisper. 'Let – me – go!'

She was afraid that he wouldn't give in. That he would actually make her stay in Aelenium by force. She prepared to hit him in the face as hard as she could.

But then his fingers relaxed, and she could move her arm freely again.

'Don't you ever do that again,' she breathed.

'I don't want to quarrel with you, Jolly.'

'You just did.'

'Come back to land. Please.' But the way he said it sounded like an order.

'No. *You* get off this ship. At once.'

Munk's hand reached round as if to bring something out from behind his back. But he was spreading his fingers towards the circle of shells behind him. A light immediately flashed.

He doesn't even have to look to make the pearl! thought Jolly. He's so much stronger than I am.

Not a muscle in Munk's face moved.

The glowing pearl rose slowly from the circle, hovering higher and higher in the air.

Had he just been playing with her all these days? Letting her think she had a chance of defeating him in their ridiculous contest? So that she would at least *try* to impress him?

'Stop that,' she said, forcing herself to keep calm.

The pearl was almost level with her eyes now.

'Munk, stop it!'

The glow grew even brighter, slowly pulsating. Now the pearl was bathing the whole deck of the *Carfax* in light. It was so bright that most of what was being done aboard could be seen. The first guards in Aelenium would probably have spotted it.

Jolly closed her eyes. In her mind she reached out invisible hands to the hovering pearl, trying to take hold of it, pluck it out of the air and . . .

'Ouch! For heaven's sake!'

Her eyes flew open as her real hands suddenly felt each other. It was as if they had come too close to an open fire.

'That hurts, Munk!' Once again she controlled herself. 'Is that what you want to do? Hurt me?'

'I want you to see reason.'

'*Your* kind of reason.'

Silently, he shook his head. The pearl rose higher and higher. Now it was hanging above them like a full moon.

Jolly made a sign to one of the ghosts. The misty phantom shot forward, making not for Munk but for the circle of shells behind him. The being's foot gained mass. Then the shells broke under its sole.

There was a shrill whistling sound, and the pearl changed colour to blood-red. Munk's eyes widened in alarm as he suddenly lost control of the magic. The pearl went into a spin, caught itself up again, darted sideways and then raced at Munk from behind like a shot being fired. He cried out with pain and was flung against Jolly, who tried to catch him. But the force of the impact threw them both backwards. Jolly gasped as she was jammed between Munk and the ship's wheel for a moment. The wood pressed painfully into her spine.

Munk slid down to the deck and landed on his knees. The light of the pearl had faded without doing any more damage. But such anger showed now on his face that Jolly flinched back in alarm, and came up against the wheel again.

'My shells,' he whispered, looking up at her. His eyes were deep, dark lakes, like shadowy holes in his face.

153

'You *would* have it that way,' she replied. 'Now get off this ship!'

He sprang up faster than she would have thought possible, and the flat of his hand shot forward and struck her breastbone hard. He was pressing her against the helm with all his might.

'If Griffin hadn't turned up,' he gasped, 'then everything would have been the same as before. You'd never have attacked me . . . this is all his fault.'

'*You* attacked *me*.'

'Just because he's the same as you . . . that's why you like him better than me.'

'This is silly, Munk.'

'I thought so from the start. Even when we first saw him on New Providence.'

'That's enough, Munk. Stop it. Now.'

She gave the ghosts her orders with her eyes alone. Half a dozen of them began to move.

Several phantom hands seized Munk. Although he hit out, cursing, the ghosts carried him off the ship and over the landing-stage, back to the pier.

'Jolly! Don't go!'

She shook her head, and watched as they threw him to the ground. The impact hurt her almost as much as him, but he had left her no choice. Why had he changed so much?

'Don't go!' he shouted again.

The anchor thudded against the hull of the ship as it was raised from the water. Cables were lashed down. The *Carfax* was shaking like an animal suddenly woken from sleep.

The ghosts held Munk down until all was ready. Then they drifted mistily over the landing-stage and back on board, bringing in the gangplank behind them.

Munk struggled to his feet, but he didn't try to follow the misty figures. His gaze was fixed on Jolly. She bent down, put the remaining shells in the leather bag lying on deck beside the broken circle, and threw it over the rail. Munk caught the bag safely, almost without looking.

High above on the masts, something was fluttering. Two dark shapes settled on the yards on both sides of the topmast. Red and yellow eyes looked down at the deck.

Jolly sensed the presence of the parrots rather than actually seeing them. She put her hands on the helm, and then the *Carfax* moved away from the starfish point, gliding out to sea.

'Let her go!'

The old man's voice came from behind the crates stacked on the pier.

'Forefather?' Munk turned, but could see no one.

'She's made her decision.'

'The wrong one.'

'She'll have to find that out for herself.'

'But we need her here!' Munk gave up trying to make out the old man's bent figure in the darkness. He looked back at the *Carfax*. She had now left the tangle of fishing boats behind, and was gliding out over the open water towards the black wall of mist, showing no lights at all.

'The guards won't stop her,' said Forefather. 'I took care of that.'

'But she . . . she doesn't know what she's doing,' stammered Munk desperately.

'Oh yes, she knows very well. She just can't foresee the consequences.'

Munk had to force himself to look away from the ship. He took a step towards the shadows, half expecting to find no one there. But Forefather really was standing among the crates. In the dark he looked even smaller and more frail than usual.

'I can't go to the Rift alone,' said Munk.

Forefather's face remained expressionless. 'You turned the magic against her. But even worse, you forced her to oppose you. She didn't want to. But you left her no other way out.'

'But just to . . . to . . .' Munk fell silent, and looked down.

'This has its advantages too,' said Forefather.

Munk snorted with derision. 'Oh yes?'

'She's not ready yet. Unlike you, Munk. There is one lesson that neither I nor anyone else can teach her. A lesson that you have already learned, and it gives you your strength.'

Forefather raised his staff, and gently tapped the ground at Munk's feet with it. 'Let her go and gather her own experiences.'

Munk could hardly breathe, he had such a large lump in his throat. 'What lesson do you mean?'

'The lesson of loss,' said Forefather reflectively. 'The experience of losing something that she loves more than herself.'

SWALLOWED ALIVE

'She's gone.'

Griffin gave a start and turned as he heard d'Artois speak behind him. He had been leaning against the parapet of the watch-tower, polishing the sword he had been given along with his new soldier's uniform. He didn't feel at ease in such clothing, but if he wanted to make himself useful and learn about sea horses and flying rays the uniform was necessary. The leather was soft, but it still pinched him under the armpits. And no one could tell him what the idea of the coral studs on it were.

'She's *what*?' He put the sword down, clinking, on the parapet of the tower. The surface of the sea shimmered a good three hundred feet below.

'Jolly's gone.' D'Artois was watching him closely.

Griffin felt dizzy. 'She can't have.'

'I'm afraid she has.'

Griffin spun round and stared into the depths, down past

the furrowed slopes of the starfish city and out over the water. From up here it looked like a pitch-black surface sparsely sprinkled with occasional fire-rafts. D'Artois had already ordered their numbers to be tripled over the next few nights.

'She took the *Carfax*,' said the captain.

Griffin still didn't understand. 'Why so soon? I mean, her training is still –'

'She isn't on her way to the Rift.'

'Where, then?'

'I don't know. I was going to stop her, but Forefather gave orders to let her go.' D'Artois came up to the parapet of the tower and stood beside Griffin. 'I very much hope he knows what he's doing.'

Griffin was struggling with his impatience. Everything in him was screaming to him simply to turn his back on the captain and run down to Jolly's room, hoping to find that it was all just a misunderstanding. But he kept his self-control.

'Someone must know what she's planning to do.'

'I thought you might be able to tell me.'

Griffin shook his head. 'She didn't say anything to me.'

The captain placed a hand on his shoulder, and half-turned Griffin to him. 'Is that true?'

'I swear it.' Griffin shifted restlessly from foot to foot. Jolly was leaving the city, and here he stood talking.

D'Artois sighed, and he too looked out into the darkness now. From up here the fire-rafts didn't look much bigger than the few stars showing in the sky.

'Have you any idea how difficult it was for me to obey Forefather?' D'Artois asked his question without expecting an answer. 'Particularly as he has no power of command. But I respect him and his decisions. He is . . .'

'Wise?' suggested Griffin.

'More than that. He's the soul of Aelenium. There's no one here who's more important to the city and its mission.'

Griffin pricked up his ears. 'He didn't seem specially . . . well, important at the Council meeting. No one paid him very much attention.'

D'Artois smiled, but he did not offer any explanation. Instead, he leaned over the parapet and stared down into the darkness.

'You know, people have been telling us for years that the polliwiggles would save Aelenium if the Maelstrom ever attacked. When the situation was serious we were all expecting them to turn up at last. There were even some people who prayed to them – can you imagine that? And then they appear out of nowhere, those two children – no offence meant, Griffin – and we're supposed to see them as our saviours. That's hard enough, I must say. Then, when we've finally accepted it and we're telling ourselves: right, they're the ones, they'll save us – one of them suddenly runs away. Just like that.' D'Artois drew his brows closer together, and his eyes darkened. 'And I could have stopped her. But now I have to let her go – and perhaps seal the fate of this city.'

'There's still Munk,' said Griffin, while an icy hand reached for his heart. 'Or did he go with her?'

'No,' said d'Artois, and Griffin could have hugged him for that. 'Munk is in the city. Forefather is taking care of him.'

'Perhaps it will be enough if Munk goes to the Rift alone. He's the more powerful of the two of them. Jolly's said so herself more than once.'

'Maybe.' The captain's hands closed on the edge of the parapet as if to break a piece out of it. 'But my intuition tells me we need *both* of them down there. Munk may have more power – whatever that means. I don't know much about magic and such matters. But I see things in his eyes that I . . . oh, I don't know . . . that I can't get my head around. Vanity and arrogance and, yes, power too of course, in a way. Whereas there's much more in your friend Jolly's eyes: humanity and warmth, and enough courage to win this whole damnable war. I said she was a child just now, but that's not right. She may look like a child, but inside . . . there's much more in her. Qualities I don't see in Munk.' He sighed again.

161

'And so, Griffin, it's all one to me what anyone else thinks of his abilities. Just lazy magic, I say. What matters is what's in here.' He indicated his heart. 'That's the power we need, and Jolly has a hundred times more of it than he does.'

'I know what you mean.' Griffin was missing her more with every word the captain spoke. The idea that she had gone almost choked him. Why hadn't she taken him too? Why hadn't she even said goodbye?

'*I* can't fetch her back,' said the captain, and this time there was an odd emphasis in his words. 'I've promised to obey Forefather, and I will. Someone else might be able to go after her, someone perhaps ready to defy my orders . . . but I can't do it myself.'

Their eyes met again. Griffin's heart was racing.

'Suppose I take over your watch up here?' asked the captain.

'You want me to . . . you mean . . .'

Another exchange of glances, and then d'Artois turned back to the nocturnal view before them. 'I need peace and quiet to think. This is a good place for it. I often come up here, especially at night. You can go to bed if you like.'

Griffin snatched up his sword, pushed it into his belt, and ran for the steps. A thousand thoughts were passing through his mind at the same time. *Go to bed* . . . he understood only too clearly what d'Artois meant.

At the top of the stairway he stopped once, stammered out an indistinct, 'Yes, sir!' and then leaped down the stairs. He had a feeling that d'Artois was watching him go out of the corner of his eye. And smiling.

The stairway seemed to have grown longer of its own accord. There'd never been so many steps over the last few days. Griffin took three at a time, and finally even four.

Down at the bottom he ran along the deserted streets, going downhill. There were no candles burning behind most of the windows. It was nearly midnight, and people had gone to bed. For most of them, tomorrow would be full once again of the thousands of things to be done when a siege threatened: filling sandbags and stacking them at the most vital defensive positions, putting up barriers, supplying the buildings and the escape chambers deep below the city with emergency rations, sharpening blades, cleaning rifle and pistol barrels.

Griffin looked neither right nor left. His thoughts were all bent on Jolly, her smile, the way her skin had felt when he was tattooing it, her voice, the sparkle in her eyes when she was teasing him. And what lay ahead of her: her journey into the dark beside Munk.

It was this last thought that made him hesitate at the entrance to the stables. He stopped, tried to get his breath back, and leaned one hand against the gatepost. Did he *want* to bring Jolly back to Aelenium? Did he really want her going down to the Rift on a mission that might cost her her life?

It was possible that she had done the right thing in turning her back on the city. It meant she'd soon be out of danger. And that was what mattered. What mattered to *him*.

But then a certainty came into his mind and instantly sobered him up. Jolly was not a coward. She didn't run away, not even from the Maelstrom and the Rift. If she had left Aelenium, there was something else behind it. Something that had nothing to do with fear, and was certainly no less dangerous.

He entered the stables and ran along the central footbridge. Although it was late at night, several grooms were at work; some of them always had to be on duty because of the patrols. They watched Griffin in surprise when he raced past them as if demons were after him, on the way to the basin where his own sea horse was sleeping with its eyes open.

He was clumsily trying to saddle it when one of the more experienced grooms came to his aid. The man asked no questions – that wasn't his place – but the frown on his brow showed that the boy's departure so late at night made him suspicious.

A few minutes later Griffin was on his way. He rode his sea horse under one of the arched gateways leading out to the sea and then swept over the dark water on its back, past the blazing fire-rafts rocking on the waves like floating pyres.

The night was warm, like most nights in the Caribbean at this time of year, but the sultry heat of the day had died down. Griffin noticed how much more easily he could breathe at this time of day. In spite of his task, in spite of his concern for Jolly, he felt a sense of boundless freedom. This was the first time he had gone riding a sea horse all by himself, and the power of the strange creature beneath him seemed to communicate itself to him. He felt newborn.

Before he reached the mist and all went dark around him, he looked back over his shoulder at the city, searching for the tower where he had been standing with d'Artois a little while ago. But he couldn't locate it quickly enough. The first wisps of mist were already blurring his view, and then it was suddenly so dark that, for a moment, panic overcame him.

The mist surrounded him not with vapour and melancholy grey, but with complete blackness. No light from the city penetrated it; even the glow of the nearby fire-rafts died away behind him like the wicks of candles burning down. The deep black gave him a foretaste of what Jolly would have to face if he brought her back to Aelenium. She might be able to see down there with her polliwiggle eyes, but that didn't mean she would not be in the most complete darkness to be found anywhere in the world.

With the deep black, fear seeped through his clothes and surrounded his body like icy armour. It wasn't a day since the soldiers had come upon the troop of kobalins in the mist. Now, in this darkness, there might be dozens of them moving around, hundreds even, unseen by anyone. No doubt they could sense the sea horse at close quarters; perhaps they were watching its mighty tail-fin from the depths below with their small, malicious kobalin eyes.

'Faster, Matador, faster!' he urged the animal on. One of the sea-horse breeders of Aelenium had given it that name. Griffin suspected that the man had Spanish forebears, and indeed most of the people of the city seemed to have had ancestors in the Old World. That was one of the many paradoxes of this place: if Aelenium had really existed for hundreds or even thousands of years, why did those who guarded it come originally from Europe and not the surrounding islands?

The mist went on and on. Griffin blindly clung to Matador's reins, and his thighs were firmly clamped to the saddle as if his life depended on it. If need be the straps that hippocamp riders must wear would hold him in place, but it was difficult for him to feel confidence in *anything* just now.

He even distrusted his own senses. Didn't he hear soft chattering in the mist, high, piping sounds? Hadn't the roaring and breaking of the waves around him grown louder and more violent? And wasn't there something huge and shapeless ahead of him in the darkness?

That last impression at least must be deceptive: he could see nothing, not even his hand in front of his eyes, let alone gigantic bodies in the distance. The darkness had surely been playing a trick on him.

Only now did he realise what confidence d'Artois was showing in him, sending him alone on such a mission when the enemy was on the way. At the same time, however, Griffin had doubts. Had the captain really *sent* him? He hadn't given an order, and it could yet all turn out to be a terrible, disastrous misunderstanding. Perhaps he really *had* just wanted to take over Griffin's watch so that he could think in peace. He might believe Griffin had gone to bed long ago, as he had advised.

The sea horse let out a whistling sound, the alarm signal given by the creatures when they picked up an unknown scent.

Griffin patted the animal's neck with shaking fingers. 'What is it —'

He never finished his question. Something rammed the sea horse from below, lifted it out of the water with monstrous strength and flung it off course. The animal's squeals grew louder and then stopped for a moment as it fell sideways into the waves. The straps cut into Griffin's flesh. A terrible jolt shook his neck and went down his backbone. Salt water streamed into his open mouth, and his hoarse scream died away unheard in the rough sea.

The sea horse righted itself so quickly that Griffin hardly noticed the movement. Driving its fins through the water in panic, it flew over the waves, while Griffin desperately tried to get his bearings in the darkness. At least his head wasn't below the surface any more. He could breathe freely and had swallowed hardly any water. The sea horse had taken over and was carrying him forward as fast as it could go. He had no idea whether it was racing out into the open sea or back to Aelenium and the safety of its stable. Griffin hardly minded one way or the other. The main thing was to get out of here. Out of the mist, to a place where there was light and he could see what had attacked them.

Something had rammed the sea horse from underneath. Something massive enough to toss the twelve-foot-long animal into the air like a toy.

Griffin closed his eyes. It made no difference in the darkness, but it at least gave him the feeling that he could get his turbulent thoughts back into better order again. The sea horse was finding its own way in any case.

When he opened his eyes again they had almost left the mist behind. A few final swirls of vapour reached out after him, and the stars were still invisible. But then he saw the open sea ahead, a network of the glittering crests of waves and faint reflections. Matador had not chosen to return but had swum on, to the far side of the wall of mist.

The sea horse and its rider came out of the last swathes of mist and plunged into the glittering splendour of the Caribbean firmament. They were riding over waves on which the stars and the crescent moon shone down, and into a cool breeze that blew away Griffin's fears.

Not that he supposed the danger was over, not for a moment. Whatever had attacked them could have followed them. It might still be lurking somewhere, hidden beneath the waves. But the familiar sight of the night sky and the great expanse of the sea calmed him enough to think clearly again. It was almost like being on board a ship, on one of those quiet night watches he had always enjoyed so much.

His glance swept over the ocean and along the dark horizon. For Jolly and *Carfax* there could be only one direction: south-west, the course that would take them back to the islands or the mainland.

Matador knew the way. The sea horses were trained to pick

up the scent of large landmasses even over hundreds of miles. That was one of the countless marvels of Aelenium, its people, even its animals. The magic concentrated in the polliwiggles touched everything there, just as if the veins of magic that Count Aristotle had spoken of ran through the floating city.

Griffin's eyes had to get used to the new lighting conditions. Then he saw the shape of sails in the distance, many miles away: grey rectangles carrying the *Carfax* landward on a strong favourable breeze.

With a loud shout, he urged the sea horse on, turning it to follow the ship's course. Matador was much faster than the sloop, and with a little luck they would catch up with her in less than half an hour.

Spray flew into Griffin's face as the sea horse raced on through the waves. His heart was beating fast. He kept looking back over his shoulder. The mist could hardly be seen now. Only a dark streak lay behind him, extinguishing the glittering surface of the water and the starry sky as if someone had taken a cloth and wiped away part of the horizon. The black rampart was several miles wide, shrouding the towers of Aelenium and the cone of the coral mountain.

Griffin didn't get far.

Ahead of him the sea rose up like a mountain, at first only

slightly, like the gentle slope of a hill, then becoming steeper and steeper. Floods of water cascaded down the sides of this rising shape.

Griffin tried to turn the sea horse aside, but once again it reacted faster. Matador darted to one side to avoid the gigantic creature now coming up through the surface ahead of them. But it was too late. The waves caught sea horse and rider alike, and this time the saddle straps didn't hold. Great masses of water washed over Griffin, a wall of salty foam. Then invisible hands forced him down beneath the surface. Suddenly he was alone, parted from the sea horse that could have carried him to safety.

Jolly! The thought of her went through him in the darkness, and he realised that he was going to die. If he didn't drown he would be swallowed up by this thing, this living mountain of darkness.

The same forces that had just held him down below the water now seemed to be hauling him up again. His face broke through the surface of the sea. He gasped for air but took in more water, and in spite of the clear night air he was now near choking. His wet uniform dragged him down, but he kicked out so violently that he managed to stay on the surface. Coughing, he opened his eyes and could see no horizon now, no sky, only something black again, but this time as massive as an island unexpectedly emerging ahead of him.

However, it wasn't an island. And the gigantic outline blotting out the stars certainly promised no safety.

Another current caught him, a mighty undertow carrying him forward along with great masses of water, as if a hole had opened up to swallow him and the whole Caribbean Sea.

The Maelstrom, he thought.

But no, it wasn't the Maelstrom.

It was a gaping throat as big as a church porch, a stinking, glittering inferno of flesh and heat and rows of bright teeth. Griffin felt their sharp tips shredding his uniform as he was washed over them on his back. Then he was cast against a soft, warm wall and into more darkness, slid further, couldn't catch his breath, and rushed on along a tunnel, downwards, sideways, forward.

It's eaten me, he just had time to think before the certain knowledge of that fate extinguished all other ideas.

Behind him, the gigantic jaws closed and the current ebbed away. The beast that had swallowed Griffin dived down into the depths of the ocean.

THE GHOST IN THE BARREL

Many legends tell invented stories but are still true in their way. Others are lies only because those who hear them close their ears to the truth. And many stories – improbable as they are, crazy and outlandish as they seem – paint a picture of reality that far outdoes it in clarity and truthfulness.

The story of Santiago and his death in the barrel had not been invented, but within a few months it had become far more than just a rumour. It was told and retold a hundred times, exaggerated and embellished.

Yet in this case reality outdid all the retellings: it was the craziest, most macabre and downright deranged scene that Soledad had ever encountered in all her years as the daughter of a pirate emperor.

On the surface there was nothing but a wide sandy beach,

a big barrel, and a pair of boots sticking out of it. But as *seen* and *felt*, it was a sight that burned itself so deep in her memory that she was never to forget it.

It wasn't just the scene itself that made such an impression on her. There was more. On the desert island, among the treeless sandy hillocks, Santiago's ghost was as palpable as an ocean breeze rising and dying away again.

'You can feel him too, can't you?' The Ghost-Trader's voice was the first to break the silence that had fallen over them since their arrival on the island.

Soledad and Walker nodded at the same moment.

'No other human being has ever died on this island,' said the Ghost-Trader, frowning. 'For a ghost, this loneliness must be a thousand times worse to bear than for a living man.'

Soledad nodded again, as if she knew exactly what the Trader was talking about. Her lips could almost taste the isolation and confusion surrounding the whole island.

The sea horses were moving through the shallow waters almost at walking pace. They took care not to touch the bottom with their sensitive tail-fins. Finally they came to a halt, and the three riders had to go the rest of the way on foot.

The air above the sand seemed to blur as Soledad reached the shore and turned towards the barrel. Only another ten paces separated her from her goal. The Ghost-Trader had preferred to stay a little way behind. He sensed that the island was entirely in the dead man's hands.

Before Soledad's eyes vague shapes formed out of the flickering air, images of ships, battles, drinking bouts. And the beach also showed distorted impressions of ragged children, men in uniform, prison cells, women laughing and screaming, fire and gold, and blood trickling into the sand. None of it was real, and when the Ghost-Trader called to her, saying these must be incidents from Captain Santiago's life, Soledad had already come to the same conclusion herself.

The images did not appear in consecutive order, but overlapped and mingled. Adults suddenly had children's faces, and vice versa. Clothes changed within a split second. Ships turned to forests, to swamps, to harbours. Everything felt like a wild dream in which what was seen and what was imagined came together as a single entity, one that had strayed far from the path of reason.

And there was death. Again and again, death.

Flickering figures fell lifeless, run through by swords, strung up to yardarms, on burning wrecks, in a hail of bullets. In her life Soledad had seen many people die in battle or of old age, or stabbed by cowardly murderers. But these pictures far outdid any experiences of her own. She couldn't be sure whether they were deaths that Santiago himself had seen, or whether they showed the fate he had intended for the mutineers. An unappetising mixture of the two, probably.

Walker came up to Soledad and took her right hand. She gave a small start, but did not withdraw her fingers.

'I know a few of them,' he said, as the visions around them became more terrible and bloodthirsty with every passing moment.

'They all look like ghosts themselves,' said Soledad, spellbound.

Now the Ghost-Trader came closer too. 'That's deceptive,' he said, and he was the only one of them to remain composed. 'These are only dreams and wishes and memories in Santiago's confused mind. There's no reason to fear them – at least, as long as they don't follow you.'

Walker looked nervous. He held Soledad's hand a little more firmly. 'Follow us? What do you mean by that?'

'If you're exposed to such images for too long they can sometimes settle in your mind. Then you'd take them away from this place, and they would follow you all your life.'

Soledad and Walker exchanged a meaningful look. 'And how long is *too long*?' asked the princess.

'You don't know that until it's too late.'

Walker bent down to Soledad's ear. 'I knew he'd say something like that.'

She nodded, looking anxious.

The Ghost-Trader put a hand under his robe and brought out the silver circlet that gave him power over the world of ghosts. The simply worked ornament had the diameter of a plate and looked like something a juggler might use to do cheap tricks.

The Trader held the circlet flat and let the fingertips of his right hand pass over it. As he did so he closed his one eye, muttered something to himself, and then fell silent again. His eye was still closed, he didn't move.

'What's he doing?' whispered Walker.

Soledad shrugged. 'Something very powerful.'

'Wrong,' replied the Trader. 'I'm concentrating on the mosquito bite on my left heel to get it to stop itching.'

'Oh.' Walker nodded earnestly.

'Mosquito bite?' repeated Soledad.

'I can't catch ghosts if my foot's itching. Please show a little more sympathy.'

'Oh, by all means,' said Walker nastily.

Soledad shook her head, looking blank.

'There,' announced the Trader, breathing deeply. 'Now I can start.'

'A good idea too,' murmured the captain.

Once again the Trader ran his fingers over the silver

circlet. The images from Santiago's crazed mind moved closer, drawing together around them in a cocoon made up of the past and the possible future. Soledad fought the urge to avoid the blows struck by the flickering figures, but didn't succeed. She closed her eyes, hoping to shut out the horrible images like that. As she did so she concentrated entirely on the touch of Walker's hand, although she found herself plagued by contradictory feelings. Annoyance with herself, but reassurance too. Shame because she was so inconsistent, but also . . . could it be affection?

Good heavens!

A little later she sensed that in spite of anything she could do the visions were getting through to her, streaming into her mind like water into the leaky hull of a ship.

Soledad opened her eyes and saw, with horror, that it wasn't Walker holding her hand any more but a fat fellow. A striped shirt strained over his pot belly, exposing his navel. He had hair on only one side of his leering face; the other side of his skull was covered by a network of old burn scars that made it look like a leather cap. Over the shirt he wore a shabby frock-coat with its right sleeve in rags. A cut on his forehead had stopped bleeding long ago, but still gaped wide open.

'Santiago,' whispered Soledad, bemused.

The fat pirate turned his face to her and opened his mouth.

An indescribable stink of rum and dead fish hit her as he bared his teeth like a wild animal. She wanted to tear her right hand away and reach for one of her throwing-knives with her left hand. But her movements were too slow and strangely indecisive, as if she shared command of her body with someone who always wanted to do the opposite of what she did.

'Soledad . . . little Soledad,' said Santiago, putting his head on one side. Only now did she notice that he was even more bloated than when they had last met a few years ago. Of course he had been alive at the time, and hadn't spent months with his head in a barrel of rum.

She very much hoped that the yellow-brown liquid dripping from his thick lips really was just rum.

'You've come to see me,' he said. 'Nice of you.' At every third or fourth word he spoke small bubbles formed at the front of his mouth, and burst a little later. 'Know what those fellows done to me?'

'They marooned you.'

'Mutinied, that's what they done. They ought to be strung up. Skinned and quartered.'

'The story goes that you tried to cheat them of their share of the loot.'

'Huh! A little mistake in the arithmetic, that's all.'

'I'm sure.'

'Skinned and . . .' He fell silent as if he had forgotten what he was about to say.

'Quartered?' she suggested.

'Quartered,' he agreed with a horrible grin. 'What d'you want of me?'

Soledad looked around at the beach of the island, but she could see neither Walker nor the Ghost-Trader. The visions had dissolved into thin air too. Only the barrel of rum still stood in the same place, but there were no boots sticking out of it now. Instead, damp footprints led to the living corpse beside her that was still clutching her hand. Santiago's fingers felt soapy.

She plucked up all her courage. 'Do you remember my father?'

'Old Scarab? Sure I do. A swine, but he kept his word.'

'And do you know what happened to him?' Her voice was husky as she remembered her father, even here in this strange in-between realm.

'Kendrick cut his throat.'

'Yes . . . he did.'

'And now you're out to get Kendrick, right? You were a little devil even as a child. I once tried buying you from your old man, but he wouldn't let you go, not even for ten barrels of rum.'

She secretly sent up a prayer of gratitude to pirate heaven. 'You know something that could help me.'

'What're you planning?'

'I have to find Kendrick. And I want to get the Antilles captains on my side.'

Santiago shook with laughter. 'What makes you think they care tuppence for you? Or your plans?' Shaking his head, he let go of Soledad's hand and trotted back to the barrel.

Soledad followed, her steps heavy and dragging.

'Wait!'

He didn't even turn to look at her. 'Why should I?'

'Because . . . because we've conjured you up and you have to obey me.'

'You?' He laughed again. 'Your one-eyed friend . . . yes, maybe. But you? Pirate throne, eh? Dream on, little Soledad, but leave me in peace.'

He moved faster than she did, in spite of his considerable weight and sodden limbs. It was infuriating to have to stare at his broad back and be unable to keep him there.

'Peace?' she said. 'You call this peace? Under siege from your own memories and nightmares.'

'What d'you know about it?' he said, shrugging, and trudged on.

'Santiago!'

'What?'

'I won't pretend to you. I can't help you. But I need *your* help!'

'Don't sound like a good bargain to me.' He reached the barrel. Its metal-clad rim came up to his belly. Instead of climbing in, he simply leaned against it with a groan and let himself tip over. Head first, he sank into the barrel until only his sun-bleached boots were sticking out.

Soledad could feel the moment slipping away from her. She couldn't simply give up.

She placed both hands on the rim of the barrel and looked down. There wasn't much to be seen; Santiago's broad backside blocked her view.

'Swine!' she swore at him.

'You leave me be,' he muttered. Coming up out of the barrel, his voice sounded hollow and muted. So there couldn't be any rum left in it. Even as he died, the old soak had drunk the lot.

She looked up helplessly from the barrel and the fat man in it, and gazed across the beach. The entire island consisted of a long sandbank with a few palm trees and bushes clinging miserably to life. It might be the unreal atmosphere of this place, but she wasn't surprised that Walker and the Ghost-Trader hadn't accompanied her to the in-between world.

After all, the whole thing had been *her* idea, so it was her mission alone.

'Have you gone yet?' said a voice from the barrel.

'I've no intention of going.'

'You're a damn pest, little Soledad. Hear that? A pest!'

'For heaven's sake, Santiago, you drank a whole barrel of rum.'

'You think I didn't notice?'

'A *whole* barrel, for God's sake!'

'Bring me another and mebbe I'll help you.' Now he sounded as defiant as a little boy demanding a second birthday cake.

Furiously, she kicked the barrel. 'Not likely!'

'Ouch!' he wailed. 'That was *loud*!'

'Oh yes?' She kicked it again. And then a third time.

'Ouch!' whimpered the ghost

'Come out of there again at once!'

'Ouuuch!'

Another kick, and yet another, followed by a particularly vigorous one.

The captain's wails inside the barrel had an eerie sound. Soledad was beginning to realise that there were far more reasons to pity ghosts than fear them.

'All right, all *right*,' he howled. 'I'm a-coming.'

Somehow he managed to clamber backwards out of the

barrel, struggling and cursing. It was not a pretty sight. His shirt slipped, then the belt of his trousers, and in the end Soledad tactfully looked away until he was standing beside her, panting, and had adjusted his clothing.

'Humiliating, that,' he said crossly. 'In front of a lady too.'

'Nice of you to call me a lady,' she said, and gave him a bewitching smile.

'Oh no!' he cried hastily, raising both hands to fend her off. 'No, no, no . . . nothing doing! That kind of thing ain't for me no more. I mean, look at me.'

Soledad switched off her seductive wiles and planted her hands firmly on her hips. 'All I want from you is some information, Santiago.'

He scratched his chin. Stubble and tiny scraps of skin fell to the sand. 'Oh, very well,' he growled, 'if you'll finally go away then.'

'It's a deal,' she said cheerfully.

He began cleaning the fingernails of his right hand with the nails of his left hand. One broke off. 'Well?'

'The secret meeting place of the Antilles captains. Where is it?'

'That's all?' Doubtfully, he raised his eyebrows. The doughy lines on his forehead were still visible long after his expression had relaxed again.

'That's all,' she assured him.

'And then you'll leave?'

'You can be sure I will.'

'And promise never to kick my barrel again?'

'I promise,' she said, raising one hand.

'Good, good.' He cleared his throat and belched up more of the aroma of rum. 'St Celestine,' he said. 'That's where they're meeting.'

Her tension instantly relaxed. 'St Celestine! That's not far from here!'

'You know Tyrone's going to be there. The cannibal king.'

'Do you know him?'

He nodded. 'You watch out for Tyrone.'

'Yes. I will.'

He let out a blubbering sigh. 'I just want 'em all to leave me alone here.'

'Don't worry. No one's going to venture to your island. There are rumours, you know. About a curse.'

He pricked up his ears. 'A curse?'

'A particularly terrible, gruesome curse.'

'What, *my* curse?'

'Why, yes.'

He gurgled again, and looked happy for the first time. 'That's what they say about me? That I cursed the whole rotten lot of them?'

'I'm telling you, yes!'

'Well, by the Lord Harry, I'll be damned!'

'You're famous, Santiago. And feared.'

'By God I am!'

'Glad to hear that pleases you.'

He grinned for a moment, full of self-satisfaction, and then turned to his barrel. 'Good luck, little Soledad.'

'You too, Santiago.'

He let himself drop into the barrel again and waved his left foot at her by way of goodbye.

She closed her eyes, thought of Walker, and at the same moment felt his hand in hers.

I know the place, she thought proudly, and repeated it out loud. 'I know the place.'

'Yes,' said the Ghost-Trader, when she opened her eyes again. 'And you stink to high heaven of rum.'

ALONE AT SEA

Jolly wiped the sweat out of her eyes. She was dead tired. Even the excitement of getting away from Aelenium wouldn't keep her on her feet much longer. She could hardly feel her hands on the ship's wheel, and her knees seemed as soft as a kraken's arms.

She had been at the helm of the *Carfax* for a day and two nights now. From time to time she had lashed the wheel in place with ropes and slept for an hour, and she had eaten and drunk something now and then. But she was still utterly exhausted, and her stomach was grumbling so loud that it even drowned out the breakers at the bows.

If it had been calm she could have left the wheel unattended, but not in seas like these. A keen east wind was racing across the Atlantic, and the waves formed hills and valleys as high as a man. Sea-spray foamed against the hull and washed over the deck. It wasn't a real storm, nothing that would have given an experienced steersman any trouble. And Jolly knew about navigation and cartography; she knew how to steer a ship, and what dangers winds of this strength meant. What she lacked was sheer physical strength. The wheel was as tall as she was, and she had to spread her arms wide to hold it. Every time the *Carfax* went down into the valley of a wave or a particularly angry breaker struck the bows, she felt as if her arms were being wrenched from her shoulder sockets. A grown man might have taken the strain well enough, but Jolly was too small and, as she had to admit, grinding her teeth, not strong enough for the task. Certainly not for a day and a half on end.

She had tried handing the wheel over to one of the ghosts, but those misty beings were no good at the job. Countless sailors had obviously died aboard the *Carfax*, but not a single steersman. The ghosts just stood there helpless, with none of the sensitivity you needed at the helm of a sloop. The steersman must judge every quiver of the hull, the impact of every wave hitting the bows, and be able to hold the ship on course. With the ghosts, though, it was as if you'd asked a wooden dummy to ride a stallion; you could tie the dummy firmly in the saddle, but at some point the horse would shake it off or smash it against a post.

If the weather didn't change soon, Jolly's plight was

hopeless. She'd be able to hold out a little longer, three hours, maybe four. But then she would finally have to give in. The wooden colossus under her was stronger than she was, and she had hugely overestimated herself in thinking she could steer the *Carfax* alone to the mouth of the Orinoco, with only the ghosts to help her.

The sun had risen some time ago, but that didn't improve Jolly's situation.

In the night hours she had kept asking herself the same tormenting questions. Why on earth had she set off alone? Why hadn't she taken Griffin with her? She hadn't seen him since that evening two days ago, but now she was all the more painfully aware of how much he meant to her. And she'd left him behind in Aelenium without a word. Without saying goodbye, without any explanation. Had she really believed that she had to go in search of Bannon by herself, or had she simply been too proud to ask for help?

She missed Griffin more than she would ever have thought possible. Missed his gibes, which usually had some truth in them, missed his laughter and the concern he felt for her. She thought of him tattooing her skin, and what he had said before Munk appeared in the doorway. If she closed her eyes she could feel his fingers passing over the picture on her back, as if his touch were caught inside the pattern, softly stroking the edges of the coral in the picture.

Jolly pulled herself together and made herself concentrate on the *Carfax* and the sea ahead of her. Grey clouds covered the sky; rays of sunlight only occasionally broke through the vapour and stood above the sea like bright columns. The Atlantic was turbulent all the way to the horizon, treacherously beautiful in its shades of colour: massifs of grey, silver and icy blue lay side by side, sharply distinct from each other, heralding capricious winds and changeable seas.

Jolly and the wheel seemed to have merged together over all these hours, as if keeping one another upright. More and more often she felt her vision blurring and her mind wandering in a way she knew only from the minutes just before she went to sleep: moments when reality and imagination mingled, and both seemed equally plausible. She thought she saw the sea around her turn black, with crests of foam made of tiny living creatures. But her senses were no longer wakeful enough for her to realise that she had seen that image once before, at the end of a bridge, in the abyss between worlds.

The sun should really have climbed higher, but for reasons she couldn't fathom it was growing darker. The glowing pillars of light that had propped up the cloudy sky just now thinned out and finally disappeared entirely. All at once darkness fell on the *Carfax*. In the middle of the morning, in broad daylight, it was night again.

The wind grew no stronger, but the hull was creaking as if something in the pitch-black, sluggish water were compressing it on all sides. Jolly's head fell forward, but her fingers were clutching the wheel so firmly that she stayed upright. Her black hair fell over her forehead and tickled the tip of her nose. She started and was suddenly wide awake again, but the darkness was still there, and the waves were no longer water but something with a life of its own. The foam spraying over the rail on both sides of the ship did not run over the planks as water, but took shape on deck as crowds of shimmering crustaceans, small as water-fleas but in their thousands upon thousands, constantly creating new formations: star shapes, jelly-like blobs, networks of pulsating patterns.

The Mare Tenebrosum has come to get me, she thought with surprising objectivity, and she repeated the words in her mind until they sounded perfectly logical and natural. It's come to get me.

Such a thing had happened before, and whenever it did the Mare Tenebrosum had swallowed up the ships that met it. But Jolly was not afraid. Not any more. The Mare Tenebrosum had come because it wanted something of her.

She doubted that it was in its power to kill her at the moment. Others, those unfamiliar with the sight of the Mare Tenebrosum, might be driven to panic by this strange and baffling unreality and sail their ships to perdition. But this wasn't the first time Jolly had seen that nocturnal sea, and although she was afraid to the marrow of her bones, her fear did not make her lose control entirely.

And there it was again, the same effect she had seen on Agostini's bridge: the surface of the water seemed to go on into infinity without blurring. It was not the horizon that bounded the view but only Jolly's vision. In the end she had to turn her eyes away to avoid being entirely lost in those endless horizons.

'What do you want of me?' she shouted at the raging sea.

No one replied. What had she expected? A disembodied voice speaking to her? A sea-monster raising its ugly head and saying something?

Only the blackness. Only the endless ocean.

'Say what you want or leave me in peace!' she cried, clutching the ship's wheel as if it were her last hold on reality.

Out to port, something happened in the distance. She couldn't tell how far away the place was, for nothing could be judged properly in the extreme clarity of her surroundings. It might be ten miles away or a hundred.

The oily waters of the Mare Tenebrosum were in violent movement, as if millions and millions of the black crustaceans in the spray were taking a particular shape on the crest of the waves. The milling, teeming turbulence became something approximately like human features, several miles high and equally wide, as if stretching above the ocean.

It was her own face.

She wasn't sure how she recognised it, for she was seeing it from a strange angle, looking at the chin and lips, the towering mountain of the tip of the nose, staring along the cheekbones to the eyebrows and the forehead. The features could have been those of any human being, but Jolly was sure that the Mare Tenebrosum had come to meet her as her own likeness, formed from the water of the primeval ocean.

The hill of the lips moved as if to speak, but only the roaring sea and flapping sails could be heard. A few lightning flashes zigzagged through the darkness, and blue-white tongues of fire flickered in the rigging.

'What do you want?' cried Jolly into the distance again.

The gigantic mouth opened and closed faster and faster before exploding in an eruption of black water. A tidal wave as high as a house rolled towards the *Carfax*, but it ebbed away before reaching the ship. The distance must be much greater than Jolly had thought – and the face unimaginably larger. Where it had been just now a whirlpool was forming, at first slowly and almost lethargically, then moving faster and faster until it was a rotating abyss spreading swiftly in all directions.

The gigantic whirlpool was soon many miles across. Now it even seemed to be sucking the lightning down from the sky, for more and more branching arms of light flashed down into the raging eddies.

But the *Carfax* lay in the water untouched – rocking, creaking, groaning, yes, but without being drawn into that dreadful current. That was the final proof. Now Jolly was sure that the only danger here threatened her mind, not her body – and that she could put an end to all this by herself. She just had to want to, she had to believe she could do it.

'That's enough,' she whispered, and then shouted it firmly out into the darkness. *'That's enough!'*

The vision disappeared, contracting for a moment to a black core inside the chasm and then dissolving into a thousand fragments that disappeared like wisps of mist in the sun. Light flowed towards Jolly from all quarters of the compass, meeting her like rolling fire. She cried out in alarm but with relief too, and then slipped slowly to the deck.

The last thing she saw was a dog's face leaning over her: the face of a pit bull terrier. Then she heard a voice.

'Oh, my goodness! Oh, dear me!' lamented the Hexhermetic Shipworm, but if he found one of his terrible rhymes for that she didn't hear it.

'If Walker were here he'd wring your neck,' said Buenaventure, looking at her.

Jolly was crouching on the bridge by the rail, only three paces from the wheel, which the pit bull man was holding easily in his hairy paws as he kept them on course. The horny plate on the Hexhermetic Shipworm's head was peering out of Buenaventure's rucksack, which he had propped against the balustrade beside her. The Worm was remarkably silent. Since she opened her eyes again he had made only a couple of remarks, and they neither rhymed nor were particularly caustic.

'Were you two on board the whole time?' she asked, bewildered.

'No,' Buenaventure teased her, moving his chops into a grin. 'I'm good at swimming backstroke, see?'

'I don't believe it.' She shook her head. 'You were below decks all the time, while up here I was . . .' Another shake of her head.

'Well, we had a few problems down there too. The Shipworm ate some of Walker's loot: one of those Spanish thrones. And the three-eyed Madonna. The captain won't be very pleased, but I couldn't let the little fellow starve.'

'And what about me?'

'You've learned your lesson, I hope.'

'I could have died out here.'

'I doubt it. We took a look at you now and then. You didn't do too badly really. Until yesterday, that is.'

Jolly hadn't told the others anything about the apparition of the Mare Tenebrosum, less for fear of conjuring up what she had seen again than because it was impossible to describe those images.

'Until yesterday? How long have I been asleep?'

'A day and a night.'

She looked incredulously up at the sun.

'Did you find the food beside your berth?'

'If I hadn't I'd probably have eaten the Worm.' She gave the little creature a wry smile, but he just responded with a cool snort. Only a few days ago such a remark would have set off a long tirade of abuse. But now he was keeping quiet.

'What's the matter with you?' she asked him.

'Hmpf,' went the Worm.

She raised an eyebrow. 'Hmpf?'

'He's taken a vow of silence,' said Buenaventure. 'He swore

it when I . . . er, got him out of a fix. Right, Worm?' He laughed quietly.

'Hmpf.'

'What kind of a fix?' asked Jolly.

Buenaventure just laughed louder and shook his head.

'That's the thanks I get for my poetic art,' said the Worm morosely, but he refrained from any further explanation.

'As you know,' said Buenaventure, 'the good people of Aelenium were crazy about our friend here.'

Jolly nodded. 'Prince of Poetic Song,' she remembered, grinning.

'Wonderful Worm,' muttered the Shipworm. 'Huh!'

'So what happened?' she asked.

'They gave him a house in the poets' quarter. And then they —'

'What does a Worm want with a house?' the Shipworm interrupted him. 'If it had at least been made of wood — but no, coral. Everything made of coral. Yuk!'

'They did bring him wood to eat.'

'Wood shavings,' the Worm corrected him. 'Measly damp wood shavings!'

'And in return he was to give them a sample of his . . . er, poetic talent every day at sunrise and sunset.'

'So?' asked Jolly. 'On Tortuga you gave the people a poem

a day too. One more or less surely wasn't any problem for the *Maestro Poeticus*, was it?'

The Worm moved a little deeper down in the rucksack. 'All very well for you to mock!'

'The problem,' said Buenaventure, 'wasn't the lack of inspiration in our highly respected bard, it was his ravenous appetite.'

'Wood shavings!' repeated the Worm with derision. '*Damp* wood shavings!'

'He spent the time between his poetic performances eating half a dozen of the barricades put up in the streets by the good folk of Aelenium to fend off the enemy. The results of two weeks' work, I may say. As you can imagine, he'd do well not to show himself in Aelenium again.'

'You mean we're not sailing back there?' asked Jolly hopefully.

'That's right,' replied Buenaventure. 'I can understand why you couldn't stand the city any more. I felt the same — and they weren't even going to send me down to the bottom of the Rift.'

'I didn't run away because I was afraid,' she said. 'I mean, yes, I *am* afraid, of course . . . but I've sworn to find Bannon.'

Buenaventure nodded without looking round. 'It's your decision.'

'Does that mean you'll help me?'

'I've nothing better to do, so it seems. And I promised Walker to keep an eye on you.' He quietly laughed his strange dog-laughter. 'Well, I would have anyway. I mean even without the promise.'

She jumped up, although that made her feel so dizzy that she almost fell over, and hugged the pit bull man from behind. It felt like flinging her arms around the trunk of a jungle tree, he was so massive.

'Thank you,' she whispered.

By the afternoon Jolly was feeling well enough to climb up to the crow's-nest. She sent the ghost on watch there back to the deck. It slid down like a blurred wisp of mist, and didn't assume the vague shape of a human being until it was at the very bottom of the mast.

Jolly let the wind blow in her face. Her black hair danced like the pirate flag in the strong breeze. From up here the waves looked small and harmless, and although the ship was still rocking quite hard the sea had grown calmer. It stretched endlessly away in all directions like a cracked mirror, shimmering in the sunlight. There was no land anywhere in sight. The *Carfax* would probably be sailing for another three or four days before the trees on the jungle banks of the Orinoco delta appeared on the horizon.

Jolly held the top of the mast with one hand. The British flag waved in the wind above her – the usual deceptive manoeuvre. The skull and crossbones, symbol of the freebooters, was hoisted only during an attack or at pirates' meetings.

She kept her knees relaxed to compensate for the rocking of the ship. It wasn't difficult, for her legs still felt a little wobbly. Her encounter with the Mare Tenebrosum had taken more out of her than she liked to admit. It annoyed her to be so susceptible, so vulnerable to the visitations of her enemies. On the other hand even that couldn't spoil her mood at the moment. She might be on the way to Bannon at last. She had never wondered whether he had really been a kind of father to her – she didn't know what it felt like to have a father, after all. He was just Bannon, the captain of her crew and one of the wiliest pirates in the Caribbean Sea. He had taught her all she knew – about the sea, about people, about the art of privateering. She loved him the way other children love their parents, that was for sure.

And she missed him.

Carefully, she put her hand in her pocket to find the little box containing the dead spider, took a last look at it and closed the lid again. The ugly corpse had come a long way with her, from the sinking of the *Maid Maddy* to the blazing inferno of New Providence harbour, then on to Tortuga and Aelenium, and even out here.

But now the hairy corpse had served its purpose: it had pointed the way to the Orinoco. And she had climbed to the crow's-nest to throw the little box into the sea – as a kind of burial, and also to mark another turning point in her life. Until a few days ago her destiny had unfolded in line with the Ghost-Trader's plan. Now, however, she had taken it into her own hands, and it was time to part from this remnant of her past as well.

She was swinging back her arm to throw when she felt something settle on her shoulder. Claws dug into her skin. Suddenly there was vigorous fluttering beside her ear.

In alarm, she looked round and dropped the little box. It fell on the floor of the crow's-nest beside her foot. With a scream, she prepared to hit out, and was only just in time to stop herself when she saw what had settled on her arm.

'Moe!' she cried in surprise.

The Ghost-Trader's black parrot hopped along her arm until he was in an upright position again. His blood-red eyes searched her face as if he were trying to convey a message through his gaze alone.

'Is Hugh here too?' She looked around her, and saw the

second parrot on the foremast. He too was looking down at her as he perched there motionless.

She remembered seeing both of them on the pier in Aelenium. During her quarrel with Munk they had flown over the ship and settled on one of the yards. But after that she had forgotten all about the parrots. Had they been on board all through the voyage? But if so, surely she would have been bound to notice them. On the other hand she had been concentrating so hard on steering the ship that she could have overlooked the birds entirely.

Moe flew back up to her shoulder, flapping his wings. It was annoying not to be able to look straight at him now, and she half expected him to whisper something in her ear. But the parrot was silent, and just perched there for another moment. Then he took off and fluttered to starboard, flew a little way out to sea and began circling there.

Jolly followed the course of his flight, frowning, until she realised what he was trying to tell her. She looked at the surface of the water below Moe.

There was something in the waves, a dark shape. An icy shudder ran down her spine. Everyone knew that the sea around the coral city must be teaming with kobalins and other creatures of the Maelstrom. They might not show themselves, but they were there: scouts and observers, the vanguard of the fighting force that the Maelstrom was about to unleash upon Aelenium.

No wonder one of these beings had followed the *Carfax*. But why hadn't it attacked before?

She still couldn't make out its contours clearly. It could be a whole shoal of kobalins or a single mighty creature. But one thing surprised her: whatever it was, it was coming no closer. Instead, it kept on a course parallel with the *Carfax* as if to observe and gather information, but not to attack. Or was it waiting for a suitable moment? No, not likely; there had been more than enough of those.

Moe flew in a final circle, then returned to the ship and settled on the foremast beside Hugh. The mysterious birds looked over to her with their red and yellow eyes.

Jolly picked up the little box, put it back in her waistcoat pocket, and nimbly shinned down the shrouds to the deck. Moments later she was beside Buenaventure, telling him what the parrots had discovered.

The pit bull man asked her to take over the wheel for a moment, hurried to the rail, and stared grimly the way that Jolly had pointed. But from down here the outline couldn't be seen; the light reflecting on the waves and the shallow angle hid it.

'There *is* something there,' Jolly assured him.

Buenaventure nodded. His dog's face didn't show how concerned he really was, but the frown on his forehead boded no good.

'We could fire on it,' suggested the Hexhermetic Shipworm. 'A few well-aimed shots and boom! We'd be rid of the thing. Simple.'

'Simple?' repeated Buenaventure. 'In the eyes of a half-blind Worm, maybe.'

'And what's *that* supposed to mean?'

Jolly got in before the pit bull man could reply. 'It means we can't afford to fire on something that hasn't shown itself hostile yet.'

Buenaventure gave her a nod. 'Even if it's a shoal of kobalins, which to be honest I don't think it is, then we ought to be wary about attacking it. As long as it doesn't come any closer it isn't bothering us.'

'A shoal of kobalins doesn't bother you?' The Worm's voice was shrill. 'By my mother's rodent tooth and the six hundred legs of her whole miserable clan, you can't be serious!'

The pit bull man looked back at the place Jolly had shown him in the sea, and then took over the wheel again without a word.

Jolly climbed back up to the crow's-nest, glad to leave the

Shipworm's complaints behind. Buenaventure was right. There was no point in risking a fight at the moment.

The strange outline was still close to the *Carfax*, not a hundred paces away. She narrowed her eyes, hoping to get a more distinct view of the creature, but that didn't help.

Hugh and Moe fluttered over and settled on the yards of the topmast to right and left of the crow's-nest. Almost imperceptibly, they followed Jolly's eyes. Only now did she realise that Buenaventure wasn't the only one who had been told to keep an eye on her.

The parrots too were here to take care of her – or keep watch on her.

THE MAN IN THE WHALE

Griffin brought up seawater. It tasted like cod-liver oil with a touch of rotten fish and a large pinch of salt. He retched and spat until his throat and stomach hurt, and even then the flavour that had settled on his tongue was so disgusting that he wished he could swap it for a new one.

He was crouching, bent double, in the middle of a jumble of splintered, broken planks, tangled black seaweed, and all kinds of indescribable objects that might be part of wrecked ships or the remains of living creatures. A little light surrounded a passageway of semicircular arches close to him — they were either the skeleton of some great fish or the planks of a wrecked ship's hull. He didn't feel very keen to find out which.

What did interest him a great deal, however, was why he was still alive. And where light could be coming from in the belly of a sea-monster.

Unfortunately he wasn't going to stay alive long enough to solve this riddle. He assumed that the stinking liquid slopping around his legs was a mixture of his own vomit and the monster's gastric juices. The idea made him retch again, but he had nothing left in his stomach.

He struggled up and tried to wipe the slime and dirt off his uniform, but gave up when he found that his hands were just slapping ineffectually at his clothes.

Only now did despair overcome him. It hit him late but all the more strongly for that, and it forced him to his knees. He buried his face in his hands and closed his eyes for quite a long time, hoping to master the nightmare that way.

A shock made his surroundings tremble – a quaking undulation that began on one side of the cavernous space, rolled towards Griffin, almost knocked him backwards, and then went on past him, flinging around bones and bits of wood as it did so. Finally it died down. When whatever lay below him was still again, Griffin listened intently to the silence. There was a monotonous rushing, like the sound of a waterfall behind thick walls. And something else too, a rhythmical thudding, muted and far away: the beat of a gigantic heart.

Leaning against one of the high arches, Griffin took a deep breath. The place stank as if the guts of an entire week's catch had been laid out to dry in a fishing port. The air here was so damp, warm and musty that it settled like an oily film on his larynx. He cleared his throat, coughed and spat, but it did no good.

Far away the mighty heart went on beating.

Griffin's hand felt the curve of the arch. Too smooth for a plank from a ship. It really was a bone, the rib of some great animal that had been stranded down here heaven knew how long ago.

Slowly, he moved forward. In the dim light filling the cavern he had difficulty making out the floor in front of his feet. He saw outlines, the black silhouettes of parts of wrecks, mountains of bones. Now and then he stumbled upon human skeletons. Nothing about them showed exactly how these poor devils had died. Had they drowned, or had they been killed down here?

He took hold of a metal bar sticking out of a pile of half-rotted wood, weighed it in his hand, and decided it would do as a makeshift weapon. His sword had gone; he supposed he had lost it as he fell into the creature's great maw. There was no sign of his sea horse Matador either, and he fervently hoped it had escaped the pull of the current that had swept him into that gigantic mouth. Even without a rider it would find its own way back to Aelenium.

How long had he been unconscious? A few hours. Maybe even days. Since his stomach was grumbling he had presumably arrived down here some time ago. And his skin was soft and wrinkled where he had been lying in water and gastric juices. Disgusting, he thought, and hoped it would soon pass off.

Not that that made any difference if he was about to be digested anyway.

What he still couldn't imagine was just what kind of a gigantic creature might have swallowed him. The picture of the Mare Tenebrosum formed before his mind's eye: movements in oily water, the sound of huge bodies beneath the surface. Was this one of its creatures? Good heavens, was he even in his own world?

Despair overcame him again, but this time he was armed against it. He gritted his teeth and dug the fingers of his left hand so firmly into the ball of it that it hurt. That briefly took his mind off his despair, and when the pain ebbed so did his panic and resignation. It was a trick he'd learned from an old sea dog on Haiti.

The iron bar in his hand felt slippery and rather rusty, but the weight of it gave him a little confidence. If there was anything here to endanger him, he'd defend himself.

But what could he do about the digestive juices? Suppose

they rained acid, and a wave of poison washed him deeper down into entrails of some kind?

'Good day to you,' someone near him said suddenly.

Griffin leaped back, came to a halt among rubble and dead fish, legs braced apart, and swung the iron bar in front of him like a sword.

'Ouf!' went the voice, and there was a clatter as its owner fell backwards. Then the light went out. Darkness enveloped Griffin from all sides.

'That . . . wasn't very nice of you,' said the voice, and there was a groan. Griffin heard the man's hands splashing around in the liquid.

'Who are you?'

'Ebenezer Arkwright. At your service.'

'At my . . . service?'

'That's what we say in my trade, young man. And a little more civility would do no harm.' Judging by the sounds, the man was hauling himself up and knocking the dirt off his cloak.

'Er . . . what is your trade?' asked Griffin.

The man cleared his throat. 'I'm in the catering business,' he explained with formality, taking an unsteady step forward.

'Don't you come any closer!'

'Do I look as if I was about to harm you?'

'It's dark. I can't see anything at all.'

'Ah, the darkness . . . how forgetful of me. When you've been here long enough your eyes get used to it. Then you can see almost as well as in daylight.' There was a rustling sound as he brought something out from under his cloak. 'Wait . . . here we are.' A hissing sound and then a flame. 'There. Is that better?'

The flickering flame leaped from a match to the wick of a candle. The yellowish light drove most of the shadows away from the man's face but deepened others. He had full, round features and large, chubby cheeks. His eyes were very pale, either blue or green like a cat's, and were in curious contrast to the rest of his stout appearance. His lips were narrow, and not very different from the folds of his many double chins. Whatever Ebenezer Arkwright was doing down here, he obviously wasn't starving.

Griffin's stomach rumbled again, but he tried to ignore it.

'I fancy a meal would do you good, boy,' said the man, who had not failed to notice the sound. 'I can offer a choice of a couple of new recipes.'

Griffin retreated. He already saw himself ending up in some madman's cooking pot – until he realised that Ebenezer was perfectly serious. He was actually inviting him to dinner.

'Both of them fish dishes, I'm afraid.' Ebenezer smiled

apologetically. 'But I'm sure you like seafood, don't you? I can offer a very tender shark's fin in a piquant marinade. Or there's inkfish, grilled rather than fried, with an excellent –'

'Wait a minute.' Griffin silenced him with a gesture. 'I'm sorry I lashed out at you just now, but –'

'Oh, you didn't hit me. I stumbled, that's all. A man so seldom meets anything alive down here, you see. That's one of the reasons why I could hardly get over it. Quite apart from this horrible smell.' He smiled with satisfaction. 'Yes, you gave me quite a turn just now.'

Griffin shook his head. Drops of water sprayed off his countless little braids in all directions. 'I . . . I don't understand. Where are we?'

'Inside a whale, of course.'

'Of course.'

'Don't say you didn't know?'

'I was swallowed by . . . by something. But a whale?' When he said it out loud it sounded a thousand times more incredible. 'I thought I . . . oh, I don't know. Perhaps I'm just imagining all this.'

'Oh no, you're not. And if you will allow me, I can certainly convince you of that with my marinade. It's my version of a recipe from a Breton monastery.'

'So we're really inside a whale?'

'We are.'

'But no ordinary whale has —'

'I never said it was an ordinary whale. Far from it.'

'What is it, then? Something from the Mare Tenebrosum?'

One of Ebenezer's eyebrows shot up. 'Certainly not. But I might have guessed you'd know about that. You seem to be an unusual young fellow, or you'd never have arrived in this place safe and sound.'

'You know the Mare Tenebrosum?'

'Not from first-hand experience, but I know the stories. In fact I know a great deal about the islands and the mainland. I've even written a book on the subject.'

'What, about the Mare Tenebrosum?'

Ebenezer dismissed that. 'About the coastal regions of the Caribbean. As a young monk I was one of the community at a small mission station. I was the first to collect data about the animal and plant world of these parts. I'd almost finished my work when a supply ship that had been taking me to visit one of the islands was caught in a storm and sank.' He heaved a deep sigh. 'God knows what became of my manuscript. But that's a long time ago, thirty years or more.'

Griffin's eyes widened in disbelief. 'You've been here as long as that?'

Ebenezer nodded. 'That's when he swallowed me. I

survived and . . . well, discovered something.'

'Not by any chance a way to get out of here, I suppose?'

'Oh, *that*! Yes, I certainly know a way, but that's not what I meant.'

'You know how to get out of this thing . . . I mean, how to get it to spit you out again?'

The fat man smiled. 'Perhaps. But first you must taste my marinade.'

Griffin looked around at his unappetising surroundings. He was ravenously hungry, but doubted whether he would be able to swallow a morsel here. Certainly nothing that smelled of fish. Or tasted of fish either.

'Come along.' Ebenezer moved away, picking up the skirts of his cloak, which Griffin now recognised as something like a monk's habit, only more colourful. He cautiously clambered over the debris and bones. 'I want to show you something.'

Griffin was about to object, but then thought better of it and followed this eccentric character. The candle gave only a small circle of light, and most of the walls of the belly of the whale – if that was really where they were – remained in the dark.

'What are you doing down here?' asked Griffin. 'Apart from cooking, I mean.' But before Ebenezer could reply Griffin stopped, rooted to the ground. Something had come into his mind. 'Wait a minute . . . it's *you*, isn't it?'

'What do you mean?'

'You're the Man in the Whale!'

'Well, I'm a man, and yes, this is a whale.'

'You're famous all over the Caribbean. I've known the stories ever since I can remember. Everyone's afraid of you. They say you make the whale ram ships and then he eats the sailors, and . . . and . . .' Griffin's voice faltered, and he raised the iron bar in front of him again, ready to strike.

But Ebenezer's voice didn't sound at all angry, quite the opposite. 'Is that what they say?' he asked sadly. 'About me?'

'On every ship.'

The man had stopped. He turned to Griffin in the candlelight. 'But that's terrible.'

'Is it true?'

'Of course not! I've never . . . no, really, never . . .' He fell silent, thought for a moment, and then slowly nodded. 'Well, there was that whaler once, about – dear God, so long ago – about twenty years back. Her captain wanted to harpoon our friend here . . . I couldn't allow that, could I? But he'd have rammed the ship anyway, even without me. Whales are very clever, you know, and this one is cleverer than all the rest. Even if he may not look like it from inside.'

'The whaler sank?'

'With all hands.'

'And that was the only time?'

'Yes, of course.'

'There must have been survivors,' said Griffin. 'One of them saw you.'

Ebenezer nodded again. 'I stood in the mouth of the whale, thinking I could persuade those men to leave us alone.'

'Well, someone survived and told other people. That's how the story must have started. Everyone's added to it, making you the bloodthirsty Man in the Whale.'

'Bloodthirsty! Good heavens!' Horrified, Ebenezer raised his hands to his temples. 'When all I want to do is . . . but wait a moment and you'll see.'

Griffin was not entirely convinced that he could trust this peculiar stranger, but on the other hand Ebenezer knew a way to get out. And Griffin had to eat something too, never mind how bad it smelled.

The monk climbed a hill made of all kinds of refuse and rubble. He had built some rough and ready steps from boards, so that his feet didn't sink into the ooze.

At the top of the hill there was a door.

It was made of massive oak beams, with metal fittings that shone in the candlelight. They ought really to have rusted in the moist, salty air, but Ebenezer seemed to polish them

216

regularly, for they were sparkling bright. The door stood in a frame anchored to the top of the hill by stout wooden struts propped against it. Griffin suspected that more fastenings went deep inside the mound of rubble, so that the frame would stay in place even when the whale dived down or came to the surface at a slanting angle.

They were approaching the door sideways on, so Griffin could see that it led nowhere. If you went through it you would come out on the other side, yes, but you would still be on the hill. He was beginning to have grave doubts about his strange host's sanity.

Ebenezer reached the door and waited for Griffin to catch up with him. Then he turned the heavy knob and opened the door. Flickering firelight met them, and suddenly there was a smell of fried fish in the air.

Behind the door lay a room. Not the other side of the horrible hill of rubble and bones, but a real room. With wood-panelled walls, an open fire on the hearth, and polished floorboards that gave it a cosy feel. And along the opposite wall was something that looked like the bar of an inn.

'Welcome to Ebenezer's Floating Tavern,' announced the monk proudly.

Griffin blinked. Then he walked round the outside of the door. It was open on the other side too, and when he looked through the frame he saw Ebenezer standing in the doorway smiling.

'It only works from one side,' said the monk.

Griffin went back to the point of departure of his round trip, and looked at the room beyond the door again.

'Come on in,' said Ebenezer, and went into the room himself.

Griffin scraped the last of the food off his plate with his fork and spoon. He had just wolfed down his second helping.

'That was good,' he said, licking his lips.

'A practical training always comes in useful.'

'I thought you were a monk?'

'The good Lord alone doesn't fill bellies. Monks have to eat too, and someone has to cook for them.'

Griffin cast a regretful glance at his plate, but it was empty. 'Then you were the cook at the mission station?'

'Cook, scientist, illustrator. You learn all kinds of things when you suddenly find yourself in the wilderness.'

'And you never wanted to go back there?'

'At first, yes. But then I told myself it was a sign from the Lord to let me survive here. After all, I'm not the first man of God to have met this monster.'

'You're not?'

'Even the Old Testament mentions him. There was a man

called Jonah, and God gave him a job he didn't want to do. So Jonah decided to run away, and he fled to sea in a ship. But God pursued him with storms and tempests. When the seamen realised that Jonah was to blame for those storms they simply threw him overboard. Before he could drown, however, Jonah was swallowed up by a giant fish, and it spat him out again on a coast three days and three nights later.'

'And you think it was this whale?'

'It's perfectly possible. There are more such stories. Have you ever heard of the Irish monks who sailed the seas in the old days? The most famous was the monk Brendan, who set out on a seven-year voyage to find the Isle of the Blessed. His story was written down at the time under the title of *Navigatio Sancti Brendani Abbatis*. Anyway, in the sixth century AD this Brendan met a mighty fish, bigger than an island, and gave it the name Jasconius. Brendan and the other monks even celebrated Mass on its back, so they say.' Ebenezer scratched his head, and smiled a little awkwardly. 'Well, it's certain that there have been others like us. And in a way I've got used to my situation. This whale is a real treasure trove. You can't imagine the stuff he swallows. Specially when we're near the trade routes. Day after day ships sink and whole cargoes go overboard. A lot of the stuff that's lost at sea ends up here sooner or later. Jasconius has developed a good instinct for it.'

Griffin shook his head. He could make nothing of all this. 'What about the door? This room?' He pointed across it. 'Are we in the belly of this whale or . . . or somewhere else?'

Ebenezer's glance followed Griffin's gesture as he waved his hand around the room. The wooden panelling, the fire on the hearth, even a handful of paintings seemed to make it an imitation of a European nobleman's country house. It didn't look like part of a whale's belly, anyway.

'To be honest, I can't give you any good answer to that,' said Ebenezer, shrugging.

'Have you tried looking behind the panelling?'

Ebenezer nodded. 'Stone.'

'A wall?'

'That's right.'

'But that's just crazy!'

'You get used to it.' Ebenezer waved dismissively. 'It's a little strange at first, to be sure, but after a while . . . well, you know what they say. Don't look a gift horse in the mouth. And it has its advantages. I'm not sure that I'd have survived for long in that damp hole out there. But in here . . . why not?'

Griffin stood up, went over to one of the walls and tentatively tapped the panelling. Then he went back to the door, opened it and looked out. The dark swamp of bones and flotsam and jetsam from wrecks still lay there inside the gigantic animal. With a shudder, he closed the door and turned to the second, which was behind the bar.

'May I?' he asked.

'Of course.'

He found himself in another room, as large as the first. Ebenezer had made this one his kitchen. There were several tables and chopping blocks of notched wood, as well as shelves and cupboards containing a haphazard collection of crockery, obviously taken from wrecks. Griffin also saw a cast-iron stove with a hotplate, and a huge fireplace with a smoke hood where you could have roasted a whole ox. He couldn't make out where the smoke went, though. It looked as if it might give Jasconius a nasty cough.

Shaking his head, Griffin crossed the room towards another door. He took every step very hesitantly, as if some incautious touch might make his surroundings burst like a bubble.

Behind this door lay a third room of the same size with an iron bedstead in it. A coat of arms that meant nothing to Griffin was let into the head of the bed. Presumably it had once belonged to a ship's captain or stood in a nobleman's cabin. An open wardrobe contained nothing but a dozen monk's habits made of various fabrics and in different colours. In the cut of their pattern at least Ebenezer had changed nothing in the last thirty years. Books lay everywhere, scattered on the floor and stacked in careless piles, some of them falling apart, others with their pages crinkled after spending time in the water. Some had no covers any more, others consisted only of bundles of loose pages that Ebenezer had obviously sorted and then tied together with string. There was a wooden globe with a dent in it roughly where Europe must be; chessmen were set out on a board in an unfinished game; several paintings hung on the walls, badly damaged by their contact with salt water; a grandfather clock was even ticking; there were yellowed lampshades, a frayed rug with an oriental pattern and a stuffed crocodile with a single glass eye, as well as a draughtsman's board and a number of cracked glass cases full of collections of butterflies and other insects.

There was no other door in this room, so Griffin went back to the first of the three rooms. Ebenezer was still sitting at the table, looking expectantly at him.

'Well, what do you think of it?'

'Rather impressive,' said Griffin.

'Yes, isn't it? Very comfortable for the belly of a whale.'

'But how . . . I mean, how did you . . .?'

'Luck. Trust in the Lord. Providence. One day I found this door lying among all the other stuff. Jasconius had swallowed it along with the remains of some ship or other. I haven't the faintest idea where it comes from, or who made it for what purpose. And I doubt whether I'll ever be able to solve the mystery. Perhaps that's just as well. Mysteries are like the glowing embers in the stove: they go out if you poke at them too long.' He grinned as if he had just uttered a wise saying of great philosophical depth. 'Anyway, the door had opened as it dropped into the whale's belly – I almost fell through it head first. I stood it up and – *voilà*!' He waved his hand all round the room with the open hearth. 'So here we are.'

Griffin had been pacing nervously up and down while he listened to Ebenezer. But now, exhausted, he dropped on a chair, rubbed his eyes and took a deep breath.

'Here we are,' he repeated, sighing, when he opened his eyes again and looked at the smiling Ebenezer. 'I do have one question to ask you.'

'Ask away. We have all the time in the world.'

'When you found me out there in the belly, you said you were in . . . in *the catering trade.* And then you spoke of a Floating Tavern.' He nodded at the bar. 'And you have that counter over there, and I'm wondering . . . well . . .'

'Whether I've lost my mind, isn't that so?'

Griffin ruefully pulled a face. 'Something like that.'

'By no means, my young friend. By no means.' Ebenezer

pushed his chair back. He went over to the bar on his short, fat legs and caressed it almost lovingly with his fingertips. A dreamy glow appeared in his eyes. 'I am perfectly serious. Tell me, boy, what's your name?'

'Griffin.'

'Good, Griffin, then you will be the first to hear my plan.' He leaned back against the counter, propping his elbows on the edge. Lowering his voice, he went on, with a conspiratorial look, 'All this will become a legend in the annals of hospitality. Something sailors talk of from the North Sea to the South Pacific. No, what am I saying? It will be the talk of the whole world, on land *and* sea!' He smiled craftily. 'But the great thing is that only very few will ever enjoy a visit to this place in person. And that's what will make it so famous!' Ebenezer raised his hands in the air as if he had told Griffin a plan to become master of the world. 'Everyone will be talking about it! Everyone will want to boast of drinking a tot of rum at this bar. The first Floating Tavern! The first and only tavern in the belly of a giant whale!' His eyes were now round as marbles and staring expectantly at Griffin. 'Well, how does that sound to you?'

Griffin swallowed. 'I . . . I'm speechless.'

'Not surprising, my dear fellow, not surprising! People will give their eye-teeth to get a chance to come in. They'll be consumed by longing for a second visit – but by then Ebenezer's Floating Tavern will have put in somewhere else. Now here, now there. It will be a *myth*! Can you imagine a better business idea?'

'The fact is, I don't know very much about the catering trade, but . . .'

'But?'

'Why would anyone give their eye-teeth to dine in the belly of a whale? Isn't the idea, well . . . disgusting?'

'Disgusting? Nonsense!' Ebenezer roared with laughter. 'It's a wonderful idea! Customers eating fish inside a whale. Where else can they enjoy such an experience? Only in –'

'Ebenezer's Floating Tavern.'

'Exactly!'

It must be the solitude, thought Griffin, full of pity. The poor fellow hasn't seen another human soul for decades, and now he's imagining a whole tavern full of people.

'Well, I wish you all the luck in the world, I really do.' Griffin rose to his feet. 'Now, please will you show me how I can get out of here?'

'But I need your help!'

'My help?'

'Of course! I've been waiting months for someone to come and take part of the work off my shoulders. Of course you'll have to begin at the bottom, so to speak, as kitchen-boy. But think of the chances of working your way up! If you do well I can promise you swift promotion. I'll teach you to make starters, and then main courses. You'll wait on the guests at table and pour the rum and beer.' He clapped his hands happily. 'It will be *wonderful*!'

The room suddenly seemed more cramped. The walls seemed to move towards Griffin as if to push him into a baking tin like dough. Behind his back, he clenched one hand into a fist. 'I'm sure that's a great offer. Really. But I have a few other things to do. And I was never any use in the ship's galley. Anything I cook is inedible. And . . . well, so I'd really like to go now.'

'Go where? There's nothing but the endless sea out there. Are you going to swim to the nearest island?'

'How far away *is* the nearest island?'

'Too far, that's for sure.'

Griffin's surroundings seemed to peel away like a banana skin. Below what had just seemed to him fantastic, strange and a little crazy, the reality now showed like a rotten fruit. The scene was the same, so was Ebenezer's cheerful smile, even the comfortable room in the light of the fire on the hearth was the same – yet now it was all quite different.

Ebenezer was insane. And he obviously intended to make

Griffin a part of his madness, whether he liked it or not.

'Are you going to keep me prisoner here?' asked Griffin.

'Do you see any bars? Or locks? Nothing of the kind, my boy. I'm only asking for your help. I'll even pay you. I have gold down here, believe me. Of course we'll earn even more from the tavern once our fame gets around. One-twentieth of the takings for you. How's that for an offer?'

Keep perfectly calm, Griffin told himself. Don't give him any reason to distrust you. And then a chance to get away will come up of its own accord.

'When are you going to open the tavern, then?' Griffin found it hard to speak seriously of an idea that was the craziest thing he had ever heard. Compared to a tavern in the belly of a whale, even the marvels of Aelenium paled to a paltry collection of corals.

'Well, we have a lot of work still ahead of us. Are you a good carpenter?'

'I've often helped with repairs on board ship.'

'Excellent! You can make chairs. And tables. There's plenty of wood out there, and you'll find nails in the jetsam from wrecks. What do you think, enough chairs for fifty table settings? Will that do for a start?'

'You want me to make *fifty* chairs?'

'Too few?' Ebenezer was tripping about the room

excitedly, already revelling in his ideas of a crowded tavern. 'More like eighty? Or a hundred.'

'Fifty ought to be enough.'

'We don't want to overdo it, right? Then let's say fifty.' Ebenezer hurried behind the bar and produced a hammer and a rusty pair of pliers. He pushed both over the counter. 'Oh yes, and you'd better take off that dreadful uniform. Have a look around inside Jasconius.' He beamed happily at Griffin. 'I think you'll find everything you need there.'

THE CAPTAINS' COUNCIL

The pirate fleet lay at anchor in a wide circle around the island of St Celestine. At night the lamps on board the ships could hardly be distinguished from the constellations of stars and their reflections in the water.

'This place will be teeming with guards,' said Walker gloomily as they crossed the beach, bending low on their way to a grove of palm trees. Their hippocamps had returned to the safety of the open sea.

'Of course it will,' replied Soledad. 'But they'll be looking for Spaniards or Englishmen in uniform. Not every pirate knows the members of all the other crews. If anyone stops us we'll just say we belong to the crew of another ship. Who's going to check?'

St Celestine was a tiny island fifteen sea miles west of Martinique. Many years ago, French colonists had tried settling there, but the changeable weather and marshy ground finally forced them to give up, and Nature had taken back what the settlers had wrested from her in many years of work.

Remains of old log cabins were covered with bushes and climbing plants. In other places jagged remnants of walls stuck out of the undergrowth like the jawbones of giants. A remarkably well-preserved church tower stood in front of one wall of rock, under a cloak of fleshy leaves and tendrils. Its spire rose above the jungle almost intact.

There was fluttering, chirping and screeching everywhere – the nocturnal hunters of the jungle had woken and were after prey. The air smelled of damp foliage and a wealth of exotic flowers.

They had gone only a short distance when Walker, who was in the lead, pointed upwards without a sound.

Ahead of them rose the slope of a volcano. In the side of the mountain, level with the top of the church tower, a huge recess in the rock gaped to form a natural platform. Voices could be heard, but too far away to be distinct. A cluster of torches lit up the back wall of the recess and the overhanging roof above the platform. There could be no doubt that this was the scene of the secret meeting.

They cautiously followed the path, and a little later reached a flight of steps carved into the rock. Some quick work was enough to clear them of twining plants and under-growth. Felled branches lay scattered around. Someone had put a single torch in a niche in the rock here. The light of its flame licked over the rampart of stone and vegetation towering high ahead of them.

'Well, no point in playing hide-and-seek any more,' said Soledad firmly. 'One way or another I must show myself, so why not now?'

Walker clasped his hand more firmly around the hilt of his sword. Soledad could see that he didn't like the situation, although it wasn't fear of discovery that troubled him but the fact that he wasn't in charge of their troop. Even the Ghost-Trader kept quiet and left the leadership to Soledad. This was her terrain.

'Good day to you!' she cried as they were halfway up the steps. 'We come in friendship!'

Two figures emerged from the darkness above them. One wore a three-cornered hat and a striped shirt, and held two cocked pistols in his hands. The other was holding a sword with a jagged blade; this man had tied a purple scarf over his long hair, and wore an ammunition belt slung over his naked torso. His muscles gleamed in the light of two torches at the top of the steps.

'Who goes there?' called the pirate with the pistols.

'Are you from Tyrone's crew? About time too.'

'No,' she replied. 'I am Soledad.' The princess spoke in a clear, loud voice. 'Scarab's daughter. Take the captains my request: by birth and name, I challenge Kendrick to a duel before the council of the captains of the Antilles.'

Walker and the Ghost-Trader exchanged a glance of alarm. The captain placed a hand on Soledad's shoulder from behind. 'We never said anything about a duel!' he whispered to her in agitation. 'Drop this nonsense, will you?'

Soledad turned and smiled briefly at him. 'I never kept anything from you, Walker,' she said. 'This is about Kendrick's throne, and that's why I'm here.'

A rough voice came from above. 'And *I* am here on *your* account, Soledad!' cried the man scornfully. He stepped out now at the top of the steps in the circle of light cast by the torches.

The princess spun round.

Kendrick the pirate emperor had drawn his sword, but it was pointing to the ground. His smile was icy, his eyes narrow with hostility. The gold ring in his left ear shone in the torchlight. His right ear had been shot away years ago in a fight, but he was vain enough to cover the scar with his luxuriant curly hair.

'Soledad,' he said, and spat on the ground in front of him.

'Your head will be on my bowsprit before the sun rises.'

'Listen to me!' cried Soledad, as her eyes went from face to face. At the moment she had the attention of the twelve Antilles captains. The only question was, how long would that last?

'The pirates of the Lesser Antilles have kept their independence for years, and I know the quarrel between Kendrick and me is not yours. Kendrick isn't your leader, nor was my father. But before you consider allying yourselves to him you should know that Kendrick's rule over the pirates of Tortuga and New Providence was built on lies, treachery and betrayal. And foul, cowardly murder.'

Her voice echoed back from the rock walls. The tables around which the twelve Antilles captains had gathered in a circle stood in the centre of the natural platform made in the volcanic rock by a whim of Nature. From here you could look out over the leaf canopy of the jungle to the sea and the night sky. The ships lying at anchor were visible in the moonlight. Only three or four paces from the edge of the rock, the half-ruined timbers of the church tower rose in the air. The other ruins of the settlement lay about fifty feet lower, hidden in the jungle undergrowth.

The outdoor hearth where flames were blazing now must date from the time of the settlers too. Torches stood in rusty holders on the rock walls. The shadows cast by their flames, intimidatingly large, fell on the rough stone.

'We're listening,' said the captain sitting on Kendrick's right. 'Go on.' He was a rugged sea dog with a voice turned to a hoarse croak by whisky and rum decades ago. He wore a dark red frock-coat with a broad collar, and a black sash across his chest. His plumed tricorne lay on the table in front of him next to a silver goblet of wine. Soledad knew his name, just as she could name all the men assembled here. Rouquette was the oldest present and thus, according to tradition, was the spokesman.

Kendrick had seated himself next to him after leading Soledad up to the table. Walker and the Ghost-Trader stood outside the circle. They had not been disarmed, but Kendrick's men were watching them with drawn swords. Soledad's throwing-knives were still in her belt too.

'We thought highly of your father,' said another man before the princess could go on. He was younger than Rouquette, with black curls and an eye patch with a ruby flashing in the middle of it, a jewel large enough to buy a small island. His name was Galliano. 'If we didn't recognise him as our leader, we never had any quarrel with him and always counted him an ally.'

'You all know that Kendrick murdered my father, and

afterwards he had the corpse dragged through the streets of Port Nassau like a dead dog.'

None of the men present moved a muscle.

'You know that,' Soledad repeated, 'and it is clear to all of you that I have a right to revenge.' She pointed to Kendrick. 'And to his place in this company.'

'There's never been a pirate queen,' said Rouquette. 'But never mind that. We respect you for your courage, Princess. But do you seriously think the pirates of Tortuga and New Providence will accept a woman as their leader?'

'If she throws Kendrick's head at their feet, they'll have to.'

'Your revenge has nothing to do with your claim to the throne, Soledad. And it can't be our business here tonight. We're not in Port Nassau.'

A murmur of agreement rose from the other captains. One man knocked his pipe on the table to show his assent. The sound was thrown back by the rocks and echoed out into the jungle.

'Perhaps you'll change your mind when I tell you that the whole Caribbean – including the Lesser Antilles – is threatened by a danger that we can face only together. All the pirates, never mind whether they offer their loot for sale on Martinique or in New Providence.'

Kendrick dismissed this with a nasty smile. 'What a cheap trick! That sort of thing should be beneath your dignity.'

'I'm not here only to demand what's mine by right,' went on Soledad, ignoring his remark. 'My warning is serious. We're all threatened by deadly danger.'

'What are you talking about?' asked a captain with a forked black beard. His right arm ended in three metal prongs which he kept running across the table top. 'Who threatens us? A Spanish armada like the one off New Providence? Maybe an alliance of the Spaniards and the English?' That was absurd, and he said it in a tone leaving no one in any doubt that he thought Soledad's warning was a ruse.

She chose her words very carefully now. At the moment no one here was going to take her tale seriously. A Maelstrom miles wide, dreadful beings from another world, and an army of kobalins on the warpath?

She had to go about it in another way. 'It is a danger that will sweep over us all like a tempest, and none of us has a chance against it alone.'

'Hear, hear,' said Kendrick, laughing.

Some of the pirates joined in his laughter, but a few of them looked expectantly at Soledad.

'I can't ask you to pay me more attention than is due to me

in this company,' she said, speaking up again. 'You will all find out – though only after I have proved it by defeating Kendrick – that I am worthy to speak before you.'

The Ghost-Trader leaned over to Walker. 'A clever plan,' he whispered appreciatively.

'One that will cost her her life,' replied Walker.

'It's just a silly trick,' Kendrick told the circle of Antilles captains. 'She's deceiving you by making you curious.'

'No,' said Rouquette. He never took his eyes off Soledad. 'She's right.'

Some of the captains murmured, but others nodded.

Kendrick, in agitation, leaned forward. 'But she –'

'She's Scarab's daughter,' the oldest man at the council interrupted him. 'You said so yourself. On the other hand you've made us a good offer, Kendrick, and we owe you our appreciation of that. None of us, I guess, would have thought you capable of such a plan. And if it's true that Tyrone will be with us in carrying it out we won't hesitate to join you.'

'What's he talking about?' whispered Walker, staring at Rouquette as if he could read the answer from his face.

The Ghost-Trader said nothing, but there was anxiety in his glance, and it wasn't just for Soledad now.

Apparently Tyrone hadn't arrived on St Celestine yet. But if Kendrick had really succeeded in winning him as an ally, then the pirate emperor held better cards than Soledad here at the Antilles captains' council.

'But,' Rouquette was going on, 'even if we were to join you it doesn't mean that we can ignore the princess's just demands.'

Galliano nodded in agreement, and one by one the other captains did so too. It was hard to tell whether Rouquette's words appealed to their sense of honour or just their anticipation of a duel.

'This is ridiculous!' Kendrick struck the table with his fist. 'I come here, I promise you fabulous riches and a victory over the Spaniards, and you want me to fight a duel with . . . with a girl still half a *child.*' He spat across the table in Soledad's direction.

'If you refuse,' said Galliano, smiling craftily, 'it could mean there's something in what she says. Think about it, Kendrick.'

Soledad took her opportunity and struck while the iron was hot. 'I tell you he's a coward! He can murder by stealth, oh yes. But you've heard it for yourself: he doesn't even have the guts to face a woman in a fight.'

Kendrick jumped up. Obviously he saw his position endangered. 'This is neither the time nor the place to –'

'That's not for you to judge,' said one of the other captains, a man with fiery red hair and jagged scars on both cheeks.

'You're a guest here at our council. It's for us to decided on the justice of the princess's claims, not you.'

Once again a murmur of agreement was heard.

'That decides it,' Rouquette told the company. 'Kendrick must accept the princess's challenge, and the fight will take place here and now. Any objections?'

Kendrick looked as if he had a great many, but narrowed his lips grimly and shook his head.

Soledad did not let her triumph show. She nodded to Rouquette, saw out of the corner of her eye that Galliano was giving her an insinuating look, and confidently planted herself in front of Kendrick.

'Here and now,' she repeated darkly.

Rouquette raised one hand and silenced the pirates again. 'As Kendrick was challenged to this duel, he has the choice of weapons.'

Kendrick pressed his clenched fists down on the table. His eyes went through Soledad like steel blades. Then he smiled.

'Grappling irons.'

THE CANNIBAL KING

'The devil!' cursed Walker, restraining himself only with difficulty from falling on Kendrick. One of the guards had a pistol pointing at him. 'He knows very well she stands no chance against him with a grappling iron.'

The Ghost-Trader too looked anxious, but he said nothing. He remained a silent observer of events. Perhaps it was a part he had already played at length, ages ago and in another place.

The captains' tables were cleared back to form a large semicircle. They now marked off one side of the duelling ground; the edge of the rock and the yawning abyss beyond it marked the other. There were no railings or balustrade, only the ruined rafters of the church tower rising beside the edge of the platform like a skeleton made of wooden beams.

Rouquette had told his men to fetch two grappling irons from one of the ships. Each of the two duellists, who had taken up their positions on opposite sides of the semicircle, was given one of the spear-shaped weapons.

A grappling iron consisted of a long wooden shaft with a steel point like a spearhead and a claw-shaped hook branching off it. Originally such irons were used during sea battles to pull the rail of an enemy ship close, making it easier for pirates to board the vessel. Long ago, however, the freebooters had begun using grappling irons in attack as well – often to devastating effect. The steel point measured a good foot and a half, and would easily go through a human body, while the sharp hook inflicted terrible wounds. Anyone strong enough could even sweep the long shaft round in a wide circle to mow down several opponents at once.

For a woman, even one as skilful as Soledad, the grappling iron was an awkward, clumsy weapon. The point and the hook towered almost a head above her, making it difficult for her to get a secure grip on the shaft and keep it well balanced – let alone make attacking or defensive movements. The effect of the grappling iron depended entirely on muscular force, and wielding it was a rough, inelegant business. With sword or sabre, Soledad could easily have been a match for Kendrick. With grappling irons, the pirate emperor clearly had the advantage.

Soledad grasped the shaft in both hands and tried to balance it as Rouquette gave the signal, firing his pistol once into the night above the abyss.

Kendrick uttered a fierce cry and rushed forward. With a few swift steps he crossed the semicircle outlined by the tables, intending to run his adversary through at the first attempt.

Soledad avoided him and ducked underneath his thrust. Seconds later, she herself was trying to sweep him off his legs with her grappling iron. Her own attempt also failed, but it showed Kendrick that he wouldn't have an easy time of it.

The Ghost-Trader placed a soothing hand on Walker's shoulder when he saw that the captain was on the point of intervening. 'No!' he said sharply. 'They'd slaughter us all on the spot.'

'I can't just stand by and watch him –'

'That's the way she wanted it.'

Walker said no more, but looked in dismay at the duelling ground. Sweat stood out on his brow. His hands opened and closed with every attack and counter-attack.

The boots of the two duellists swirled up dust. Now and then an 'Oh!' or an 'Ah!' went through the Antilles captains when one of the fighters – usually Soledad – was in difficulties. But most of the time the men kept silent. They all led a life full of fighting and bloodshed, and each of them had watched hundreds of such duels. Yet they couldn't tear themselves away from the spectacle.

Soledad was doing better than the pirate emperor had obviously expected. At first Kendrick bellowed and snorted to shake her confidence, but when he saw that his menacing behaviour didn't affect her he too fought in silence, face grim, teeth gritted.

Kendrick might be a coward but he wasn't a bad fighter. He hadn't won his position among the pirates by cunning and deceit alone. He moved fast and sure, and his attacks were often unexpected, or aimed at places that Soledad could protect only with difficulty.

The princess had just one advantage: she was more agile than Kendrick, and what she lacked in sheer strength she made up for in speed. That gave her little chance to attack, but plenty of opportunities to avoid his heavy blows. She made him stumble into empty space several times, carried on by his own impetus, which almost knocked him off his feet. Each time that happened she tried to follow up with her grappling iron, but he kept managing to avoid her thrusts and blows.

They were both bleeding from small wounds. Kendrick's velvet breeches were torn at the knees, while the back of Soledad's jacket hung in rags; one of his thrusts had almost smashed her backbone.

In the end it was just a question of time before the strength of one of them ebbed away. It was already obvious that not skill but exhaustion would decide the outcome of the fight. And none of the spectators, not even Walker and the Ghost-Trader, doubted which of the duellists must inevitably be worn down first.

The weight of Soledad's unwieldy weapon was sapping her strength. By now she could barely feel her arms. Her fingers clutched the shaft so firmly that she didn't know whether her hands would ever open of their own accord again.

Kendrick was handling his grappling iron as surely as ever. Every time she managed to parry one of his blows the force of the impact went right through her, threatening to knock her off her feet.

She had to do something before it was too late, find some way of breaking through the storm of thrusts and blows that he was raining down on her.

She could think of only one possibility.

With a few great bounds she leaped out of reach of his weapon and ran to the edge of the rock. For the first time in many minutes Kendrick uttered a triumphant cry. He thought he had put his opponent to flight.

But Soledad had something else in mind. She made at full speed for the abyss – and the ruinous timber framework of the church tower. Nine feet of nothing gaped between the rocky platform and its rafters.

Even as she ran Soledad swung back her arm and flung the grappling iron at the roof of the tower like a lance.

A murmur passed through the ranks of captains.

The steel point passed through the wood and stuck in a rafter, vibrating. The roof creaked alarmingly. A flock of birds that had been roosting there, invisible in the shadows, fluttered up screeching, hovered like a flickering cloud above the void for a moment, and then shot away towards the jungle.

Soledad took off from the edge of the platform and, with a great bound, leaped across the chasm. With a bloodcurdling oath she slammed into the rafters, swiftly flung both arms out to steady herself, and whipped round. She had landed right beside her grappling iron where it stuck in the rafter. The creaking of the timbers became the sound of rotten wood desperately breaking apart. But the roof frame held. Instinctively, Soledad glanced down: on one side of the overgrown wall of the church tower she vaguely saw treetops in the darkness, on the other there was nothing but a pitch-black shaft.

Kendrick came to a slithering halt just before the abyss. He stared grimly across it at her, unsure for a moment whether he should venture to follow. Soledad put one leg round the rafter, silently hoping it would give her enough support. Then, with both hands, she pulled the grappling iron out of the wood. She whirled it round in her right hand, now holding it like a spear, took aim, and flung it over the chasm straight back at Kendrick.

The pirate emperor let out a shriek as the point hit his thigh, smashed the bone and came out again on the other side. The force of the impact flung him back. The steel head of the grappling iron hit the rock and struck sparks. Yelling, Kendrick lay on the ground, holding his leg in both hands and rolling from side to side in pain, while the shaft of the weapon swept aimlessly through the air above him.

The spectators held their breath. Rouquette rose from his chair.

Soledad was hanging in the rafters of the church tower, gasping for breath as she looked across at the rocky platform. Her long hair, damp and matted, hung over her face, and sweat burned her eyes. Kendrick's pain gave her deep satisfaction, but she felt insecure too. She wasn't going to get down from here by herself. Would the Antilles captains acknowledge Kendrick's injury as a defeat, even though it wasn't a mortal wound? Or was neither of them the victor while Soledad was stranded here, as helpless as the pirate emperor himself?

'Our decision,' shouted Rouquette, to drown out the screams of the injured man, 'our decision is that –'

'*Stop!*' A voice interrupted him, a cutting voice as sharp as a sword-blade.

The heads of all the Antilles captains swung round. Several men jumped up. Rouquette's eyes narrowed with anger at the interruption. The Ghost-Trader too turned to the man who had appeared at the top of the steps cut in the rock. Only Walker was still desperately trying to find a way to save Soledad. And the pistol held by the man watching him was still pointed at his chest.

'Patch that man up!' ordered the newcomer, and immediately two figures emerged from the darkness behind him and hurried to the injured pirate emperor.

Kendrick was still writhing on the ground. The shadow of the shaft of the grappling iron in his leg swept over the rock wall like a pendulum. The two men knelt down beside him. One of them pressed Kendrick's shoulders down on the ground, the second set about putting a tourniquet on the twitching leg above the wound.

'Tyrone?' asked Rouquette, coming round from behind his table. 'We expected you earlier.'

The man at the top of the steps walked forward into the firelight. He was wearing wide black trousers, boots with broad tops, and a black frock-coat adorned with fine silver. But his face was in complete contrast to his elegant clothing: a network of designs covered his features and indeed his whole skull. Archaic patterns and undulating lines surrounded his eyes and lips, probably the ritual markings of the cannibal tribes he had brought under his rule. A long black ponytail grew from the back of his head. The rest of his scalp was hairless, and even his eyebrows were shaved.

When he spoke, Tyrone bared teeth filed to points as sharp as needles. And Walker, standing only a few paces from him, saw that the cannibal king's tongue was split and dyed black at the ends.

'I was delayed,' he said, looking round. His split tongue made his voice hiss slightly. 'And I see I've just missed the most interesting part of the meeting.' He went over to Kendrick, who had now had the grappling iron removed from his leg. The wound was neatly bound up and bleeding less freely, but the pirate emperor had lost consciousness.

One of the two men who had tended the injured man on Tyrone's orders looked up. 'He'll lose that leg. The bone's splintered.'

'Get him on board his ship,' commanded Tyrone with a wave of his hand. 'Let his crew see to him.'

Soledad was both fascinated and repelled by the nightmare

figure of the cannibal king. The air of effortless superiority with which he faced the mighty Antilles captains was impressive. His appearance and his tone of voice immediately made one thing clear: when he spoke no one interrupted, neither Rouquette nor Galliano nor any of the others. He drew all eyes until he was the centre of everyone's attention.

The princess was still clinging to the rafters of the church tower. Her arms were beginning to go numb. However, she didn't move. Whether she got down from this tower alive wasn't up to the captains now. Tyrone would decide.

'A plank!' he cried, without deigning to look at her. 'It's not right or proper for a princess to crouch up there like a monkey.'

No one laughed. No one contradicted him. Two pirates immediately hurried off, came back with a good stout plank, and laid it over the gap between the edge of the rock and the roof of the church tower. Soledad wasn't sure that her legs would carry her, but she had to risk it. Swaying, she made her way over the plank. The abyss pulled at her; the darkness reached for her feet with shadowy fingers. When she reached firm ground, teeth gritted, she fell to her knees.

No pistol could stop Walker now. He raced straight across the duelling ground, took Soledad in his arms and helped her up. 'Are you hurt?' he whispered anxiously. 'Did he injure you?'

'I'm all right,' she said with an effort, adding more quietly, 'so far.'

Tyrone smiled. The two rows of sharply filed teeth flashed behind his lips like saw-blades. He made no comment on the couple at the edge of the rock, but instead looked at the Antilles captains one by one. Finally his gaze settled on the Ghost-Trader. The two men stared at each other in silence. The Trader didn't move a muscle or show the slightest sign of uncertainty.

Tyrone's smile grew yet broader.

Soledad was fighting her dizziness. The figures before her blurred. Did those two know each other?

The silent moment between the two men passed, and Tyrone turned back to the assembled captains. Behind him, two of the unconscious Kendrick's men picked him up and carried him to the steps.

'It's a shame,' said Tyrone without any sympathy in his voice, 'but we must do without him at this meeting.'

'Kendrick is no longer leader of the captains of Tortuga and New Providence,' announced Rouquette. Obviously he wasn't willing to put up with the cannibal king's lordly manner any more. 'Princess Soledad has defended her right to the throne. Let her conduct negotiations instead of him and speak for her people.'

With a slight shudder Soledad realised that he didn't mean Walker and the Ghost-Trader, but all the pirates between the Bahamas and the Virgin Islands. She had defeated Kendrick in a duel. But he was only injured, and she wasn't sure if that would be enough. Would they accept the outcome of the fight in Port Nassau or Jamaica?

'Princess Soledad was going to warn us of something before you arrived, Tyrone,' Galliano put in.

'She was? Looked to me more as if she was about to break her neck.' With a shark-like grin, he turned to Soledad and Walker. He frowned as he saw Soledad right behind him, no longer needing support but standing squarely on her own two feet.

'Tyrone,' she said coolly, looking him in the face. 'You're as much a guest here as I am, and I ask myself what authority you have to speak for Kendrick or any of these other captains. If they're happy with it – well and good, that's none of my business. But you will not speak for *me*.'

It was a rash and perhaps unwise attack, but Soledad was sick and tired of Tyrone's domineering tone. On the mainland he might command a few thousand cannibals, but out here on St Celestine he was only a pirate like all the others.

Tyrone sketched a mock bow, but the sharp retort she had expected didn't come. 'Then tell us your plan. What about the attack on Caracas? That's what has brought us all here?'

Caracas? Had Kendrick seriously been planning to attack one of the richest and strongest of the Spanish coastal fortresses? Had he lured her here for *that*? By all the saints, he was even crazier than she'd supposed.

'I'm not here about Caracas,' she said, 'but to warn you all of a danger that will face us in a few days or weeks.'

Tyrone kept calm. He listened.

Soledad exchanged a quick glance with the Ghost-Trader, and saw him almost imperceptibly nod.

'The kobalins have united into a mighty army.' Now there was no going back. 'They're gathering out in the Atlantic to the north of the Lesser Antilles. I've seen them with my own eyes, thousands of them. It's said they are commanded by something that calls itself a Maelstrom.' She deliberately kept that part vague so as not to ask too much of the captains all at once. She was on thin ice here, and she felt as if Tyrone's looks alone were lighting a fire under her feet.

'Kobalins?' Galliano stared at her, and to her horror she saw the disappointment in his eyes. He had obviously been expecting something more convincing. 'Everyone knows that the Deep Tribes hate each other's guts. They'd never unite, not for any reason.'

Some of the other captains nodded. A dark-skinned man

snorted derisively. 'So that's your great danger, Princess? An old wives' tale?'

'It's no old wives' tale,' she said firmly. 'I myself have seen the Deep Tribes moving east. The kobalins are gathering and will attack. I've heard that they've already left the water and gone on land once. And they'll do it again.'

'Kobalins *never* leave the water,' cried Tyrone, not in reply to what Soledad said but appealing to the captains. 'Even their chieftains fear the air. They'd never go on land. It's utterly out of the question.'

'Yet it happened.'

'And what guarantee do we have of that? Your word?' Rouquette looked her up and down suspiciously. She was on the point of losing the last of their sympathy.

'The word of the rightful queen of the pirates,' she said with emphasis, and then something else occurred to her. 'Hasn't it been said that the cannibal tribes were always at odds with each other too? Yet Tyrone has succeeded in uniting them. Why shouldn't the same thing happen with the kobalins?'

The muscles of Tyrone's face twitched. 'Cannibals are only human,' he said coldly. 'Human beings fear each other, and that makes them weak and malleable. But kobalins? What's a kobalin afraid of?'

'And what are cannibals afraid of?' she countered him.

Now there was an intent silence among the Antilles captains. A new contest was shaping up, one that none of them had expected. Not a fight with grappling irons and bloodshed, but a contest of words to find out whose will was stronger.

Tyrone's eyes bored into the princess. It was difficult to withstand a gaze that had seen so much cruelty and horror. But she kept her composure.

The cannibal king spun round. 'Captains!' he cried to the company. 'This girl promises you a war with the kobalins. But *I* will give you the treasure-chambers of Caracas.'

Soledad was about to protest, but this time Rouquette interrupted her. 'Quiet, Soledad! It's Tyrone's turn now.'

The cannibal king smiled at her with relish – it was the smile of a beast of prey – and then turned his back on her and began pacing up and down in front of the captains. 'In two weeks' time there's to be a great attack on Caracas by the Caribbean pirates. You will say it's been tried before, and all who attempted it failed. Very true. But today the situation is different. Back then the assault on Caracas came only from the sea, but with my help they – and *you*, if you'll join us – will take the city from both sea and land.'

The whispering among the captains became a murmur

and then turned to loud discussion. Soledad cast the Ghost-Trader a desperate glance, but his expression was as inscrutable as ever. Walker was standing somewhere behind her, near the edge of the rock but keeping his distance, in case any of the captains might think she needed a man's support.

Tyrone waited until the talk had died down and then went on with his speech. 'She gives you kobalins,' he repeated, relishing every syllable, 'but I will give you gold! If all the pirates of the Caribbean come together in this attack, dozens of ships will have their guns trained on Caracas harbour – a whole armada! At the same time I and my men will strike from the landward side. We'll take the city in a lightning attack.'

'How many men are you speaking of?' asked Galliano.

'Yes,' the dark-skinned captain wanted to know. 'How many men do you command?'

Tyrone dropped the answer into the silence as if driving a stake home. 'Five thousand!'

Soledad's heart was hammering. One thing was clear: even if she told the captains that the world was about to end, it would get her nowhere in the face of their greed for gold.

'Five thousand,' the captains echoed.

'Eighteen of the largest tribes of savages obey my orders,' Tyrone confirmed, 'and a few more scattered groups as well.

More are joining me every day.' He paused to let his words take effect.

Soledad intervened. '*Tribes of savages*, he says. But what he means is *cannibals*!' She fixed her eyes on Rouquette and Galliano. 'Is that what you want? An alliance with *five thousand man-eating savages*?'

The two captains exchanged a glance, but then attended to what Tyrone was saying again.

'And the best of it is yet to come,' announced the cannibal king.

'Go on!' cried the captain with the forked beard. They could hear the greed in his voice.

'I'll give you five thousand men – and none of them will cost you a single doubloon!'

Silence again. Open mouths, wide eyes. Then someone burst out laughing, while others clapped their hands. The captains' enthusiasm washed over them like a tidal wave.

Soledad stood there as if turned to stone. Suddenly Walker was beside her, speaking softly in her ear. 'Come on! Quick!'

'But –'

'No. It's over. They won't listen to you any more.'

She knew he was right. She was powerless against such arguments. The Maelstrom? A war against the kobalins? Of no importance compared to five thousand warriors who would make every one of these captains many times richer than before. A fighting force, moreover, for which they wouldn't have to pay anything.

Soledad said goodbye to her idea of returning to Aelenium with a great fleet. Even her victory over Kendrick suddenly meant nothing any more. If they were in luck they'd get off this island alive. The Antilles captains would eat out of Tyrone's hand and give him anything he wanted. Soledad's head on a golden platter? Just a question of who had the sharpest blade, she felt sure.

While the captains leaped up from their seats talking excitedly all at the same time, Soledad moved towards the flight of steps with Walker. The men who had been guarding him and the Ghost-Trader showed no more interest in them now.

'Let's get away from here,' said the Trader when they reached him.

And next moment they were hurrying down the steps. Soledad looked back just once, and saw Tyrone turn her way.

He opened his mouth and laughed. Torchlight fell on his lips.

His gums were as black as a dog's.

Walker and the Ghost-Trader were arguing. That is to say,

Walker was arguing – the Ghost-Trader was considerably more self-controlled. The captain wanted to know why the Trader hadn't simply called up all the ghosts on the island to put a stop to the farce on the rocky platform. The Trader replied – not for the first time – that the meeting had to go as it did and in no other way. That was not, of course, an argument that appealed to a man like Walker. But the Ghost-Trader stuck to his point, as if he knew something that would affect the fate of them all.

'It was important,' he said, 'for us to meet Tyrone like that. And it was just as important for Soledad to have a chance to humiliate Kendrick before all eyes. You'll understand that sooner or later, Walker.'

Soledad paid attention only when she heard her name, but then she sank back into her own gloomy thoughts, leaving the men to themselves.

They had gone almost half the distance back to the shore when two pirates came out from the trees and barred their way.

'What's going on up there?' asked one of them. He carried a long-barrelled shotgun, and the other drew a sword from his belt. However, the pair didn't seem particularly anxious to start a fight with Soledad and her companions. Their attention was mainly on the platform in the rock wall. Seen from down here and lit by torches, it shone like another half-moon in the darkness.

'We're celebrating Captain Tyrone's arrival,' said Walker quickly, before Soledad's hesitation could make the guards suspicious. 'He brought good news.'

'*He* did? Good news?' The man with the shotgun frowned. 'Looks like a madman to me.' But then he quickly added, 'Don't tell anyone I said so.'

Walker shook his head. 'The captains are going to have a feast in his honour. They've just tapped a barrel of rum up there.'

'Rum?' said the pirate with the sword.

'For everyone.'

'Us too?'

'Not while you're standing guard down here.'

'You mean . . .?'

Soledad nodded. 'We're on our way to let the men on our ship know. And if they get there first, there won't be much rum left for you.'

The pirates exchanged a glance and then hurried off. 'Thanks!' one of them called back over his shoulder, with a grin. 'You're real friends!'

Soledad and her two companions, bending low, disappeared into the undergrowth. As they did, they heard one of the pirates tell the other, 'Hey, I think I knew one of those fellows. Looked like Walker.'

'*The* Walker?' asked the other, but whatever answer he got was lost in the rustling of the leaves as the three friends hurried away.

They came upon two more groups of guards, but managed to avoid them in time. Soon after that they reached the belt of palms surrounding the island. Here the trees grew further apart, with no undergrowth to protect them. Their outlines looked like silhouettes against the snow-white sand. The companions quickened their pace. Walker was left a little way behind, cursing when he trod in a nest of hermit crabs, and all the rest of the way to the water he was busy plucking the little creatures off the leg of his breeches.

A keen wind was blowing over the sea. The breakers foamed at their feet, and even in the moonlight they could see tall, mountainous waves towering up in the open sea. It was as if Tyrone had brought the heralds of a storm to St Celestine with him – in more than one way.

The Ghost-Trader raised a whistle made from a shell to his lips and blew it to summon the sea horses. Then they waited in silence for the hippocamps to arrive.

The idea that the Antilles captains were seriously going to join the cannibal king gave Soledad no peace. It was one thing to storm a Spanish fortress, even at the cost of dozens or even hundreds of lives, quite another to let five thousand man-eating savages loose on the inhabitants of Caracas.

In her thoughts she saw Tyrone's sharp teeth and the black-dyed ends of his tongue. She knew what awaited the people of Caracas if that brute moved in on the city. And although Soledad herself had taken part in raids and had seen pirates attacking the women and girls of Spanish settlements, the idea of a hungry army of cannibals invading conjured up scenes of pure horror in her mind.

Suddenly it all seemed to her hopeless. Her entire mission had failed: the cannibals were wreaking havoc on land, the kobalins were at large in the sea. And somewhere in the distance the Maelstrom was turning.

She wondered if it hadn't been also pulling the strings here, and for quite some time, in the shape of men like Tyrone and Kendrick. Was there some link between them and the Mare Tenebrosum? Was the whole raid on Caracas nothing but a ruse to keep the pirates and the Spaniards occupied, while the Maelstrom extended its sphere of influence day after day?

She was about to share her thoughts with the others when Walker suddenly pointed to one of the ships that were carrying lights.

'That's Tyrone's ship – the *Quadriga*!'

Before the starlit sky and the rough seas on the horizon lay a four-master, a former Spanish frigate with a tall superstructure at her bows. Only a few lanterns were burning on the rail and the bridge. It was almost as if the men on board wanted to hide what was happening on deck from any prying eyes.

Soledad shuddered as she thought of the men in Tyrone's service. His companions up on the rocky plateau had not been savages, and she suspected that the rest of his crew also consisted of men from the Old World. But who would willingly volunteer to follow a monster like Tyrone? What bait did he dangle before his men? Wealth? Fighting? Or was it sheer fear of him that made them obedient?

A good hundred paces from the *Quadriga*, Kendrick's brigantine the *Masquerade* lay at anchor. While the *Quadriga* was best suited to battles at sea, the small and racy *Masquerade* was an excellent ship for a fast voyage.

'The ship's boat!' Walker pointed out to a narrow shape on the dark water. 'They're taking Kendrick back on board. Whether the other Caribbean pirates follow him or you in future, he won't forget this defeat.' He was going to put an arm round Soledad's shoulders, but she took a step aside as if by chance.

'I'm not afraid of him,' she said.

'The man who bandaged him up was right,' said the Ghost-Trader. 'Kendrick will lose that leg. The wound was too bad, and they'll only be able to give it rough and ready treatment on board. He's done for as a leader.'

She shrugged, although she was shivering inside. She had killed many men in her time – but never before had she maimed one and left him alive.

'Whatever happens I'm with you,' said Walker.

She was preparing to make a sharp retort when she suddenly realised how seriously he meant it. She'd never known him like this before. He was a cut-throat and a rogue, a man who didn't find it easy to accept anyone else as an equal – until the moment up on the platform when he'd taken her in his arms. A change was coming over him, and it moved but also alarmed her. This time it was her own courage she feared.

'There they are!' said the Ghost-Trader, pointing to the three sea horses gliding through the water towards the shore.

Soledad went into the surf first, wading out to the hippocamps. The sea horses stopped a stone's throw from land, where the water was still deep enough to leave room for their long fishtails below the surface. The animals lay low in the water, as if instinctively feeling that the ships meant danger.

A little later Soledad, Walker and the Ghost-Trader were in their saddles. They turned the sea horses and rode out into the open ocean.

The Trader brought his mount close to the other two. 'I think it would be a bad idea to go back to Aelenium now.'

Soledad looked at him in surprise. Secretly she had been thinking the same thing, but she hadn't ventured to say so out loud. She had defended her father's throne and was the rightful leader of the pirates, whether or not Kendrick accepted it. Her place was with the Caribbean freebooters; the raid on Caracas was a bad plan at the wrong moment, and it was up to her to prevent it. But at the same time she felt a confusing sense of obligation to Jolly and the others. She was part of this group now whether she liked it or not.

Walker looked from one to the other of his companions in the faint moonlight. 'I know what you two have in mind. I'm just wondering why.'

'Let us follow Tyrone in secret when he goes back to his base,' said the Ghost-Trader. 'We shall serve the cause of Aelenium best by thwarting his plans.'

'You felt it too, didn't you?' asked Soledad acutely. 'There's more to Tyrone than meets the eye.'

The Ghost-Trader nodded. 'I was aware of it when he

stood there talking to the captains. The words were his, but the plan behind them . . . I'm not so sure.'

'You think Tyrone is serving the Maelstrom?' asked Walker.

'That's what we'll find out.'

'Good,' said Soledad. 'I agree.'

Walker nodded. He would probably even have followed her straight into the Mare Tenebrosum, which made her feel guilty, but also roused a new and unexpected emotion in her. It wasn't just gratitude to him for standing by her any more.

'When the *Quadriga* puts out to sea,' said the Trader, 'we'll follow her.'

Walker looked grimly from him to Soledad. 'Well,' he said, 'you know where that will take us.'

She patted the head of her nervous sea horse as if that would give her courage too. 'Yes,' she said. 'Into the heart of the cannibal kingdom.'

OLD FRIENDS

'I don't understand it,' said Jolly, looking out over the Caribbean Sea. In the early morning light it shone like dull silver. Whatever was pursuing them under the waves had disappeared a day ago, leaving no trace. 'Something happened on Agostini's bridge that I simply can't grasp.'

The Hexhermetic Shipworm was sitting in his rucksack. By now he hardly left it; he was like a snail in its shell. Perhaps even he was affected by her deep sense of insecurity.

'No one in Aelenium could tell me anything about it. Not Munk, not the Ghost-Trader, not even Forefather.' She frowned. 'Perhaps no one *wanted* to tell me anything about it.'

Jolly was standing in the bows of the *Carfax* with one hand on the rail, as if the cool wood under her fingers could help her to see the world around her as reality and not another illusion conjured up by the Mare Tenebrosum. Every night now she dreamed of that black ocean, as if she were coming closer and closer to it, although she must be moving further away with every sea mile they sailed.

'The Maelstrom is the gateway to the Mare Tenebrosum, and that's why we have to seal it – I can understand that. But what about the bridge built by Agostini – I mean the shape-shifter? Griffin and I crossed it. The bridge itself was something like a gateway. If it's as easy as that to open one, why is the Maelstrom so important?'

'Hm, well,' said the Worm in his rasping voice, 'I can't say I know much about the Mare Tenebrosum.'

'But that's not true! You told me more about it than the Ghost-Trader did – at least until we reached Aelenium. You even knew about the Rift!' She cast a glance over her shoulder and up at the helm, where Buenaventure stood at the wheel. She was beginning to wonder whether the pit bull man ever needed to sleep. He spent the few breaks he allowed himself dozing but always on the alert, ears ready to register every gust of wind, any unusual creaking of the planks. For days it had seemed as if he and the ship had merged together, the body and mind of a single being. Buenaventure was here to protect Jolly – but his concern was also for the *Carfax*. She was like an old and dear friend to him.

'Come on,' Jolly challenged the Hexhermetic Shipworm. 'Talk to me!'

'The bridge, then,' he murmured, sighing, and nodded his head back and forth as if a fakir with a flute had conjured him out of the rucksack. 'You said the kobalins attacked it. But they withdrew once the soldiers from Aelenium appeared and set fire to Agostini's structure, right?'

Jolly nodded.

'Doesn't that strike you as strange? The kobalins are under orders from the Maelstrom. And the Maelstrom itself is a servant of the Mare Tenebrosum. Why would the masters attack what they had made, let alone destroy it?'

Jolly frowned. 'No idea.'

'Well,' said the Worm slowly, 'we may have been on the wrong track all this time. Perhaps the Maelstrom now has other aims. Aims of its own.'

'But the Maelstrom is the gateway for its masters.'

'Then why doesn't it just open? So far we've been assuming it may be too weak. But then how can it command thousands of kobalins and do all kinds of other damage? I have another suspicion. I think that for some reason or other the bridge was a danger to the Maelstrom, and that's why it had it attacked.'

'You really think the Maelstrom would turn on its masters?'

'Yes, I do. The Maelstrom must have freed itself from slavery to them. That's the only explanation for the way the kobalins acted on the bridge. Perhaps it's become aware of its own power. Why share that power with its masters if it's the mightiest being in this world? It could make itself the ruler over everything.'

This idea of the Worm's turned a great many of Jolly's own assumptions so far upside down. But yes, it was the only way to make sense of the whole thing. The bridge must have been built because the Maelstrom was closing itself to its masters, and they needed a new way of access to the world. The only question was why they hadn't simply come over the bridge when Agostini had finished it . . .

'You're expected,' she murmured under her breath.

The Worm put his head a little further out of the rucksack. 'What?' he asked, intrigued.

Jolly pushed a strand of hair back from her face. The wind had freshened, and the *Carfax* was gathering speed.

'That's what the shape-shifter told me when he was on the bridge with us: "You're expected," he said.'

Jolly stepped back from the rail and began pacing up and down the deck in agitation. Why hadn't she thought of that before? It was about the polliwiggles. Ultimately, it always came down to the polliwiggles.

'The bridge wasn't intended for the masters of the Mare,' she said out loud. 'Agostini built it for me. It was to take me to them in the Mare Tenebrosum.'

The Worm nodded thoughtfully. 'I've been thinking something like that too,' he said pensively.

Jolly stopped in front of him. 'But what interest could the masters of the Mare Tenebrosum have in me?' she asked. 'Why didn't they simply tell the shape-shifter to kill me? After all, I'm their worst enemy.'

The Worm hauled himself a little further out of the rucksack with his front pair of legs. 'Are you? Are you really their mortal enemy?'

Jolly was about to answer when Buenaventure's voice rang out over the deck.

'Land in sight!' he called down from the bridge. 'The coast is in view, Jolly!'

On the horizon she saw a long line of shapes like hills. The mainland. Somewhere far away there was the mouth of the Orinoco River – and also, she hoped, another clue leading her to Bannon and the men of the *Maid Maddy*.

She pushed aside all other thoughts about the bridge, the Mare Tenebrosum, and what the Worm had said. She had to concentrate on what lay ahead of her now.

'Everything all right?' called Buenaventure.

'Yes . . . yes,' she said uncertainly, and drew herself up straight, although she was thinking that nothing at all was all right. More clearly than ever before she saw that she had made a terrible mistake. In fleeing from the starfish city she had let everyone down: the people of Aelenium, her companions and, worst of all, Griffin. His face appeared before her mind's eye, and this time it was superimposed over everything else so strongly that she felt a pang of pain and longing.

The Hexhermetic Shipworm said something, but she didn't hear his words and just looked through him.

'Jolly!'

That was Buenaventure.

She pulled herself together and turned to look at him. 'What?'

'We're not alone any more. Over there – on the horizon behind us!'

She ran for the bridge, passing through several ghosts that didn't get out of the way quickly enough, leaped up the steps and looked intently over the rail. The two parrots came fluttering up and settled on the balustrade beside her.

A ship had appeared in the distance, a ship with many large sails. 'Looks like a Spanish frigate!'

Buenaventure said nothing. But after a few minutes, when it was obvious that the pursuing vessel was much faster than they were and was coming closer and closer, his dog's eyes narrowed as he looked back.

'That's the *Quadriga*,' he said. 'Tyrone's ship.'

'Can we make it to the coast before them?' asked Jolly, although she knew the answer.

Buenaventure shook his head, and his drooping ears flapped. 'No. If they want to stop us they will.'

Jolly called out orders to the ghosts on board. With lightning speed, the cannon were manned and made ready to fire. Torches flared up, barrels were filled with gunpowder, iron cannonballs rolled into place in the guns.

'There's no point in it,' said Buenaventure, and for the first time Jolly heard the strange undertone in his voice. The pit bull man was afraid – not for himself but for her. And for his ship. She had never before seen him so much at a loss, and that scared her even more than the appearance of the *Quadriga*.

'You don't want to fight?' she asked, dismayed.

'I didn't say that, but there's no point. The *Quadriga* is a warship. She has three times as many guns as we do. And if they're going to board us the ghosts won't be much help.'

In her heart, she knew he was right. But she wasn't ready to accept it. Not so close to . . . yes, to what? Her destination? But what was that?

'Jolly,' said Buenaventure, 'bring the Worm here.'

She ran to the bows, picked up the rucksack with the Worm

chattering angrily inside it, and carried it up to the bridge. Buenaventure strapped the rucksack firmly to his back.

'Keep your head down, Prince of Poets!'

'Would anyone be kind enough to tell me . . .' The Worm fell silent as he saw the ship, now only a few hundred paces away and following fast in their wake. 'Oh,' he said, and without any more fuss crept into the rucksack.

'Jolly, I want you to go below decks.'

She stared at the pit bull man. 'Certainly not!'

'Please do as I say!'

'I'm the only one who can give the ghosts orders. They won't obey you. And I've no intention of crawling away to hide.'

The Shipworm showed a tiny part of his horny plate. 'Crawling away to hide isn't a bad idea at all.'

'I'm staying here,' she told Buenaventure.

'And suppose it's you they want?'

She thought. Was that possible? What interest could the cannibal king have in her?

'I'm not going below decks,' she said at last.

Buenaventure made a kind of puffing sound that in an ordinary person would probably have been a deep sigh. 'Then at least hide behind the crates on the main deck.'

The monotonous roar of the sea behind them was broken by the thunder of guns.

'Oh, my goodness me,' whimpered the Shipworm, deep inside his rucksack. 'They're firing at us!'

'That was only a warning shot,' said Buenaventure. 'They want us to heave to.' His right eyebrow rose on his flat, hairy brow. 'Well, *Captain* Jolly?'

'Do what you think right.'

'Then get out of here.'

She ran down the steps to the deck and got into cover behind some crates standing close to the mainmast of the *Carfax*. 'Make ready to fire!' she called to the ghosts. When she saw Buenaventure nodding at her from the bridge she gave the order to heave to, and the *Carfax* slowed down.

A little later the *Quadriga* came into Jolly's field of vision on the port side. She had to duck her head further down so as not to be seen.

'*Carfax* ahoy!' someone called. Jolly dared not raise her head. A vessel like the *Quadriga* carried a crew of well over a hundred men, and as many pairs of eyes were now staring at the deck of the *Carfax*. The risk of being spotted was too great.

'*Quadriga* ahoy!' replied the pit bull man. A long pause followed, and Jolly began to wonder whether Buenaventure, standing up there, had seen something that took his voice away. There was a lump in her throat that she couldn't swallow.

Then, at last, the pit bull man called, 'We're carrying no cargo, if that's what you're after.'

'Commander Tyrone wants to know if you have a young girl on board with you.'

By now Jolly was sure that the voice didn't belong to Tyrone himself. Indeed, it sounded familiar to her. Where from was hard to say, however, as long as the man was shouting across the gap between the two ships with the wind distorting his words.

Buenaventure let out a bark of laughter. '*Commander* Tyrone? Promoted himself, has he?'

'Answer, dog!'

'The *Carfax* has no children on board!' said the pit bull man grimly.

'We'd like to convince ourselves of that.'

'Are you going to board us?'

Jolly changed her position slightly so that she could look up at the bridge. Buenaventure's left hand was resting on the wheel, but his right hand held a cocked pistol. There was something wrong. He wasn't acting as he usually did, he was much more restrained. Was that just to avoid provoking the crew of the *Quadriga*?

'We certainly will board you if we don't get permission to pay you a friendly visit,' called the voice.

'Friendly! A word of great importance, and one that you use lightly, traitor!'

Traitor? What on earth was going on? Damn it all, she had to see why Buenaventure was behaving so strangely.

Very slowly, she raised herself among the crates and looked out to port.

The rail of the *Quadriga* towered some six feet above the *Carfax*. Dozens of figures stood up there, staring down at the smaller ship's deck. They all wore the motley assortment of garments favoured by the Caribbean pirates, although some of them were island savages. She avoided looking into any of their faces. Hastily, she went to the steps and climbed to the bridge.

'Jolly, you shouldn't have –'

'This is my decision, Buenaventure. Or they'll sink the *Carfax*.'

He sighed. It was almost like a dog's whine. 'I'm sorry.'

Only when she turned to look at the bridge of the other ship and saw who was standing there did she understand what he meant.

With a cry of surprise, she flinched back. It was as if her head had come up against an invisible wall.

'I really am sorry,' said Buenaventure again.

'Jolly,' cried the man. 'It's good to see you again.'

She couldn't reply. Her jaw felt as if it had been screwed up; her tongue wouldn't obey her.

'Bannon?'

He gave her the beaming smile she'd always liked so much. His fair hair, yellow as straw, was fluttering in the stiff breeze, and his white shirt billowed out like a sail in the wind. A silver amulet hung on his chest. His father, who had been first gunner on board a freebooter in the pay of the British crown, had given it to him before he was finally strung up in Maracaibo harbour. Bannon had been going to hand it on to Jolly some day, so he'd always said. *One day this will be yours.*

'But . . . how . . .' She spoke so softly that not even Buenaventure could hear her.

The pit bull man lowered his gaze. Anger and pity flared up in his eyes in equal measure.

'Jolly, come on board with us,' called Bannon. 'We've missed you. Look – we're all here!'

Her eyes wandered over the faces looking at her from the rail of the *Quadriga*, some smiling, some grave. She recognised about every third man. There was Trevino, cook on board the *Maid Maddy*, who had designed the tattoo on her back; she saw the steersman Christophorus; Abarquez, who had taken her up to the crow's-nest with him her very first time; Long Tom, who wouldn't fit into any hammock on the *Maddy* and had made himself a bigger one of plundered brocade; Redhead Doyle; old Sam Greaney; Guilfoyle and the black giant Mabutu; the silent German Kaspar Rosenbecker; Lammond and Lenard, the best gunners on the *Maddy*; and Zaragoza, who swore blind he was no Spaniard, although everyone knew better.

Jolly recognised them all, and several more too.

She took a deep breath. She had achieved her aim. More than anything in the world she had longed to find Bannon and the crew of the *Maddy* again. But this was nothing like the reunion she had pictured, and for which she'd given up so much – maybe everything.

'What . . . what are you doing on that ship?' she called, and her voice didn't sound half as steady as she could have wished. 'I saw the spiders . . . and . . .' Once again she stopped. Tears shot into her eyes. She just hoped that at this distance no one noticed.

'We're fine, Jolly!' Bannon replied. 'Come on board the *Quadriga* and I'll tell you all about it.'

She looked helplessly at Buenaventure, who almost imperceptibly shook his head. Why the devil didn't he say anything?

'What are you doing on the *Quadriga*?' she called. She was

too upset to hear any answer he might give, but she needed time. Time to think, time to work it all out, to . . . Suddenly she didn't know anything any more. She doubted whether she was capable of making a decision at all, even if she thought about it for hours.

And she didn't have hours. She didn't even have minutes.

A man in black appeared behind Bannon, towering almost a head above him. His skull was shaved bald except for a long black ponytail which he had brought round over his right shoulder to hang on his chest – a touch of vanity there. Painted markings adorned his face, and there was something odd about his mouth, though Jolly couldn't make it out properly at this distance. Something about his teeth.

Bannon and Christophorus moved aside to make way at the rail for the man.

'We're all deeply moved by this touching reunion,' he said in a tone that gave the lie to his words. 'But we're wasting our time here. Either you come over of your own free will, girl, or I'll send someone to fetch you.'

At a sign from him, a plank was pushed over to the *Carfax* from the main deck of the *Quadriga*.

'And hurry up!' the man called to Jolly. 'I've heard so much about you that I'm keen to meet you myself.'

'It's Tyrone,' Buenaventure whispered to her. 'The cannibal king of the Orinoco delta.'

So this was the man who had cut the ring fingers off Munk's mother many years ago, and ripped her ears because she didn't take her jewellery off fast enough. The man said to command thousands of cannibals, having won their respect through deeds so horrible that they inspired terror in even the most bloodthirsty tribes of the Orinoco.

But more than anything she was shaken by Bannon's subservience to him. Tyrone's appearance on the bridge seemed to have paralysed all his men, and Bannon, who had never taken orders from anyone, was acting like a cabin boy.

Perhaps it was this observation that finally brought Jolly out of her trance. Her aim of finding Bannon and the others, perhaps even freeing them from the clutches of some tormentor, had gone like a cloud of smoke blowing away in the wind, leaving a great emptiness inside her. An emptiness that only gradually filled with the realisation that she ought not to be here at all. Her place wasn't with Bannon, who had betrayed her. Her place was with her real friends. With Griffin and Soledad and Walker and . . . yes, with Munk too.

She looked at Buenaventure again, and this time he couldn't help seeing what was going on in her mind. He nodded again, assenting with almost nothing but his eyes.

Do we need more time? she wondered.

No, the ghosts were in position and the cannon were ready to fire.

'Don't do it, little girl!' said Tyrone. He didn't have to shout to make himself heard over the gap between the ships, as Bannon had done. He spoke quite calmly, as if they were face to face, yet she didn't have to strain her ears to hear him. His voice easily halved the distance between them. 'We're ready to fire a full broadside at you,' he added quietly.

'Jolly,' called Bannon again. 'Be reasonable.'

'Do you still remember what you taught me?' she replied, her voice shaking. 'Never own yourself beaten. That's what you were always telling me, Bannon. Never give up, no matter who your enemy is and how poor the chances are.'

'There's no chance at all,' said Tyrone, with relish. 'Not for you.'

There was about fifteen feet between the two ships, and the sloping plank linking them scraped against the rail. Several men on board the *Quadriga* had grappling irons on ropes in their hands, ready to be thrown across to the *Carfax* when Tyrone gave the order. With the help of the grappling irons the ships would be firmly lashed together, allowing the pirates to move easily from one to the other.

Once the hooks were in place it would be too late to fire

the cannon. In fact even now the vessels were too close for an exchange of fire. Tyrone and Bannon must know that. If a cannonball hit the magazine of the *Carfax* the explosion might well be large enough to do the *Quadriga* serious damage too.

Did Tyrone think he could fool her by bluffing like that?

'The commander gave us the antidote,' said Bannon, for the first time ignoring the glance that Tyrone cast at him. 'He saved us. And he won't hurt you either, Jolly. Don't forget, we're pirates – you too! We're on the side of whoever promises us the richest booty. That's how it's always been in our trade.'

'I learned from you that piracy is more than just a trade, Bannon.' Jolly shook her head sadly. 'And as for the antidote: yes, perhaps he did give it to you. But he was surely the one who lured the *Maddy* into the trap in the first place! Isn't that so, Tyrone? The galleon with the spiders was your idea.'

'It was indeed.' The cannibal king grinned coolly. His features looked like the face of a hungry beast of prey.

'Who sent you to capture me?'

The cannibal king reached out an arm and pointed his bony forefinger her way. 'I'm not here to talk to a child! Either you come over to this ship or my men will fetch you.'

'Was it the Maelstrom, Tyrone?' Her knees were shaking,

but no one could see that from the deck of the *Quadriga*. 'Tell them. Tell them what it is you serve!'

Bannon frowned, but dared not look at Tyrone.

'Go on, men!' cried the cannibal king. 'Fetch her!'

But Jolly moved faster. Before the first grappling irons could come flying over, she ran to the small gun on the bridge of the *Carfax*, reaching right through the ghost in position there, and moved it to point straight at Tyrone. The arm-length barrel of the gun was mounted on a swivelling joint and slid around with a creak. Jolly snatched the torch from the ghost and held it to the touch-hole.

Up on the bridge of the *Quadriga* several men shouted all at once. They scattered, and even Tyrone stepped back in surprise. Whatever he might have been expecting it wasn't that Jolly – a child, as he had called her – would go on the attack.

'Show 'em!' shouted Buenaventure grimly, swinging the wheel round.

The backlash of the cannon as it fired almost dislocated Jolly's right arm. She was flung back, and a shock wave struck her in the face. For a moment smoke blurred her vision, and involuntary tears ran down her cheeks.

Yells and screams rang out from the enemy deck, but through all the gun-smoke she couldn't see whether she had hit the cannibal king.

She didn't wait, but shouted orders to the ghosts – the orders she had learned from Bannon long ago. The *Carfax* rapidly got under way again.

'They'll shoot us to pieces,' cried Buenaventure grimly, 'but they won't forget this day in a hurry.'

At first she didn't know what he meant, but when she looked back at the *Quadriga* it was clear as day. To starboard, the rail of her bridge had almost disappeared. The shot from the *Carfax* had made a wide breach in the planks, tearing away the cabin below the bridge. Men had fallen into the hole and found themselves a deck lower down. She saw Bannon staring at her with a grim expression, perhaps of anger, or perhaps because he knew that, with her attack, she had signed her own death sentence.

Where was Tyrone?

She saw him a few seconds later among the men who had fallen into the now open cabin. He was struggling up among the debris and mopping blood from his face with his forearm: obviously not his own blood, for soon he was standing there four-square, roughly pushing aside the injured men who were stumbling about. He stepped into the breach that Jolly's shot had made in the superstructure of his bridge.

He called something after her, but she couldn't make it out.

Bannon was still standing above the edge of the hole,

leaning on a splintered wooden post and shaking his head. He knew what was going to happen now, but before Jolly could see whether his face showed any sorrow or at least pity a cloud of smoke drifted between the ships, hiding her view.

She didn't have much time to see what her former friends were doing, all those men who had brought her up as if she were their daughter. Instead, she wiped the tears from her cheeks, swallowed her pain, and turned to Buenaventure.

'They're going to sink us,' she said in matter-of-fact tones.

'Yes,' he replied, to all outward appearance unmoved. 'But it was worth it. Almost.'

Only now did he bare his chops in a sad smile. He might have the face of a dog, but his smile was more human than the cannibal king's.

She suddenly thought of Walker. The *Carfax* had belonged to his mother, the first woman pirate in the Caribbean. This sloop was her memorial, her legacy, and the urn with her ashes in it even stood in the captain's cabin.

She had staked all that. And lost.

'I'm so sorry . . .' she was beginning when the thunder of the guns drowned out her voice. The *Carfax* shook, and Jolly was knocked off her feet. Cannonballs shredded the sails, and a split second later the air was full of iron. Cables torn loose whipped around like snakes. Wooden splinters rained down on the bridge and the deck. The foremast collapsed like a felled tree, and the ghosts merged into a nebulous swirling mist that seemed to be everywhere at once, yet they couldn't keep the sloop from sinking now.

'Jolly!' cried Buenaventure. He was still holding the wheel. 'Overboard! Fast!'

'Not without you.'

'Stop argu –'

Smoke drifted up to the bridge, separating them. Fire had broken out somewhere, presumably among the guns. Once again the cannon roared, and next moment more shots struck the ship.

The *Carfax* was sinking. She cried out and moaned and groaned like a dying animal as her planks and masts reared up one last time.

Jolly groped her way through the smoke to the helm, but the wheel was gone. Instead there was a deep cleft of devastation.

'*Buenaventure!*'

Panic-stricken, she looked round, but she couldn't see him anywhere.

'Buenaventure!'

The bows were going down. Water roared and splashed as the stern was raised from the waves. The sloop might break apart at any moment now.

'Say something!'

But there was no answer. Not from the pit bull man, not from the Hexhermetic Shipworm. Both of them had gone.

She would go down with the *Carfax*. What had happened was all her fault. If the other two were dead, she wanted to die too.

'Jolly!'

Someone was calling her name. Bannon? Tyrone? The *Quadriga* was out of sight now on the other side of the billowing gun-smoke.

'Jolly! Down here!'

Perhaps she was just imagining the words. The noise around her was deafening. The ship beneath her reared, wood was breaking apart everywhere, and she had to duck out of the way of remains of the rigging to avoid getting entangled in it.

All the same, she heard something again.

'Jolly! Jump!'

In one last moment of clear thinking she remembered what she had learned in Aelenium. The stern was now up in the air at such a steep angle that she had to fight desperately against the slope to reach the rail. When she reached the place, there was no balustrade any more, only a row of splintered wooden stumps.

Jolly flung herself into the depths. Head first, arms outstretched, she dived. It was her only chance. As a polliwiggle, she would break all her bones on the surface of the water if she jumped in any other way.

She broke through the waves in her dive, trailing air bubbles behind her. The noise around her was immediately cut off. How far down she went before she remembered her arms and legs and began moving them she didn't know. There was blue-grey twilight around her. Turbulent water. Debris drifting down.

And then the pull of a murderous current.

Right beside her, less than twenty feet away, the *Carfax* was sinking. Once her shattered, broken hull was entirely under the water there was no stopping it. The cavities inside the ship filled up at once. The wreck sank in a chaos of ropes, scraps of sails and splinters as sharp as knives, carrying everything around it down too.

Jolly struggled desperately against the undertow. She could breathe under water, yes, and her hands could part the water as if it were air, but even so she couldn't hold out against the force of the sinking ship. She saw the light below her rapidly fading. The depths clutched at her clothes and her limbs with invisible fingers.

Jolly shot downwards half lying on her back, almost

horizontal, her face turned up, her hands outstretched, as if she might be able to cling to something above her.

But there was nothing there.

Only emptiness, and the fading daylight.

THE WATER WEAVERS

The current carried Jolly on through a dismal void.

All around her was the monotonous grey that her polliwiggle vision saw. It showed her the hopelessness of her plunge into the abyss more distinctly than ever.

If she didn't drown she would probably be buried under the wrecked ships down there. Or impaled on a mast.

It was strange that she could still think so clearly. She supposed she was the first shipwrecked sailor ever to experience this fall into the depths without being driven mad by panic. The wreck of the *Carfax* was sinking faster than she was and was somewhere below her now, enveloped by air bubbles. Again and again debris came loose and shot up towards the surface, so that she had to take care to avoid it.

She could change position within the current and turn over on her front – but she couldn't escape the force carrying her inexorably down. Like a nail attracted by a magnet, she was following the wrecked ship as it fell.

How deep was the sea here? Five hundred feet? Five thousand? No, not as deep as that, they were too close to the coast. It probably wouldn't be long before she reached the sea-bed.

She saw no fish during her fall. They kept out of the way of the colossus dropping into their realm from above. Later, when the *Carfax* was lying on the bottom, they would venture curiously closer, explore the wreck, and gradually make it a part of their world. Moray eels would settle in the shattered hull, seaweed would cover the planks, crustaceans would go hunting in the cracks and crevices. Some day the shapeless mound would be no different from its surroundings, overgrown by plants, half buried under sand and silt.

These images raced through Jolly's head at high speed, flashing into her mind and out again. She had a feeling that the suction of the current wasn't quite so strong now. The stream of air bubbles died down, and then she could see the wreck below her again, surrounded by undulating ropes and billowing sailcloth.

And she could hear! Her ears were fast getting used to her new surroundings. When she and Munk had dived down to the underwater city of Aelenium they had been able to talk to each other, but she had been too excited to notice the sounds of that underwater world itself.

Silent as a fish, people said. But that was nonsense! In the distance, Jolly could hear a confused whistling and piping and roaring in the chaotic rhythm of birdsong, except that it wasn't birdsong but the voices of fish somewhere just outside her field of vision.

And the noise of the wreck breaking up also reached her. Pressure was crushing the wooden interior. The cabin with Walker's mementoes of his mother must have been destroyed long ago. Once again Jolly felt such a pang that she thought for a moment a piece of the debris had struck her body. But it was only her conscience hurting her. The certainty of being dreadfully guilty.

And still she fell.

Now she was crying – there was no one she had to pretend to any more. Her tears would mingle with the water anyway as soon as they rose to her eyes. She didn't need to keep wiping them away, for even when she was crying she could see as clearly and distinctly as if she were on the surface.

At every moment she waited for the impact that would probably break all her bones, so fast was the speed of the current. She wouldn't drown, she wouldn't be crushed by the pressure – she would simply be left lying there, unable to move. Good heavens, she would be the first human being ever to die of thirst on the sea-bed.

Suddenly a second current caught her. It tore her away from the first, pulling her aside much faster, as if she were gliding through a narrow tunnel. Perhaps she lost consciousness for a moment, perhaps for hours. Or had she merely blinked her eyes?

When she opened them again she was somewhere else.

She had only just seen the *Carfax* below her, a tangle of wood and rope and bent iron. But next moment the ship was gone as if it had dissolved into nothing within a split second.

The stream of debris had dispersed too.

Below her Jolly now saw the sea-bed, a grey wilderness that reminded her of descriptions of the Rift. But this couldn't be the Rift, or even anywhere near it. She was thousands of sea miles away from it, quite apart from the fact that there wasn't any sign of the Maelstrom.

Was she dreaming? Was this the first step into the next world? Could she be dying faster than she had feared?

The current ebbed away. At a height of about fifty feet above the sea-bed she found that she could control her fall. She hovered where she was and looked down.

She saw something that puzzled her.

At first glance it looked like three dark patches marking

the points of an equilateral triangle on the grey sand. Only when she slowly let herself sink lower did she see the three figures. Three old women sat there, faces looking outward, their long white hair divided into two strands each at the backs of their heads. They were connected by these strands of hair, stretched taut between their heads and joining so that Jolly couldn't see where the hair of one old woman ended and the hair of the next began.

The three women were sitting on low stools, and each had a spinning wheel in front of her. Jolly rubbed her eyes, she distrusted them so much. But on closer inspection there was no doubt: the women were sitting at spinning wheels on the sea-bed.

Jolly was now floating a few yards above them, part of her still very much on her guard, another part so fascinated by the strange sight of the weavers that she couldn't tear herself away.

Why did they have their backs to each other? Why were they tied together by their hair? And what, for heaven's sake, were they doing down here?

'Greetings, young polliwiggle,' said one of them, without raising her head. Jolly couldn't see which of the women had spoken.

'What . . . what is all this?' she asked uncertainly, and

immediately felt rather foolish. It must be a hallucination to make dying easier for her.

'You are not going to die,' said one of the women.

'Not yet, anyway,' added a second.

Jolly looked from one to another, but she couldn't make out which of them had opened their mouths. 'Where's the *Carfax?*' she asked, feeling a little calmer.

'Far from here.'

'Or maybe not.'

'Depending on how you look at it.'

Had they spoken in turn? If so, then they spoke with a single voice.

Jolly hesitated to let herself sink further down. However, when it was clear to her that this conversation would lead nowhere until she could see into the three women's eyes, she overcame her timidity. She moved a little way aside so as not to land in the centre of the triangle, and then finished her descent.

Sand swirled up when her feet touched the bottom of the sea. One voice cried, 'Careful, child! Don't tread on the yarn!'

Yarn? She looked down and saw that the ground was covered with a kind of net. Countless strands were entwined in a densely woven tissue. They came in star shapes from all directions, and ended at the old women's spinning wheels.

'What is it?' She crouched down and reached her hand out to touch one of the threads. Each was as thick as a finger. She half expected the women to stop her, but they did not object.

A tingling went through her hand and shot up her arm, but passed off again just as quickly, as if it were streaming out of Jolly's fingers and back into the yarn. The material was soft and smooth and as clear as . . . water?

Yes, it was. The old women were spinning threads out of water. Or something that was in the water anyway and became concentrated in their hands.

'Magic,' said one of the old women. 'You would have worked that out for yourself, wouldn't you?'

In amazement, Jolly looked at the expanse of the great network. Its ends were lost on the edge of her field of vision. 'Are those the veins of magic?'

'We call it yarn,' said the old woman sitting closest to Jolly. Her lips hardly moved as she spoke.

'But it probably comes to the same thing,' said another of them.

'Who are you?' asked Jolly.

'Weavers.'

'I can see that. But I mean . . . what are you doing down here?'

She knew the answer before the women gave it. 'Spinning the yarn.'

'Weaving the net.'

'What do you want of me?' Jolly no longer had any doubt that her presence here wasn't just chance.

'We have been watching you.'

'You and the other polliwiggle.'

'Did *you* make us?' Once again Jolly looked down at the magical strands of water that never lost their shape, although they were surrounded by more of the same element. It was as though they were firmer and thicker than ordinary water. Or just more magical.

'The yarn made you,' said one of the women.

'We didn't.'

'But that doesn't matter.'

'It's time for you to learn certain things.'

'We thought others would explain them to you.'

'But no one did.'

'So we will do it now.'

All three nodded, and the strands of hair between their heads were stretched nearly to breaking point. It didn't seem to hurt them.

Jolly slowly walked in a circle around the three women. The sand swirling by her feet wiped out her prints in seconds.

'First tell me what kind of a place this is.'

'It has no name.'

'We are weavers.'

'And this is where we weave.'

Jolly bit her lower lip. Instead of asking more questions she looked closely at the women as she passed them. All three wore long robes that hid their feet even when they were sitting. Like everything here, the fabric of their garments was a uniform grey. The old women's long, fleshless fingers worked the spinning wheels with agility and no wasted movements. None of them looked up at Jolly as she passed. But they spoke in turn, although she couldn't see in what order.

'You were made of the sea, little polliwiggle.'

'Of the magic of the yarn and the power of the water.'

Jolly stopped. The yarn – it was the veins of magic she'd heard about in Aelenium. And this was where they came from. She felt quite dizzy at the thought of how much power must be concentrated here. It was said that the Rift, where several veins crossed, was full of strong magic. But this was its origin, the root of the whole network of veins. And the three old women had made it.

So strictly speaking they had also made Jolly and Munk.

No, she contradicted herself. They didn't make me, only

the polliwiggle magic in me. But somehow even that thought couldn't reassure her.

Who were these three women? Enchantresses? Witches? Goddesses? Or something that came even earlier than the gods?

Moments later she discovered how close her guess came to the truth.

'It is from the sea that all life comes,' said one of the women. Her fingers danced around the spindle and the yarn like nimble insect legs. 'Every creature, every human being has its beginnings in the ocean. The first living creatures were born of the water, and the water made them what they are today.'

Jolly nodded impatiently. She had heard something like that before. Was it the cook Trevino who had told her during one of his lectures about this, that and everything, always delivered in a state of total intoxication?

'The gods too once came from the sea.'

'Not all from *this* sea.'

'Or from *this* water.'

Jolly crouched down in front of one of the women to look into her face. She wasn't afraid any more, she didn't even feel shy with them. Like a young animal still recognising its mother by her scent even months after birth, Jolly suddenly had a sense of deep familiarity. The strange aura surrounding the old women was like something she knew from her dreams.

'Not from this water,' she echoed in a whisper, and then her eyes widened. 'From the Mare Tenebrosum? Is that what you mean?'

'The oldest sea of all,' said the women in front of her, and another added, 'The mother of all oceans.' The third said, 'The father of all waters.'

Jolly tried to follow what the weavers were saying. What was all this talk about gods? She didn't even believe in one god, let alone several.

'They all lived.'

'And still live.'

'But they are not gods any more.'

'Or what you humans understand by gods.'

'They have become like you.'

'Almost like you.'

'They have lost their power since they made all this.'

'This world cost them all their strength.'

'It sucked them dry.'

'But so that none more powerful might follow them from the sea of seas, they sealed the entrance and kept close watch on it.'

'For many aeons.'

'They withdrew, mourning for their old days of power. To be close to the water from which they were born, they settled in a city on the sea that served them as both a hiding place and a fortress.'

'A city that seals the entrance.'

'Aelenium.'

Although Jolly could breathe under water, this took her breath away for a moment. 'You mean the people of Aelenium aren't . . . aren't human at all? They're gods?'

'Not all of them.'

'Only a few.'

'They were too weak even for the simplest things. Many passed away. They just vanished.'

'Like a dream in the first rays of the sun.'

'No one remembers them any more.'

'They needed help, and lured humans through the mist to Aelenium. Humans to take on the task for them.'

'But those human beings had children. And they in their own turn had children. Generation after generation.'

'And while the old gods who had withdrawn to Aelenium died, the number of human beings grew. Today only a few of the original inhabitants are left.'

'Forefather?' asked Jolly, hesitantly.

'The oldest of all. The creator.'

Jolly raised her hands as if that could fend off the things the weavers were saying. 'But Forefather's only an old man with a lot of books!'

'So he is, today.'

'But he wasn't always.'

'He had a name then.'

'Many names.'

'But he was always the same. The creator. The first who came over from the sea of seas and kindled a light in the darkness.'

Jolly suddenly felt the weight of the sea above her, a column of water as broad as her shoulders and many thousands of feet high. She sank faintly to her knees, let herself drop back and drew her legs up to sit cross-legged.

'Forefather is *God*?' she asked.

'Not *the* god. Only *a* god.'

'The oldest.'

'What about the others?' asked Jolly. 'Count Aristotle, and d'Artois, and . . .'

'They are human beings. Busy hands with a spark of reason.'

'. . . and the Ghost-Trader?'

'The one-eyed god.'

'The raven god.'

'Once his birds had other names. One was Hugin, the other Munin. They were ravens then.'

For a moment there was silence, as if the three weavers were aware that even they had already forgotten things. That their power too was waning, like the power of the gods.

'Never mind,' said one of them at last.

'Never mind, never mind,' the other two agreed.

'But the masters of the Mare Tenebrosum,' said Jolly, still trying to find a meaning in all this, something she could grasp and understand. 'The masters are . . . bad.'

'What does that mean?'

'Who says so?'

'Most of all they are young. And powerful. Just as the gods of this world once were, infinitely long ago.'

'They are curious.'

'Greedy, perhaps.'

'Or envious.'

'But bad? What does bad mean, Jolly?'

It didn't escape her that the women had called her by her name for the first time. And she knew what that meant. The weavers expected an answer from her. Not something that someone had told her, not something learned by heart, but *her* answer.

What does bad mean?

The Acherus had murdered Munk's parents. That was bad. Wasn't it? Was it bad when Spaniards killed the English?

All a question of your point of view, thought Jolly, feeling uncomfortable and guilty about it. But that made no difference to her answer. All a question of your point of view.

No, she thought suddenly. Killing is bad, whatever the reason for it. Perhaps that was the solution. But how could she presume to judge the masters of the Mare Tenebrosum when she herself had been on countless raids and privateering expeditions? There were certainly people who would have described her, Jolly, as bad for doing that. It couldn't be so simple.

'If the masters of the Mare Tenebrosum aren't bad,' she said thoughtfully, 'then why are we fighting them?'

She got no reply but silence.

'Why?' she asked again, jumping up. She was on the point of seizing one of the women by the shoulders and shaking her.

'Those are the facts,' said one of the weavers. 'Make up your own mind.'

Laboriously, Jolly tried to put everything she had just learned into some kind of order that made sense. Forefather had been born of the water of the Mare Tenebrosum. He had *kindled the light*, as the weavers had put it, and made this world. Jolly's world. And life had risen from the new oceans in its own turn. Other gods, then animals, then human beings. And when the gods had finally used up all their power and grown weaker they withdrew to Aelenium, using the city to seal the gateway to the Mare Tenebrosum. They weren't strong enough now to enjoy the fruits of their creation, but they wouldn't let anyone else have them either. They weren't ready to share with the powers of the Mare Tenebrosum, not even Forefather, who had once come from there himself. They jealously guarded what was theirs, but it wasn't humanity they were protecting, they were defending their possessions. Like a child who won't let another child have a toy even when he doesn't want to play with it any more himself.

So that was the secret of Aelenium. A city of gods who had ceased to be gods a long time ago. Some gone and forgotten, others still alive but already on the way to oblivion.

What did that mean for Jolly? For her friends? For the struggle against the Maelstrom? She was far too confused to find answers herself, so she asked her questions out loud.

'It means nothing,' said one of the women.

'Or everything,' added another.

Anger rose in Jolly. Anger over everything that the Ghost-Trader hadn't been telling her all this time. Anger with herself too, because she felt so terribly helpless. And anger with these three women, who were certainly far from being ordinary old women. Why were they telling her these things if they couldn't give her any answer to take away with her?

'Because you will not find the answer until you reach the end of your journey,' said one of the weavers. 'Perhaps.'

'You thought it was all simple. You go to the Rift, shut the Maelstrom up in its shell again, and everything's over.'

'Nothing is over.'

'Nothing is ever over.'

Furiously, Jolly stamped her foot in the sand. The dust of the sea-bed rose, and had surrounded her like mist before she knew it. She quickly took a few steps aside, but that only made matters worse.

Not until the swirling dust died down again did she see what it had done.

The water weavers had gone. The sea-bed was smooth; the magical strands had disappeared.

The wreck of the *Carfax* lay not fifty paces away, and that was what had churned up the sea-bed so violently. Debris was still raining down and landing in the sand close to Jolly.

A dream, then? A trick of the senses, the result of her fall into the depths?

No, she thought. Certainly not that.

Her legs felt weak, but she bent her knees, gathered herself together, and pushed off. Like an arrow, she shot up in the twilight towards the crystal roof of the distant surface.

306

*

The brightness of day was coming closer. Sunlight breaking on the glassy crests of waves. White-gold rays pierced the surface and were not lost in the depths until they had gone a long way down.

From here it looked as if someone were passing a golden brush through the waves, and its sparkling bristles combed the water now this way and now that.

A few feet from the surface Jolly slowed her climb. She wondered if the spectacle of the battle had enticed any sharks here yet. While she was walking on the water she was safe from them, but when she was swimming she was vulnerable to the predatory fish, like any other shipwrecked mariner.

Buenaventure! Seething hot, the thought shot through her mind. How could she have forgotten him and the Hexhermetic Shipworm while she talked to the weavers deep in the sea? Had she wasted valuable time? But she had hardly been given any choice. As so often in the past few weeks.

Cautiously, she went the last part of the way and put her head up through the surface. The glitter of the waves with the sun on their crests dazzled her for a moment. The unusually low angle from which she had so seldom seen the sea made her uneasy. For the first time, hemmed in by such masses of water, she almost felt something like claustrophobia.

The *Quadriga* was gone.

Jolly's first thought was: how long have I really been down there? And her second was: where are Buenaventure and the Worm?

Flotsam from the wreck could stay on the surface for days, or even longer, depending what it was made of. The fact that parts of the ship had still been reaching the sea-bed until a few moments ago didn't prove that the wreck of the *Carfax* was recent. Anything was possible.

Nonsense! Don't get obsessed with your fixed ideas. It's only a few minutes ago you were talking to the weavers. Only a few minutes ago.

And then Jolly saw them: three outlines standing out against the horizon, narrow and tall and curiously shaped. About two hundred feet away. Not ships, certainly not. For a moment she thought the weavers themselves had risen from the depths.

A minute later she saw what they were.

Riders on sea horses! Human beings mounted on three hippocamps.

'Ahoy!' she shouted as loud as she could. 'I'm here! *I'm here!*'

She leaned her hands on the water beside her as if it were the edge of a solid surface and hauled herself out. Soon she was standing upright on the waves. She immediately realised that there was no going back now: for miles around there was no high point from which she could venture to dive head first – and without diving she could never get below the water again. That meant she was at the mercy of the riders, whoever they were.

'Jolly?' cried an incredulous voice. And then, cracking with delight, 'Jolly! There she is! Jolly's over there!'

'Soledad?' She raced towards the riders. 'Walker? Is it really you?'

The hippocamps were coming closer so fast that Jolly could hardly follow their movements. Soledad was beside her first, making her sea horse sink lower in the water so that her face was level with Jolly's. With a cry of joy, the princess held her close. 'Devil take it, Jolly! We thought we'd lost you!'

Walker and the Ghost-Trader guided their animals to Soledad's side, and now she saw who was sitting behind the captain in the saddle of his hippocamp.

'Buenaventure!' Jolly let go of Soledad and ran over to the pit bull man. He looked relieved, as if he'd have liked to jump off the sea horse and run to her over the water himself.

'Jolly! You're alive! By Poseidon's seaweed beard!' They hugged as best they could. The pit bull man was in such high spirits that he didn't seem to want to let go of her. His bark of laughter echoed over the water, and he bared his teeth in his relief.

'Good to see you, Jolly,' said Walker. He too was relieved, although dark shadows lay over his face, shadows of grief and loss. His ship, his mother's ship, was sunk. The *Carfax* lay at the bottom of the sea.

'I'm so sorry,' stammered Jolly. 'I . . . I really . . . oh, I don't know what I can say.'

'I'll tan your hide for it later, I'm sure,' said Walker gloomily. As if numbed, he looked at the isolated bits of flotsam still drifting on the waves. Then he quickly shook his head. It was obvious that he was trying to pull himself together. 'But for now –'

'– for now we're just glad to see you alive,' said the Ghost-Trader, finishing Walker's sentence. Jolly turned to look at him. The words of the water weavers rose in her mind as she saw him sitting on the sea horse, a dark silhouette against the setting sun. His robe billowed out in the wind over the sea. Above him the two parrots fluttered, beating their wings fast.

She straightened her shoulders and looked from one to the other. 'I was stupid. I'd like to apologise to all of you and . . . Wait a minute! Where's the Shipworm?' Her glance had fallen on Buenaventure's rucksack, which was hanging flat and empty on his back. 'Oh no!'

Sadly, the pit bull man shook his head. 'He didn't make it, Jolly! I looked for him as soon as I went overboard . . . but all of a sudden the rucksack was empty. He must have slipped out and . . .' He fell silent, lowering his eyes.

Jolly spun round to go and search the debris, but the Ghost-Trader's voice kept her back.

'No, Jolly. It's useless. We haven't found a single trace of him.'

Jolly's eyes passed over the sea and the drifting remains of the *Carfax*, moving on far out to the horizon and the distant coastline.

Once again Soledad was beside her first, gently placing a hand on her shoulder. But this time the princess said nothing, and only listened to the whispering of the winds with her.

Jolly felt salt tears on her lips, and for the first time in her life it occurred to her that sorrow tasted of the sea.

THE ENEMY FLEET

Half the mountain on which the cannibal king's fortress stood had fallen into the sea long ago, leaving a steep rock wall that dropped some sixty feet to the ocean, ending in a foaming rampart of breakers. The winds here blew keenly from the north-east, driving the waves mercilessly against the coast. Remains of the submerged mountain showed above the surface as rocky islets surrounded by sea-spray. From the north and east it was almost impossible to manoeuvre ships between these rocks, but to the west a passage led through the reefs to the shallow waters of the Orinoco delta.

On one branch of the river, below the fortress on its rocky height, there was an extensive settlement of huts and wooden houses with a large tented camp on its outskirts. It had spread all over the area cleared for it long ago, and now merged with the dark green thickets of the jungle.

'Where's the harbour?' asked Walker when they saw the fort and the settlement in the distance. He was still having difficulty keeping the sea horse under him calm. Unlike Soledad, who controlled her mount as confidently as if she had years of experience riding hippocamps, Walker was obviously uncomfortable with his mount even after several days, and the weight of Buenaventure in the saddle behind him did nothing to make him feel better.

The Ghost-Trader narrowed his single eye as if to see the coast more clearly. 'Yes, this is certainly strange,' he said. 'Where are all their ships?'

Walker scratched his head. 'Perhaps Tyrone was telling the truth after all. If his cannibal tribes are really going to attack Caracas from the land, they don't need ships.'

'They'd march on foot from here to Caracas?' Soledad shook her head emphatically. 'Very unlikely. It's several hundred miles through dense jungle.'

'The savages know their way around these parts,' said Walker, but his voice showed that he himself was far from convinced.

'We're in the east of the delta, aren't we?' asked Jolly.

The Ghost-Trader nodded. 'The river mouth there must be its eastern arm.'

'Then I know where the ships are lying.'

They all turned their heads to her in surprise. Soledad glanced at Jolly over her shoulder. 'You do?'

'I told you about the book where I found the drawing of the spider. It had maps of the Orinoco delta in it too. I tore one out.'

'Do you have it here?' asked the Trader.

'No, it sank with the *Carfax*.'

'Like so much else,' said Walker grimly.

Jolly still couldn't look him in the eye, she was so ashamed of herself for losing the ship. 'Anyway, I had enough time to look at the map and compare it with the charts in the cabin,' she said in a small voice. 'I think I know the course of the arms of the Orinoco pretty well.'

'So?' said Walker.

'The fortress itself wasn't marked on the map, of course, but the rocky height where it stands was. The rest of the coast around here is rather flat. I think there's a lake beyond that steep rise, linking up to the delta. We can't see it from here because the mountain and the fortress are right in front of it.'

The Ghost-Trader looked back at the coast. 'That would mean the fortress itself stands on a kind of promontory, with the sea on one side, the river on the other, and a third side inland bordered by the lake.'

Jolly nodded vigorously.

314

Soledad was obviously impressed. She gave Jolly a smile and then turned to the men. 'Tyrone's a pirate. He wouldn't build himself such a fort if he had no chance of offering several ships a sheltered place to lie at anchor near it. What Jolly says sounds sensible.'

Walker couldn't help agreeing. 'Anyway, we ought to take a closer look.'

'That's what we're here for,' said the Ghost-Trader firmly, urging his sea horse on. Next moment all three animals were racing towards the coast in a wide arc, to avoid being seen from the towers of the fortress.

They landed about two miles east of the rocks. The hippocamps went back out to sea while the five companions waded through the breakers to the shore. Ahead of them lay a narrow, sandy beach that stretched thirty or forty feet before disappearing into the shadows of the forest. A few crabs were crawling through the sand, and coconuts lay under the palms on the outskirts of the jungle. Walker sliced several in half with his sword and they drank the sweet milk, ate the flesh of the nuts, and shared out some of the few provisions that the Trader, Walker and Soledad had brought in their saddle-bags.

Not really fortified, but with something inside them, they set off. Jolly stuck close to Buenaventure, and saw in surprise

315

how close to each other Soledad and Walker seemed. During the ride to the coast the princess had told her the story of Tyrone's plans and the fight on St Celestine, but she had said nothing of what had passed between her and Walker.

But Jolly's thoughts were elsewhere anyway. She was grieving for the Hexhermetic Shipworm, and she could see from Buenaventure's face that he felt the same. The little creature might have been a pain in the neck, but they had grown fond of him during their voyage on the *Carfax*.

And then there was Bannon. Every memory of him was like a slap in her face. The man who had brought her up, the man she had loved like a father, had joined her enemy. An enemy who – if Soledad's suspicions were right – was not just a man-eating monster but in league with the Maelstrom.

The Ghost-Trader too believed that Tyrone merely wanted to distract the pirates' attention with his plan for them to unite and take Caracas by storm. The truth was obvious enough: the Spanish armada and the pirate fleet were to keep each other occupied off Caracas, while the armies of kobalins attacked Aelenium undisturbed. And now the reason why the Maelstrom had delayed its attack on the starfish city appeared in a new light.

How important in all this, though, was what Jolly had heard from the water weavers? Now that she was back with her friends again her meeting with the three old women seemed more improbable than ever – and was blurred like a dream. But could she make it so easy for herself? It was tempting to go on dividing the world into good and bad – Aelenium on one side, the Mare Tenebrosum and the Maelstrom on the other – but reason told her that it was nothing like so simple.

The mere fact that the Maelstrom might have broken away from the masters of the Mare Tenebrosum altered the picture she had formed of events so far, though without making it any less terrible. She didn't even wonder what would have happened if the bridge had not caught fire and Griffin hadn't dragged her back.

One thing was certain: the answers to these questions could be found only in Aelenium. Whether the gods who had withdrawn to the city were acting solely in their own interests or not, they had the knowledge that could save humanity. The kobalins had to be stopped before they set off on their campaign of annihilation. And the Maelstrom had to be halted in its tracks.

What is bad? the weavers had asked. Now Jolly saw that the answer didn't really matter. The aims of the people of Aelenium weren't important so long as their struggle served to protect the whole Caribbean. Jolly didn't mind whether jealousy or the gods' ancient claim to ownership was their driving motive.

What was Griffin doing now? Was he still safe in Aelenium? When would the Maelstrom's great attack begin, and how long would the city be able to hold off the kobalins?

And what about Munk? She shook her head so hard that Buenaventure, who had been going thoughtfully along beside the others, turned to her.

'Don't blame yourself for the loss of the Worm,' he said.

Gratefully, she let him take her mind off Griffin and Munk for a moment. Not that remembering the Shipworm was any relief. 'If only I hadn't gone off in the *Carfax* you wouldn't have had to follow me,' she said sadly. 'And the Worm would still be in Aelenium now.'

'Where the good folk of the poets' quarter would probably have roasted him on the spit, they were so furious.'

She gave the pit bull man a half-hearted smile. It was nice of him to try to make her feel less responsible for what had happened. All the same, she knew the truth. It was her fault, all her fault.

They lapsed into silence again as they walked westward among the trees on the outskirts of the jungle, just far enough from the shore to be out of sight of anyone looking from the sea. In other circumstances it wouldn't have taken them as much as an hour to walk to the steep cliff. But the soft sand delayed them, and they were all going cautiously and concentrating hard, for the danger of coming upon enemies increased with every step they took.

For the time being, however, they met no guards posted to keep watch. The land soon began rising and became stonier. The sand here lay only in light drifts, and then they left it behind altogether. There were no paths in the forest; they had to use their swords to hack themselves a way through the dense undergrowth, past creepers and twining plants. Walker and Buenaventure went ahead, cutting a path for the others. Every time they slashed at the plants the sound seemed to Jolly loud enough to give them away, and she feared that the birds flying up would alert Tyrone's guards.

The climb was more and more difficult now. They were going up a natural rocky ramp that fell steeply away to the sea on their right. The fortress must be somewhere ahead. But what lay on their left? Jungle, certainly, but if the lake was to the south then the terrain in between ought to begin sloping downhill.

They had the answer a little later, when Walker and Buenaventure stopped. The jungle was thinning out before them. The red-gold light of the setting sun fell in narrow rays through trees, tingeing their faces with red. They had turned away from the steep cliffs some time ago and gone further left, always taking whichever path seemed easier and less likely to make much noise. Like this they had reached the western side of the rocky ramp.

Before them an abyss opened up, as steep as the cliffs behind them and equally impassable. A hundred feet down another strip of jungle clung to the rocky wall. Behind it, shining in the evening light like a plain of gold, lay the lake.

'Jolly, you little devil, you were right!' Walker took a deep breath. Here on the edge of the precipice the air was clearer and more refreshing than under the oppressive leaf canopy of the jungle. Jolly too felt that she could breathe more easily.

Tyrone's fleet lay at anchor in the lake.

There were at least two hundred ships.

For some time no one said a word, but the same thoughts were going through all their minds. Everyone could see how hopeless a battle against such superior numbers would be.

Finally Buenaventure spoke. 'Where did he get them all?'

'Built them,' said Walker. 'Take a look. Most of them have never been on the high seas yet.' He pointed to a row of landing stages, ramps and wooden huts on the distant southern bank of the lake. 'Those must be the shipyards.'

'But I don't see any unfinished ships,' said Jolly. 'Do you think they were really all built here?'

The Ghost-Trader nodded in the shadow of his hood. 'The fleet is ready. Those vessels are just waiting for the order to put to sea.'

'Even if all the pirates of Tortuga, New Providence and the Lesser Antilles unite they won't get such a huge fleet together,' said Soledad. Her voice faltered. 'It must have taken years to build so many ships.'

As far as they could see in the dusk, the jungle to the south had been extensively cleared. They couldn't see where the forest began again. Mist was rising from the ground, veiling the horizon.

'He can't have done it without help.' Walker said what they were all thinking. 'The savages aren't ship-builders. He must have hired master builders, carpenters, sail-makers.'

'Spaniards,' said Soledad.

'Spaniards?' repeated Walker. Then he understood. 'Of course! He's betraying two sets of people at once, not just one! The hell with him!'

'Two?' asked Jolly.

Walker ran a hand angrily through his long hair. 'That devil! He tells the Spaniards he's going to lure the pirates into a trap. And he promises the pirates an easy victory over the Spaniards. In gratitude for the double game he's playing, the Spaniards supply him with men and materials to build a fleet of his own. Perhaps they're planning to leave him part of the Caribbean later, or support him when he goes raiding British strongholds.'

Jolly stared at him. 'And don't forget the third move in the game,' she said quietly. 'He's betraying the Spaniards by planning to use the fleet for an entirely different purpose.'

'The destruction of Aelenium,' murmured the Ghost-Trader. 'Tyrone is just another of the Maelstrom's henchmen. He'll send his ships to Aelenium to support the kobalins.'

'And I'll bet you,' said Soledad, pursuing this idea further, 'that the Spaniards anticipate an attack by the pirates of Tortuga and New Providence, but they don't expect to see them allied to the captains of the Lesser Antilles too. There'll be a far larger fleet facing the Spanish armada than they thought. Tyrone has seen to that as well. This way he'll play off our own people against the Spaniards, and vice versa. And by way of thanks for his efforts he has this mighty fleet for himself.'

'It's despicable,' growled Buenaventure.

'Clever, though,' Walker acknowledged.

'Indeed it is,' the Ghost-Trader agreed. 'Tyrone and the Maelstrom will take Aelenium in a pincer movement. The fleet above water, the kobalins below the surface. And who knows what further surprises he has in store for us?'

Jolly said nothing. As the others went on discussing Tyrone's plans, she was looking into the future. Forefather and the others had been right from the start. There was only one way to avert disaster now: she and Munk must go down to the Rift and face the Maelstrom.

She went closer to the edge of the precipice and looked westward, past her companions. A few dozen paces away rose the outer wall of the fortress. Further west, a winding path led through the rocks to the huts and tents on the banks of the lake. Only now did she see that a deep, broad channel of water divided the settlement in two – it was the way out of the lake leading to the Orinoco delta and the open sea.

'Do we go on?' asked Walker. 'Or do we turn back to warn Aelenium?'

'We go on,' said the Ghost-Trader. 'Perhaps we can find out more down there.'

'In that hornets' nest?' Soledad frowned. 'Is that really a good idea?'

'Do you have a better one, Princess?'

Before Soledad could answer, noises suddenly rose to their ears. First they just heard a few screams, but then came the sound of wood breaking up.

'Over there!' cried Jolly excitedly, pointing down. 'Look, the ship in front, next to the *Quadriga*!'

Next moment they all saw it.

One of the ships had tilted over and was sinking. It must have sprung a huge leak, for it was going down at such speed that within a very short time water was lapping over the rail. Two more ships began to list, followed by a fourth. And a fifth.

'What's going on down there?' asked Walker.

'Sabotage,' growled Buenaventure with satisfaction. 'Someone's sending their ships to the bottom.'

'Someone?' cried Jolly, breathlessly. Then she suddenly gave a cry of joy. 'Heavens above, you're right! And I know who it is!'

How did they get past the wall of the fort unnoticed by the guards on watch? How did they manage to climb down the path unseen, in spite of the troops of workers and tribal warriors coming their way? How, against all reasonable expectations, did they pass the outer buildings of the settlement and get into its maze of streets without anyone spotting them and unmasking them as spies?

Later, Jolly couldn't find a satisfactory answer to any of those questions. Their way past the rocks was just a blur in her memory, a confused impression of ducking low as they slunk along, surreptitious glances cast in the darkness, avoiding places where guards were stationed, quiet whispers, fingers clutching sword-hilts, trickles of sweat running down her forehead and into her eyes.

But none of that really counted. Her relief outweighed all other feelings, even her fear of falling into the hands of Tyrone's cannibals.

The Hexhermetic Shipworm was alive! No one could doubt that now. *He* was responsible for the leaks in the ships around the *Quadriga*. After the sinking of the *Carfax* he must have eaten his way through the hull of Tyrone's flagship just above the waterline, so close that the vessel had hardly leaked at all on the short voyage to this harbour. Jolly was astonished: she would never have credited him with so much foresight. He could easily have sunk the *Quadriga* out there at sea, but instead he had let the ship take him into Tyrone's harbour where he could do even more damage.

She pictured him winding his way through the water from ship to ship. He wasn't a very good swimmer with his stumpy legs – indeed, when they first met Jolly had saved him from drowning – yet somehow he seemed to have made his way from hull to hull.

Dear, good, wise Worm!

Jolly and Buenaventure exchanged glances. Both felt the same relief. The others might not appreciate what the Worm had done yet, perhaps didn't even believe he had really been responsible for the sabotaging of the fleet. But Jolly and the pit bull man were agreed. Nothing would keep them from saving the little fellow now – although they might wait until he had sent a few more ships to the bottom of the lake.

And while Jolly was still feeling elated, the Ghost-Trader suddenly said, 'It won't be enough.'

Jolly looked up at him. 'What?'

He shook his hooded head. 'There are at least two hundred ships out there. How many hulls can he eat holes in before they catch him? Seven, eight? Maybe a dozen. And they'll even be able to save some of those ships if they plug the leaks quickly enough. The fleet itself won't be weakened much. And Tyrone won't have to alter his plans.'

The alleyways among the huts and wooden houses were full of men. Many were savages with teeth filed to points like Tyrone's, but even so most of them wore European clothing and had obviously been trained in seamanship by Tyrone's subordinates. So he wasn't manning his vessels solely with Spaniards and the scum of the Old World, but with cannibals too. Jolly shuddered to think how long Tyrone must have been working on this plot. Many years, she felt sure. And none of the pirates had known anything about it.

Except for Kendrick, the pirate emperor himself. Or had he

too fallen into a trap? Did he really believe the raid on Caracas had any prospect of success? It was almost to be feared he did. Kendrick was a fool if he trusted a brute like Tyrone.

The companions reached the banks of the lake and made haste to skirt it to the south. If they looked over their shoulders and up at the rocks, they could see the cannibal king's fortress dominating the landscape. It was a plain building, like the defensive forts the Spaniards had built on many of the islands of the Caribbean: high, sandstone-coloured walls, with room on their long parapets for many guns; no towers, but low structures protected on the seaward side from cannon fire by the parapets. There would be few ways in, probably just a main gate secured by a moat and a drawbridge.

Tyrone had got more from his Spanish allies than just help in building his ships – on this rock at the end of the world they had built him a fortress that could compete in strength and defensive power with any governor's palace.

It gradually dawned on Jolly that Tyrone was far more than a crazed despot who had forced his command on the savage jungle tribes. He was equally good at influencing the authorities from the Old World.

The friends had almost reached the place where the sinking ships lay at anchor. Workmen and sailors were

327

running hither and thither in agitation. Overseers were desperately trying to bring order into this chaos. Commands were being bellowed and instructions issued everywhere. Men with knives held in their teeth plunged into the water to look for the saboteur. They had all swiftly realised that it must be someone diving down to move from hull to hull, hiding in the maze of narrow channels between the ships.

Curses rang out from dozens of throats, some in English, Spanish or French, others in languages that none of the companions knew. The noise was deafening. One of the ships listed to port and rammed her masts into the rigging of a frigate next to her. Yards splintered, ropes tore. Men who had been on the deck of the sinking ship jumped overboard, screaming, and met those who were already looking for saboteurs in the water. Soon it was so crowded down there that any attempt to catch the culprits was doomed to failure.

Jolly felt hope for the Hexhermetic Shipworm revive. If he didn't drown, it was most unlikely that anything bad would happen to him now. No one would be expecting such an insignificant-looking creature to be responsible for all this destruction. She hoped that, small as he was, he could make his way through this excited crowd of men.

'God damn it!' exclaimed Walker. 'Look at that!'

They were standing in the shelter of several crates and

woodpiles not far from the quay where the damaged *Quadriga* lay at anchor. Before them they saw frantic coming and going, yet they now clearly heard the yells ringing out over the moorings from Tyrone's flagship. The cannibal king and Bannon didn't seem to be on board any more, but among the men now hastily making for land Jolly recognised several of her old crew. The sight of their familiar faces hurt her. She quickly stepped back into the Ghost-Trader's shadow.

'Serves them right,' murmured Soledad, as the *Quadriga* too listed over and slowly sank.

'Bannon's over there,' said Buenaventure, placing one of his great paws on Jolly's shoulder as if to keep her from running to him.

Bannon and some of his men were making themselves a way through the crowd milling about frantically on the quayside. Obviously no one had yet worked out how to stop the ships sinking, so they were all following different orders or standing around uselessly, getting in the way.

Bannon shouted commands, gesticulated wildly, and tried to get some of the seamen who had just left the *Quadriga* back on board to plug the leak. The stink of hot tar came from somewhere, but it was obvious that neither that nor any other measures would save the *Quadriga*. Bannon and his crew were forced to watch helplessly as the ship sank in the lake. She did not tip right over but went straight down with majestic calm until water was lapping over her decks. When she finally sank to the bottom, only her masts still rose above the choppy surface. The rest of the ship had disappeared into the lake.

Jolly counted thirteen ships that had already sunk or were past saving. More and more were added to their numbers, for the Worm was clever enough not to work his way along a row but was moving back and forth, apparently at random, among the crowd of ships lying at anchor close together. Many sank as quickly as a stone; others went down in a more leisurely manner.

'This is getting too dangerous,' said Walker. 'We must be off.'

Men now came streaming up from all directions. There were already several hundred on the quayside, and others stood in crowds on the decks of those ships that hadn't yet suffered any damage. And still no one seemed to know who or what was responsible for the catastrophe. Many of the ships let their boats down into the water. On others the crews simply jumped overboard to get away fast enough from the undertow of their sinking ships. And the vessels were still inflicting further damage on each other when they collided, or masts broke off and shredded the rigging of a neighbouring ship.

'Walker's right,' said Soledad. 'Even in all this turmoil someone's going to recognise us sooner or later.'

Jolly's heartbeat was racing when she protested, 'I'm not going without the Worm!'

'You don't even know if he's really responsible for all this,' said Walker, but a growl from Buenaventure made him raise his hands defensively. 'All right, all right! So it really is him. But how are we going to get him out of the water?'

Jolly came out from behind the Ghost-Trader. 'I'll do it!'

'No, Jolly! Wait!' But Soledad's cry came too late.

Jolly shook off the pit bull man's hand, ducked under the Trader's arm and raced away.

Walker was beside himself. 'That . . . that *brat*!' she heard him curse, but then she disappeared into the crowd on the quay, wriggling past seamen, savages and harbour workers and coming closer to the water with every step. Was that someone calling her name? As she ran, she looked in the direction from which the voice had come. But she saw no familiar face. Nothing would be worse than crossing Bannon's path now.

No sooner had she thought of him than he was actually standing in front of her.

'Jolly?' he asked incredulously, and for a split second she even considered stopping. But then she simply ran on, ramming her shoulder into his stomach, and saw him fold up like a puppet with its strings broken. She jumped over his hands as they reached for her, avoided another man's grasp, and two steps further on she reached the harbour wall. Without a moment's hesitation, she took off and jumped.

Instead of sinking, she landed hard on the waves with both feet. Jolly stumbled, and was only just able to catch herself. What had happened? Polliwiggles could walk only over salt water, and this was a lake! She had assumed she would go under the water like anyone else, and be able to look for the Worm unnoticed amidst the tumult. But obviously enough salt water flowed through the channel leading from the sea into the lake to bear a polliwiggle.

Make the best of it, then, she thought. Get moving!

She ran on as fast as she could. The surface seemed to be boiling with all the uproar, the currents created by the sinking ships and the air bubbles rising from the wrecks. There were people in the water everywhere, many of them splashing about in panic like children. Others reached deliberately for her, as if guessing that the polliwiggle running past them had something to do with this disaster.

She heard a whistle behind her. Was it an alarm signal? Or was the Ghost-Trader trying to call up the sea horses?

Jolly didn't look round. She didn't want to see whether

Bannon was giving orders for his men to train pistols and shotguns on her. And if he wasn't, if in spite of everything he remembered how much she had meant to him until a few weeks ago – well, that was all to the good.

Acrid smoke was stinging her nose and throat. Fires had broken out on at least two of the sinking ships. Before the water closed over the flames and put them out the fire had already caught masts and sails. Flying sparks and torn rags of burning cloth carried it in all directions. Soon two nearby ships, until now lying at anchor intact, were burning too.

Shots whipped around her, whether on Bannon's orders or from somewhere else Jolly didn't know. She just hoped that her friends hadn't been seen. The water ahead of her was flowing over the deck of a sinking ship, and she had to swerve fast to one side so as not to be caught in the suction as the wreck went down. There was a strong current flowing beneath her feet, and for a moment she ran into the raging waves and got nowhere. But then she reached a broad channel between two undamaged ships that gave her cover from the marksmen on the bank. She was making for a sloop about fifty paces from the quay, one of the last ships to begin sinking, and hoped to find the Worm somewhere near it. Her advantage over the pirates and the savages was that since she was running over the surface she could move faster than they did.

There was a hollow thud beside her, and suddenly a feathered spear was sticking into a ship's side to her right, quivering. Several cannibals appeared on the ship to her left, not in seaman's clothing but wearing loincloths, with strange ribbons wrapped around their arms, legs and stomachs.

A second spear missed her. A third splashed into the water beside her, grazing her leg, but only with its shaft. Then she was past the two hulls and running in a zigzag as she approached the ship where she thought she might find the Worm.

'Worm!' she called over the water. She couldn't see more than ten paces ahead of her now, for the smoke in the air shrouded the entire harbour. But that helped to protect her from the men on the bank.

'Worm!' she shouted again, and looked round.

A ship beside her was listing to port. She was only just in time to jump out of reach of the masts as they went over. Again and again she called to the Hexhermetic Shipworm, at the same time ducking away from a new hail of spears coming from another ship. Somewhere or other a marksman with a pistol now opened fire, but after two shots he gave up. Now and then she still saw men in the water, but the further she moved from the banks of the lake the fewer there were.

'Worm! For heaven's sake, where are you?'

She was slowly coming to see how crazy her plan was.

How was she to find the tiny Worm somewhere out here in the water, among the ships and the waves, in the smoke and under fire from her enemies? But she wasn't going to give up hope.

The Hexhermetic Shipworm was doing Tyrone's fleet more damage than Jolly and the others would ever have thought possible. Whatever the Ghost-Trader might say, the mere fact that Tyrone was suffering such a setback in his own harbour would do his reputation among his men no good. Tyrone, deranged ruler of the Orinoco delta, suddenly seemed only half as powerful as before.

'Jolly,' came a plaintive cry somewhere to her right.

There was something in the water that looked like a piece of wood rocking up and down in the waves. It wriggled as it moved forward, but it was obviously too weak to resist the surging waves much longer.

'Worm!' Beside herself with relief she ran to him, pulled him out of the water and held him close. She cradled him in her arms like a newborn baby, and even dropped a big kiss on the horny plate on his head. His breath was rattling, and his short legs hung from his body like lifeless appendages.

'So . . . tired . . .' he gasped. 'All that . . . eating.' And he gave a loud belch. It echoed back from the hull of a nearby ship.

'Don't worry,' said Jolly, running on. 'I'll get you to safety.'

'I don't think . . . I could have gone on . . . much . . .' He fell silent. She felt he was a little heavier in her arms. He had gone to sleep, and he was snoring.

At first she was still drunk with delight, but only too quickly reality caught up with her. She couldn't go back to the quay and her friends. The place was swarming with enemies now. Perhaps Tyrone himself had come down to the harbour.

She thought briefly, then decided against going back to the bank and ran further out on the lake, away from the burning, sinking ships. She hoped with all her heart that the others could manage to get away in time. If she could somehow make it to the delta herself, away from the town of tents and huts at the foot of the fortress, then perhaps . . .

She stumbled, and forced herself to concentrate. Every step mattered, every minute taking her further from her enemies' eyes and their bullets.

Having eaten his fill, the Hexhermetic Shipworm was sleeping peacefully in her arms while she raced over the water, taking great strides. There were ships at anchor everywhere, but not as close together out here as near the bank where the moorings lay. She saw only a few men on board them, and in the gathering dusk they were not much danger to her.

Jolly was gasping with exhaustion when she finally reached the channel leading into and out of the lake. Torches burned to left and right on the beaches of the tented town. She still had enough strength to run on. People were watching from both sides of the bank now. Some even began wading through the water to reach her, but after a few steps the channel was too deep. Now and then a few bullets whistled round her ears, but most of them were fired so wide of her that they didn't even make her jump.

She reached the eastern arm of the delta and followed it out into the Atlantic Ocean. The Worm moved in her arms, purred, growled something, and went to sleep again. Breathing heavily, she carried him on over the water, skirting the fortress that towered dark and menacing above her. At a distance of about a stone's throw from land she followed the coastline south-east.

The sun had set at last, and night fell rapidly over the jungle and the sea. Tyrone's fortress merged with the sky, and could soon be seen only as a few lights in the distance. The noise from the lake on the other side of the promontory came over the ocean to her ears. On the way, Jolly had several times seen dark shapes under the surface of the water racing past her in the opposite direction. She clung to the hope that they were the hippocamps responding to the Ghost-Trader's signal.

The fortress was far behind her now. The black wall of the jungle gave way to the sandy beach where Jolly and her companions had landed. In the dark she could make it out only as a ghostly line, shimmering faintly in those places where the sand cast back the moonlight.

With the last of her strength, she staggered towards the shore, sank to her knees, exhausted, and let the breakers carry her the last of the way to the beach. Holding the Shipworm in her arms, she rolled away from the foaming surf into the sand and lay there. She couldn't feel her legs any more; she lacked the strength to drag herself into the shelter of the palm trees.

She drew up her knees, curled herself protectively round the Worm, and went to sleep on the spot.

At some point, perhaps quite soon, perhaps much later, the sound of several voices woke her. The night was black as pitch. Clouds must have come up, for neither the moon nor the stars could be seen. She had sand between her teeth. The Worm moved too, and without a word snuggled closer to the warmth of her body.

Jolly sat up in the sand. She was dizzy and her legs ached. She felt cramp coming on in her left foot, and quickly moved it back and forth a little to loosen it up.

The voices were coming from the sea, carried on the salty

wind. She jumped up, moved slowly towards the palms, and got behind a tree for makeshift cover.

There was splashing and the sound of lapping water. Something was moving out there. A dark tangle of shadows drifted apart, itself little more than a dark patch against the darkness of the nocturnal ocean.

'It's not them,' whispered the Shipworm grumpily.

Jolly put a finger to her lips. Her heart was thudding so hard she was afraid it would make the whole palm tree shake.

'Jolly?' Little more than a whisper, but easily identifiable. Soledad's voice!

Jolly ran out from behind the palm, stumbling over the soft sand. 'Here we are!' she cried. She had difficulty keeping her voice down; she was so relieved she could have shouted out loud. The Worm relaxed too. He had been curled up in a tight ball just now, but he stretched again and almost slipped out of her hands.

She could hardly make out the princess's face in the dark, but there was no mistaking her slender figure or the sound of her voice.

'Hurry up, Jolly!'

'I'm so glad you made it!' Jolly looked past Soledad. 'Is everyone here?'

'Yes, don't worry.' Soledad briefly hugged her, making the

Shipworm grunt indignantly when he was squashed between the two of them. 'And our little friend is all right too, I see,' said the princess, glancing at the cursing bundle. 'By the way, well done, little man.'

'Man?' groused the Worm. 'Men are human beings. I'd rather be a *rock* than a human being.'

'We're not sure if we're being followed,' Soledad told Jolly.

'By Tyrone?'

'Not himself. His men have their hands full putting out the fires on their ships. And it's too dark for them to take a vessel out to sea.' She led Jolly down to the water with her and waded into the surf, while the other girl walked over the waves beside her.

'Who, then?'

'Kobalins.'

Jolly felt an icy chill. She uneasily remembered the night when the *Carfax* had been followed. Her eyes went to the surface of the sea, but it was too dark to make anything out there.

'We're not sure,' said Soledad as she struggled against the waves towards the place where the others were waiting for her on their hippocamps.

'Don't you ever do that again, Jolly,' was the first thing Walker said when they were close enough.

'Take no notice of him,' protested Buenaventure from the saddle of the sea horse. 'He's glad to see you, he just won't admit it.'

Jolly grinned, even though she could hardly see either of them. She hurried over to her friends. 'Guess who I found.'

In the darkness Buenaventure reached out his paw, ruffled her hair appreciatively, and fished the Shipworm out of her embrace.

'Looks as if we have something like a genuine hero here,' he told the Worm.

The strange little creature stretched out proudly to his full length. Parts of the horny plating of his skin scraped against each other. 'Very true. I think someone ought to celebrate this great deed in verse. A mighty epic about the heroic fight of the Hexhermetic –'

'With a tragic ending,' Walker interrupted him, 'if I hear a single rhyme.'

'Fish-brain! Philistine!'

Jolly helped Buenaventure to stow the indignant Worm in his rucksack. The hero slipped into it, fell silent at once, and uttered only a happy sigh. She noticed that something was clinging to her fingers, something fine and soft as a spider's web, but wiped it off on her trousers and thought no more of it.

'Quick!' The Ghost-Trader guided his sea horse to get in position beside Soledad's. The princess got herself into the saddle. Jolly jumped up behind her and put her hands and feet into the safety loops.

With cries of encouragement, they urged the hippocamps on. Soon they were racing over the black sea.

'We spoiled Tyrone's little game for him,' Soledad called cheerfully over her shoulder when they were out of hearing distance of the coast. The sea wind blew her hair into Jolly's face.

'I thought a few wrecked ships weren't going to be enough to weaken him,' said Jolly.

'No, not that. But he knows we'll warn the people of Aelenium. So now he has no choice but to put to sea tomorrow morning and begin attacking as soon as possible.'

'You mean that's good?'

'Well, he'll have to pass through the waters of the Antilles captains. They won't fail to notice such a large fleet, and they'll wonder what happened to the great land campaign against Caracas that he promised them. Then the captains will realise that Tyrone was stringing them along.'

'So no raid on Caracas now?'

'I doubt it. Without the Antilles pirates, our people in Tortuga and New Providence will think three times about their chances. And the Antilles captains won't let Tyrone's fleet pass through their seas. They're proud men, and Tyrone's betrayal will wound their honour deeply.'

'Does that mean they'll attack him?'

'It's possible. They have no chance against such numbers, but I suspect they'll still harry his flanks and his rearguard. With a little luck they'll weaken Tyrone a good deal. And that in turn will be to Aelenium's advantage.'

Jolly leaned forward to look into Soledad's face. 'How do you know all this?'

The princess laughed, and for the first time in days there was no bitterness in her laughter. 'They're pirates, Jolly. And men. If there's one thing I learned from my father, as I've told you, it's how to think like one of them. Believe me, it's much easier than it seems.'

Soledad had said something like that to Jolly once before, about Griffin and Munk, and that time too she had been right.

'Kendrick was wrong,' said Jolly.

'What do you mean?'

'When he said no pirate would follow a woman. I think you'll make rather a good pirate queen some day.'

The princess shrugged, but even in the dark Jolly could guess at her proud smile.

*

They saw no kobalins that night or the following day. The friends did not talk much, and gave the sea horses no rest. The Shipworm stayed hidden in Buenaventure's rucksack. Jolly suspected that he was already composing his heroic epic. She thought of the substance that had stuck to her hands with vague uneasiness.

When the wall of mist appeared on the horizon early on the morning of the third day, the companions breathed again. The parrots fluttered above them, and for the first time those mysterious birds seemed almost exuberant.

Although Jolly could hardly wait to see Griffin again, she was the only one to feel no real relief. Her heart sank at the thought of meeting Munk. But even these fears paled in view of the task awaiting them. She looked past the mist to the north-east, across the expanses of the endless ocean, and suddenly felt panic seize her.

Somewhere out there lay the Rift, many thousands of feet under the sea, in icy cold and eternal night. She had recognised her enemy and made her decision. Aelenium was just a stop along her way, not her destination.

The rising sun filled the sky with gold, and the companions were riding straight into the light. But Jolly's descent into the shadows had begun.